WIRED FOR SOUND

David Ferrier

Battle Press
SATELLITE BEACH, FLORIDA

WIRED FOR SOUND

Battle Press books may be ordered through booksellers or by
contacting:

Battle Press
1-919-218-4039
steve@battlepress.media
www.battlepress.media

ISBN: 979-8-9887651-2-7 (softcover)
ISBN: 979-8-9887651-3-4 (eBook)
LCCN: 2024901602

First Edition.

To get your FREE copy of the first book in _The Mountaintop Series_:

1. Click on (or type into your internet browser) the link below.

2. Enter your **name** and **email.**

3. Click **Send** and the book will be emailed to you.

Enjoy!

Free Book Link:
https://battlepress.media/?page_id=13

Book One of _The Mountaintop Series_

OTHER BOOKS BY DAVID FERRIER

THE MOUNTAINTOP SERIES:

Born On A Mountaintop

Raised On Rock

Forged In Fire

California Dreaming   **Coming in 2024**

After Your Military Service

A Cry For Mercy In The Night

Self Inflicted Wounds

If you enjoy **Wired For Sound**, *I would really appreciate a short review, your help in spreading the word is highly valued and reviews make it much easier for readers to find the book.*

Table Of Contents

Sing In Me Muse
Of Choices Once Made
That Did Not Last.
And a Future That will later be Past.

Dedication:

TO THE SEEKERS & THE TRYERS

THE ONES WHO MAKE THE EFFORT

NEVER LET GO OF THE ROPE

All that is gold does not glitter,
Not all those who wander are lost,
The old that is strong does not wither,
Deep roots are not reached by the frost.

From the ashes in fire shall be woken,
A light from the shadows will spring,
Renewed shall be blade that
was broken,
The crownless again shall be king.

J.R.R. Tolkein

Prologue

Coming home. Being home. Leaving home. Searching for home.

These are the matters to be discussed in this collection of twenty stories. Once again David, Margaret Mary and Teddy face changes and challenges on the road from childhood to maturity.

Their world is at war. Their country is divided. Their leaders are confounded.

As always, the radio whispers musical messages in their ears. Not just happy tunes but songs of protest, songs of desperation and despair, songs of protest and unanswered questions.

Such were the times. The late fall of 1969 through the late summer of 1974.

Struggling to survive it all while being Wired For Sound.

Youth is the first victim of war; the
first fruit of peace.It takes 20 years
or more of peace to make a man; it
takes only 20 seconds of war to
destroy him.

— Baudouin of Belgium —

Chapter One

Don't Let The Kid Drive The Truck

The first thing I notice about being home from Vietnam is how small everything in my hometown seems. How trivial and unimportant the daily activities are. How meaningless and inconsequential I was becoming. I feel empty inside, hollow. The one strong feeling I can manage is how much I miss being part of the 571st Medical Detachment. And no one back here is going to understand how I feel about back there, back then.

I realize, of course, that the change is in me, not them, not the place, not the doings, me. I watch the way people around me behave and feel empty inside. Empty of empathy, empty of spirit, empty of fellowship. I feel, most often, alone. I stand among them and feel like an outsider. At home, with my family, I am alone. I fear that if they could know what is going on inside me, they would shun me.

I am alert to dangers they do not see. Wary of situations, they glide through every day, fearful of things I cannot name and secretly long for a life I no longer have. A life far away in an Asian jungle. A life with a purpose, with a value I cannot find here.

I am alone, among them. And the radio whispered…

To think that only yesterday

I was cheerful, bright and gay,

Looking forward to, who wouldn't do,

The role I was about to play,

But as if to knock me down,

Reality came around,

And without so much as a mere touch

*Cut me into little pieces. **

I've been back from Vietnam for five months. Five dreary, snowy, cold, New England winter months. In the White House Richard Nixon skulked about, secretly ordering the bombing and invasion of Cambodia and Laos. Aided by a collection of thugs like John Mitchell, Charles Colson, John Dean, H.R. (Harry Robbins) Halderman and John Erlichman the ruling coven amassed a presidential "Enemies List" which grew to contain over five hundred names. Journalists, college professors, clergyman, professional athletes and movie stars who publicly disputed the pro-war line were deemed enemies of the country and earmarked for "special attention." Such was the country's leadership when I returned home from my far away Asian War.

Movies glorifying war or portraying combat's lighter side proliferated. "Patton" went full Technicolor, Widescreen, Academy Award glorious, while "Catch 22" and "M.A.S.H." combined Hollywood heartbreak with hilarity. "Kelly's Heroes" gave us the Man With No Name masterminding a military heist caper set to a snappy, upbeat soundtrack. I recall walking out of the theatre roughly ten minutes into "M.A.S.H." too much, too soon, too cute for my amusement levels. Movie War was all laughter and loyalty, except for my war, the one still raging in Southeast Asia.

I wandered around in this fog, day after much the same day for months as my personal bitterness and the national cynicism poisoned the air around me. Making miserable matters worse, anti-war protests and pro-war rallies rocked the nation on a daily basis. One sunny weekend over 100,000 demonstrators assembled on the National Mall to protest the war in Vietnam while hard hats on construction sites battled with hippies and the nightly news totaled the war dead like football scores.

Just when it appeared that nothing could make matters worse, less than a month after I got home a journalist named Seymour Hersh published an article revealing an unspeakable atrocity in a village called My Lai, in Quang Nai Province, Vietnam. More than three hundred villagers, men, women and children were executed by members of our own Americal Division. No explanation was ever given for this outrage which was covered up and denied by the military for over a year. Twenty-six soldiers, including the Commander of the Americal Division were eventually charged with war crimes for the incident. Only one, Lieutenant William Calley, the on the ground platoon leader who supervised the killings and, according to eyewitness testimony, murdered several villagers himself, was ever tried. He was eventually found guilty of the atrocities, sentenced to life in prison and subsequently fully pardoned by President Richard Nixon.

Overnight the shame of the war was shifted from the politicians and generals to the soldiers fighting in Vietnam. The actual reason we were losing the war, the official line now proclaimed, was because of the poor quality of the soldiers fighting the war. We were labeled as "baby killers" and drug addicts, losers creating a losing cause. Honorable soldiers, like Woody, Harry, Don, Major Cronin, Sergeant Major Hoadwonick and all the men of the 571st Dustoff were to blame. It was not a good time, to say the least, to be recognized or to proclaim you were a Vietnam veteran. The My Lai Massacre, as it came to be called, hung in the air like poison. As the nation recoiled from the horror of the incident, I turned up my collar, grew my hair long and tried to erase any notion of having been in the war. Except inside my head.

I tried to shelter from my thoughts with some good old Rock & Roll, as I had years before in happier times. Gone were the toe-tapping, finger popping sounds of Blue Suede Shoes, Bye Bye Love, The Twist and Jingle Bell Rock. My dashboard radio echoed Sounds of Silence, Suspicious Minds, Hard Day's Nights and Can't Get No Satisfaction. Hardly uplifting, rather depressing. Which I was supplying plenty of for myself.

I was still living with my parents which was strained by the oppressive, lingering anger of my Mother, who had never forgiven me for voluntarily extending my tour in Vietnam a year before. All my life my Mother struggled to express her concern or caring through the veil of her unnamed sadness. Her temper was quick, foul and long lasting. Forgiveness came only with time, and though she never understood my sense of loyalty and obligation to the men I served with, she eventually relented. Meanwhile I slept in my childhood bed, dreaming an old man's dreams.

I slept late most mornings, lollygagged around the house until noon and eventually ventured out into the wintertime, wasting time. Lunch, far too often, found me at the Whipple Café drinking twenty-five cent pony beers and munching a hand-made hamburger. The mid-day Whipple is manned by a cast of semi-benevolent alcoholics, disgruntled townies, bar stool philosophers and drifters, like myself. I'm getting more comfortable there every day.

"Buncha' shit, letting those guys go!" Ralphie something or other, belched as he sat at the bar nursing a midday bourbon and water while fingering a greasy bag of potato chips.

"Yeah, that little shit Abie Hoffman guy, they shoulda' kicked his ass, that Jerry Rubbin' guy too." Mike, "Permanently Unemployed" Sullivan chimed in from the next stool.

"Them guys was like riotin' in the streets, breaking the law all over the place. It was on TV for Christ's sake!" Ralphie wasn't letting this one go.

"Chicago 7 they calls 'em, Chicago assholes is more like it." Mike finished his beer, waved for another.

I keep my head down, chewing and swallowing with no place better to go than here. It's time for a change.

Behind the bar a small black and white TV screen flickers, giving the latest sports scores, the Bruins and Celtics highlights, like they really mattered, like someone really cared. During the umpteenth Super Bowl highlight show Mike changed gears, "Fuckin' Vikings laid down I tell ya', the game was fixed all the way."

Drunken heads nod in agreement around the room. I throw two bucks on the bar and get up to go.

"Got a hot date, Dave?" Ralphie asks as I wonder why I ever told these mutts my name.

"Job interview," I answer. Everyone at the bar looks down. I leave.

That was pretty much what my days were like before I started working.

Then they got worse.

My Dad got me on where he worked at Haartz Auto Fabric. They made convertible tops, rolls and rolls of rubberized vinyl to keep Detroit autos topless. My dad worked upstairs, way upstairs, in the testing lab. I was down in the basement, in the dryer room where the hot rubber met the textile cotton. There the fabric cooled and spooled onto wooden spindles before being taken upstairs to the inspection tables then being shipped to Detroit. The temperature in the dryer room was a couple of degrees less than hell and the smell defies description unless you have ever had your sneakers catch fire. Eight hours a day, three spools an hour, twenty-five or so a day. Monday thru Friday.

"Stormy Lady to win in the third, three-six on the Daily Double, four-six, deuce perfecta in the fifth, Wild Child in the tenth, across the board."

This was the lingo I was learning down in the dryer room. I worked with three other guys, Lenny Watlins, Doug Shapiro and Wally Branca. They were all in their late twenties or early thirties, married, semi-married and divorced and had worked at Haartz Auto for ten years. Ten years! In the basement, in the dryer, in the heat and the smell. They liked it there, joked around all day and bet on the trotters at Rockingham Park, the pups at Wonderland, the Red Sox, Celtics, Patriots and Bruins and almost any other foolish notion that popped into their heads. My old pal, Eddie Legrand, would have loved these guys. These guys would have loved Eddie. As far as I knew though Eddie was still up in Canada, Montreal his mother told me, dodging the draft, taking foolish chances with secret visits to Southie where there was a federal warrant for his arrest.

"Dave, you want in on this? Sure thing, it's a lock." Wally had at least one lock a week, very few of which ever came through, but he kept on believing. So did the other guys.

"Pass, Wally, I'm still saving for the Corvette." Which I was not going to buy but made a great place to tell these guys my money was going besides into a savings account which I am not sure they had ever heard of.

"Your loss, man. Easy money."

Yeah, easy money, the kind that keeps you working in the dryer room for ten years. Among other things I'd never say to these guys. These were not bad people, your car breaks down, they are there to help. Moving? They'll tote furniture, just buy the beer. But they had already gone as far as they were going to go in life and didn't even seem to notice, or care. As a far, far better man than I once noted, they sailed from "Tedium to Apathy and back," over and over. Not the life for me.

I had spoken with my Dad about this. He understood, and said he felt the same way when he came home from World War II. He eventually married my Mom, started night school and worked a variety of jobs for six years until he got his degree in Textile Engineering and began working at Haartz Auto. Six years of night school, factory jobs during the day and a wife and three kids. Not the life for me. But knowing what was not the life for me was not getting me any closer to discovering what the life for me was.

I had also spoken of this with Margaret Mary, of course. She was finishing her junior year at Loyola. We spoke by phone every weekend, she alternately sounded enthused and troubled, but she assured me she was well and over the whole

Kendall thing. She was lying of course. I was too bewildered to notice.

Teddy was due home from the Marine Corps in three weeks. His four-year term of service was up. He was still down at Quantico punching officers but was prepared to give it up for a return to Lowell to work with his Dad at the garage. Partners. I was happy for him.

Peter Rayburn was finishing up his novitiate in Washington, D.C. and was going to Rome to study Papal Law at the Vatican. Peter, a priest and a lawyer. The world did not know what it was in for.

My friends were moving forward. Meanwhile I pushed spools of vinyl up a ramp from the basement to the loading dock at Haartz and positioned them in the back of a bobtail truck. The truck would then take them around to the other side of the building where they were off-loaded at the inspection tables. Three, sometimes four trips a day, six or eight rolls a trip, over and over. The truck never left the parking lot, going from one side of the building to the other. And this became the reason I quit Haartz Auto.

"Inspection just called down; they need more rolls now!"

Hank Izzaria was the dock foreman, the boss of the basement. He was calling for Rick Gerreau, who usually drove the truck. I had just finished placing the last roll in the back of the truck. Rick Gerreau was, for the moment, nowhere to be found. Hank was getting irritated, the inspectors needed work, so I jumped in the cab and drove the truck around to the front of the building. I off-loaded the rolls of vinyl and returned the truck to the basement loading ramp, backing it into the dock. Hank came out when he saw me get out of the cab, he was pissed.

"Who told you to take the truck?" He demanded.

"Nobody told me to take it, it was loaded, you wanted the rolls upstairs, so I drove it around. What's the big deal?"

"It's not your job is what's the big deal. I say who drives the truck. Where the hell is Rick?" Hank was steaming. Right then Rick strolled out onto the dock not knowing anything was wrong or supposed to be wrong.

"Where the hell have you been?" Hank repeated, louder.

"Upstairs, in payroll. They called down for me, I had ta' straighten something out." Rick answered.

"You're supposed to let me know when you ain't around," Hank said, "and don't let the kid drive the truck!"

Hank stomped off. Now I was pissed. I followed Hank to his office, went in and closed the door behind me.

"Can I have a word with you, Hank?" My turn to be steaming. Hank was back to his usual, mellow self. I was way far from mellow. Hank nodded, more curious than apprehensive.

"Six months ago," I began, "I drive a two and half ton truck loaded with medical supplies and ammunition fifty miles north from Danang to Phu Bai. That's in Vietnam, Hank. There's only one road, Highway One. The VC mine the road, shoot at the trucks and try to blow up the bridges, usually while the trucks are on them. I did this several times during my tours Hank. I never lost a truck, so you might consider that the next time you need a truck driven around the parking lot and you don't want 'the kid' to do it."

Some experiences are harder than others to put behind you.

I didn't finish my tirade. My anger had morphed into sadness, that goddamn lump in my throat I hated swelled up once again. My eyes started to tear up. I didn't know why. I turned on my heels and stomped out of Hank's office. I was going to go back to the dryer, but I turned to my car instead. I got in and sat behind the wheel and a dam burst inside me. I was crying, trying very hard to stop and having no success. This crying business was really starting to annoy me. I started the car and drove away.

My coming home business wasn't going well. I didn't know where I was going as I drove away from Haartz Auto. Of course, I didn't know where I was going when I drove to Haartz Auto either. As I drove aimlessly around, I punched the car radio listening to Bridge Over Troubled Water, Sons of a Preacher Man, and ear poison like Psychedelic Shack and Yummy, Yummy. Nothing to soothe my mind, raise my spirits or ease my confusion. Rock and Roll had changed radically and, not it seemed, for the better. Toe tapping and finger popping had been replaced by mournful, preachy, pontificating poets with guitars, or so they saw themselves. Right now I didn't need angst, I needed rhythm and blues. No such luck.

The Beatles, once the shaggy headed mop tops of many years ago, were no more. They yodeled "Let it Be" and shouted, "Instant Karma" and they now resembled bored billionaires who became gurus to a movement I could neither fathom nor adopt. The rest of the Top 40 crew consisted of flowery hippie imitators chanting about peace, love and dope.

Meanwhile ten thousand miles away the "dirty little war" raged on. Casualties mounted and were counted and forgotten on nightly newscasts. Anger, frustration and confusion pretty much described my mental health at the time. And I was getting worse.

The mushy music on the radio was making my heart ache so I pulled over and was surprised to find myself on the side street that ran alongside the Immaculate Conception Church in Lowell. This was the place I had learned to yearn for a better future, to aspire to being a better person, to be part of something I didn't feel a part of anymore. I wasn't really aiming for this place but here I was. Karma or coincidence?

I hadn't been to church much since I'd been home. Midnight Mass at Christmas, a stray Sunday or two here and there but somehow the habit had faded along with my faith. I read somewhere that war could do that to you but at this point I had no idea why religion had dropped out of my life. Lots of things had dropped out of my life lately and here I was parked outside the cathedral of my childhood. There had to be a reason, I hoped.

I went into the empty mid-day, mid-week church. This was the main expanse of the basilica, fifty-four rows of straight-backed wooden pews on each side of a wide center aisle. There were towering stained glass windows depicting saints, suffering and salvation, a magnificent, elevated altar of gleaming marble ringed with tall brass candlesticks and snowy white wax candles. Along the walls and in lofty alcoves were life sized statues of virgins and apostles, and bloody crucifixes, lots of bloody crucifixes. It was hushed quiet in there, cooler than the outside world, cleaner than the thoughts in my head. I moved to a pew, far in the rear of the church and sat and stared.

As a boy I had served mass here, an altar boy, mouthing Latin I did not understand, praying prayers I magically thought would bring me happiness and begging forgiveness for sins so trivial I could now recall not one of them. I prayed, implored and chanted at the ceiling, knowing in my heart that God was here and listening. Today it felt like nobody was home.

The silence enveloped me, the stillness seeped into my bones and the anger and hurt I was feeling began to subside. As it did, I knelt to pray. I folded my hands and bowed my head and strained to pray, though my mind turned away. I tried harder, the supplications would not come. "Hail May full of grace," I began and then nothing. Solemn verses I had mumbled a thousand times deserted me. "Our Father who art in heaven," I tried, same result, emptiness, hollowness, despair. Nobody home but us hopeless.

"Hey, God," I shouted in my head, mixing reverence with respect. "How come all those guys got killed and you didn't do anything about it? How come all those guys are losing arms and legs and eyes and ears and you just sit in here and do nothing?"

It was a good thing I had the sense to keep this dialogue in my head because I did not notice the priest sorting prayer books behind me as I ranted on.

"You gonna' answer me?" I demanded, silently. "You gonna' do anything about that?"

Still thinking I was alone I shot to my feet and shouted, aloud, "Well, are you! Huh?"

Which got the attention of the bible stacking priest.

"Are you alright, my son?" The priest asked as he hurried over to me.

I was surprised and embarrassed. How did I miss this guy? I was sure the place was empty when I came in. So much for my surveillance skills. Now the priest was at my side.

"Sorry father," I began, "I just lost it there for a second."

The priest was a kindly looking old guy. I didn't recognize him from my old altar boy days. He smiled and answered in that churchly whisper we had both adopted,

"Would you care to tell me what it was you lost?"

I didn't know what to say. I didn't know this guy and felt foolish for shouting out in church. It was time for a fast retreat. But to where?

"My faith," I stammered, not knowing where that answer came from.

The elderly priest smiled. "Why don't we sit down and talk about it. Maybe we will learn how you lost it." Which was better than my idea of driving around some more in my car.

"What is your name my son?"

"Dave," I answered wanting to get away from the whole fatherly bit. "And yours Father?"

"Coogan, Daniel Coogan. Sometimes referred to as Father Coogan," He said with a smile I didn't return.

"Are you from around here?" he asked.

"Born and raised. I was an altar boy right here. Graduated from the Immaculate Conception School."

"And what is it you are doing now?"

"Nothing much, ranting and raving," and that damned lump came back in my throat and my eyes began to fill with tears.

He noticed.

"Would you like to talk about it? I'm really quite a good listener you know."

I didn't know, but I also didn't have much to lose. "I just got out of the Army," I began, "Couple of months ago. I was in Vietnam. Two years. Flew Dustoff."

"I'm not quite sure I know what that means," the elderly priest answered. "What exactly is a Dustoff?"

"Med-evac, in helicopters. We flew wounded guys to the hospital."

"Ah," he replied, "God's own work that."

"I was just sort of wondering where God was while we were doing it." I answered angrily.

"Perhaps he was right by your side, and at the side of those you carried to safety."

"I was more wondering why so many of them need to be carried to safety. I saw a lot of badly wounded people. Where was God while they were being wounded?" More anger, more confusion.

"God did not wound those people; people wounded those people." The elderly priest answered quietly.

"And God just let it happen?"

"The ways of man are the ways of man, those of God are God's." Father Coogan's answers really hit me the wrong way.

"Then why all this?" I spat, "Churches, altars, candles, prayers, what's the point if God can't be bothered to do something every now and then? You ever see a war, Father?"

"There was a time, many years ago, when I was assigned to the Fifth Army under a General named Mark Clark. Did you ever hear of a beachhead named Anzio?"

"Invasion of Italy, January 1944," I answered, I knew this military stuff.

"A disaster, poorly planned, poorly led. Generals were relieved, others vilified. Before the campaign was over almost 44,000 Allied soldiers were killed. A failure at all levels. I know because I was there."

"You were at Anzio?" Respect overwhelmed my anger.

"Was, am, whenever I think about it. War is something that stays in the mind my son."

"And you still believe in God?" He did, I didn't.

"I believe in many things I cannot fully understand. War is one of them, God is another."

"You believe in war?"

"My war, perhaps more than yours, though I must admit I know little of your war."

"Jungle fight, kill more of them than they kill us. Over and over, day after day."

"Sounds rather pointless." The elderly priest shook his head sadly.

"Which is exactly how I feel, pointless." And then I understood or began to understand why I felt the way I did.

"And you came here, to this church looking for answers?"

"I came here because I didn't know where else to go."

"The answer is not here," Father Coogan said, "This is a building, a magnificent building in its way, but a building, nevertheless. The answers you seek are within you, not within this edifice. Many people come here to pray, to ask God for answers. I believe God answers by inspiring you to look within yourself."

"Sometimes when I look inside myself, I don't like what I see."

"Then you know what you must change. Being willing to look inside and know what is good and what is not is the beginning of healing."

Reluctantly, through my skepticism, I realized what this guy was saying made sense. Now if I could just get over the anger part. "I guess maybe I'm still pretty angry with God," I admitted.

"Anger is often a substitute for hurt, Dave. God did not hurt you, your fellow man hurt you, the war hurt you. But perhaps war and your fellow man taught you something else as well, as it did for me. On the beaches at Anzio I saw confusion, terror, cowardice, and incompetence at every level. I also saw courage, sacrifice, camaraderie and heroism. I saw them at a level I perhaps would never have seen them without war. Those qualities are the ones I choose to remember, the ones you might have been able to exhibit yourself."

The lump again, a big one. I couldn't swallow, the tears started. Father Coogan smiled. "You are on the right track Dave, and in the right place to do it. Use what you have found, come back anytime."

With that the elderly priest walked away toward the sacristy. I was alone again in the church. Silence, peace, even tranquility as my anger softened, and my hurt diminished. I sat for a long time. It felt good, as good as I felt since I got home.

A song entered my head…

When the night is come,

And the land is dark,

And the moon is the only light we see,

No, I won't be afraid,

Oh, I won't be afraid,

Just as long as you Stand By Me.**

Isn't that what God is supposed to do?

I sat for a long time in the serenity of the church, and I never went back to Haartz Auto.

Margaret Mary sat in her room seeking solace for her sorrows.

Although she had re-enrolled at Loyola University and was warmed and welcomed in her Aunt Rose's home, nothing Rose nor Sean could do would shake the pain of Tuloc Meadows. The terror lingered, the humiliation of the Denver courtroom throbbed, the shame of her memories burned inside her. She felt alone and helpless as she heard miserable music in her head.

Hello darkness my old friend.

I've come to talk with you again.

Because a vision softly creeping.

Left its seed while I was sleeping

And the vision that was planted in my brain.

Still remains.

Within the sound of silence.***

In the silence, however, she found not peace but a roiling anger, an unquenchable hurt and deep shame. Which lingered on. "Will you be coming to your dinner, Daughter?" Sean asked through the closed and locked door of her bedroom. Sanctuary, the room promised. Solitude and sadness it delivered.

"In a moment," she answered, pushing away the sadness that smothered her. Stirring from her window seat she whispered a silent prayer and breathed three deep breaths as she created a smile. False courage, she reckoned, was better than none at all as she crossed to open the bedroom door.

"Your studies, they go well?" Sean asked as they sat at the supper table, Margaret Mary, Aunt Rose and Sean, the woven cloth of her family.

"Too often I look to the poets for inspiration and find only despair," Margaret Mary answered with barely concealed dismay.

"Perhaps this is what you bring to the looking," Rose suggested gently.

"I bring who I am, who I have become," Margaret Mary answered, sodden with sadness.

"Was it not our own Mr. Yeats who observed, "Being Irish, he had an abiding sense of tragedy, which sustained him through temporary periods of joy," Sean added, hoping to lighten the mood.

"Mine is not a sense of tragedy, Father. Mine is a sorrow I cannot master."

"Yet master it you shall child," Rose suggested, "Your spirit is too strong, too good to be burdened by this for very long."

"It already feels very long, Rose."

"Then perhaps you are closer to the ending of it," Sean prayed aloud.

"I'm trying Da, I really am. When I am awake, when I stay busy, I am fine. But a sound like his voice, or a smell like wet, damp clothes, when I sleep and dream, it all comes back."

Margaret Mary put her head in her hands and sobbed. Though she had re-enrolled in school, continued to see a counselor each week and in some ways moved past her horrific experience, her suffering continued.

Sean and Rose watched and wept within themselves at Margaret Mary's suffering. They offered all they could, all they had to lighten her burden, yet the burden remained.

"Your counselor, this woman you are seeing, does she help?"

"She helps when she is there," Margaret Mary answered.

"And after, how is it you are to help yourself?" Sean asked.

"My counselor talks a lot about forgiveness, she says my healing starts there. But forgiveness I cannot find, not for Kendall, not for myself." There was a bitterness in her speech and an anger her family had never heard before.

"This Kendall person, what do we know of him?" Sean asked.

"He smiled at me Da, smirked as he walked out of the courtroom. That's what I keep seeing and that is what I cannot forgive."

"Will not forgive, my child," Rose commented, "the decision to forgive is yours as is the decision to hate."

"A wise man I cannot name once said hate harms the hater more than the hated," Sean said.

"How do you know it was a man?" Margaret Mary asked with a whisper of a smile.

"Because a woman would have put it more elegantly," Rose replied.

"The message is true, even without the elegance," Sean suggested.

"I cannot forgive him; I won't forgive him. I thought there was no place in me for hate, now it fills me up."

"Perhaps forgiving him is not where to begin Daughter. Perhaps begin by forgiving yourself."

"That is the same thing Ms. Adams tells me. I'm trying, trying as hard as I can."

"Then you are sure to succeed," Rose surmised. And the family weave, for now, wove tighter as a far-away ghost of song whispered…

Them that's got shall get.

Them that's not shall lose.

So the Bible says.

And it still is news.

Mama may have.

Papa may have.

But God bless the child

Who's got his own.**

"Brother Rayburn, you missed Vespers this morning," Newly ordained Father Kurt Valden whispered after finding Peter deep in prayer in a small Vatican chapel.

"Overslept," Peter replied, returning to the present.

"Monsignor Specio was not there as well so your absence was unnoticed, save from your friends." Kurt smiled.

"And my enemies as well, I fear," Peter replied.

Since beginning his pastoral studies in Rome Peter's inquiring mind had not always sat well with some of his fellow novitiates. Peter had long ago determined to put aside his yearning for "Why?" but as of late he often wondered, "How?" regarding the inner workings of the Church, the history, machinations and politics, the extravagance and wealth of its surroundings.

While others memorized prayers and incantations Peter made timelines, researched sources, questioned accounts and examined the history of the Church and its teachings. He read of its Inquisitions, purges, condemnations, selling of indulgences, pacts with dictators, the triumphs and tragedies of the Church of Rome. Sometimes this was not all for the good.

"I may have noticed a frown or two," Kurt acknowledged. "Have you eaten breakfast yet, Peter? I'm starving?"

Breakfast it was then in the sumptuous dining hall of the Vatican proper. Waiters took orders, chefs prepared the dishes, busboys hovered about as clusters of clergy began their day.

"The gospels themselves do not agree on the events of Christ's life, Kurt. Mark and John for example, differ on…" Peter was beginning an all too familiar tirade when Kurt held up his hands in surrender.

"Peter, please, may I have peace with my eggs? I am aware of the inconsistencies of which you speak. These are ancient, oral traditions, not perfect scripts."

"Ah!" Peter proclaimed, "Now who is being the heretic?"

"Peter, if heresy will grant me eating my eggs while hot, I confess and will make amends later."

"The day Christ died is an important day, is it not?" Peter demanded over his French toast with strawberries. Kurt nodded, knowing this was the beginning, not the end of this topic.

"Yet in his Gospel Mark says that he died the day <u>before</u> Passover, John, writing of the same events says it was the day <u>after</u>. Mark says Christ died in the morning hours, 9AM, John in the afternoon!"

Peter was revving up, just getting started. Diners at other tables noticed. Kurt tried to shush him, always a bad idea.

"And what of the total eclipse of the sun that three apostles wrote of, but no other historical source noticed?! Luke claims it was dark for three hours! This is during times when scholars were obsessed with astronomy. John never mentions any darkness at all! No independent or contemporary accounts exist of this eclipse."

Peter was on a roll. Kurt patiently buttered one.

"Throughout the New Testament the gospels are recognized as firsthand accounts of the life of Jesus Christ, yes? But they contain not just inconsistencies, many of the gospel stories draw almost verbatim from earlier sources, earlier religions."

"Peter, my good friend, can you not focus on the good the Church does rather than the discrepancies of its history?"

"There is much good, yes," Peter replied, "But the myths, the creed, these do not stand up to scrutiny."

"And that is where faith must begin, Peter. I have heard you say so yourself."

"Faith is coming harder for me, Kurt."

"And perhaps stronger when it triumphs." Kurt prayed.

Peter nodded, helping himself to more strawberries. And a hymn hovered in his head.

Amazing grace, how sweet the sound,

That saved a wretch like me,

I once was lost but now I'm found,

Was blind but now I see.***

Peter was beginning to wonder if blindness was essential to the vision of religion.

Lyrical Aspirations:

*Alone Again, Naturally, Gilbert O'Sullivan

**Stand By Me, Ben E. King

***Sounds of Silence, Paul Simon

****God Bless The Child, Billie Holliday

*****Amazing Grace, John Newton

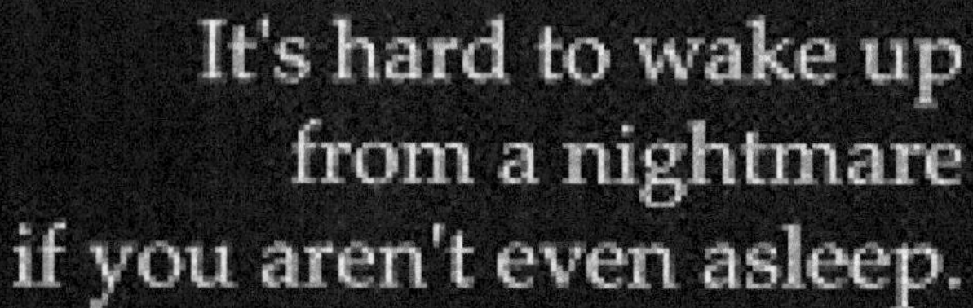

It's hard to wake up
from a nightmare
if you aren't even asleep.
J.S.

Chapter Two

Imaginings

Margaret Mary wakes up screaming. She kicks the blankets from her bed and rolls onto the floor. Again.

Sean hurries into her room, as he has done many nights before. He holds his sobbing daughter in his arms and waits for the terror to pass. Again.

Sean's sister, Margaret Mary's Aunt Rose, turns on the bedroom light and sits down beside Sean and his beloved daughter on the floor. They hold each other silently as the midnight hours creep by. Again.

"You've got to speak of this child, it's the only way you are going to get any help," Rose says softly the next morning as she and Margaret Mary sit over tea in the sunroom of her home.

"I have," Margaret Mary replies, "I've talked and talked and just when I think I'm getting better the dream comes back and I feel just as terrible as I ever have."

"And the medicine is not helping, dear?" Rose reaches across the table and takes Margaret Mary's hand.

"All the pills do is make me feel groggy and tired. I can't study, I can't concentrate. I don't feel bad because I don't feel anything at all."

"Then we will get you better medicine and more help if that is what you are needing." Sean joins them in the sunroom. He kisses his daughter on the head and takes a seat at the table. "This counselor you are seeing, Miss Adams, is she helping?"

"She is," Margaret Mary replies, "I feel better whenever I see her but the dreams won't go away." She sounds helpless, lost, sad and weary. As they, all three, are.

"Whatever it takes child, we shall do. I promise you this will pass. Hear this:

All the words that I gather,
And all the words that I write,
Must spread out their wings untiring,
And never rest in their flight,
Till they come to where your
sad, sad heart is,
And sing to you in the night.

"That's Yeats!" Margaret Mary brightens.

"William Butler his very self, speaking what my heart feels for you," Sean replies.

"We're Irish, lass. We survive. We have the souls of poets," Rose adds as sunshine fills the sunroom.

Margaret Mary's Dream

She is trapped. Kendall sits on her chest, pressing her arms to her side, a wicked, evil smile on his face. He is forcing her legs apart, tearing at her clothes. Grinning happily as she struggles.

"Stop moving!" He commands, slapping her across the face. He raises his hand to hit her again and she freezes, terrified. Kendall begins opening his pants. Then there is more pain, grunting, heaving, climaxing. He rolls off her and laughs as Margaret Mary curls into a fetal ball, crying. "I'll be back," he says standing up, "We'll do this again sometime."

And that is when her screaming starts.

Dave's Dream

I'm back. Phu Bai. The 571st unit area. The sun is shining, a sultry, tropical breeze is blowing. For some reason I'm carrying the small black cardboard suitcase I used to keep my altar boy suit in. Guys wave hello, as they go about their business, Woody, Don, Harry, Steve, Johhny K, Danny H. I'm wearing my very best faded green jungle fatigues, stylishly scruffy boots and fatigue hat with my aircraft crewman's wings embroidered on the front. I'm happy, more than happy. I'm home. I go to my hooch, toss my case on the bed. Everything is the same. Tiny four track tape cartridge player and two speakers on the makeshift desk, Sanyo three speed rotating fan (a treasure) on the corner shelf, extra uniforms, flight helmet, M-16, locked and loaded in the corner. Major Cronin pops his head in the door, smiling, "About time you got back.""

Yeah, it was. I fight hard to stay asleep, not wake up, not rejoin the back in the world day.

And then awake, despairing.

"Look at you, man, chest full of medals, arm full of stripes, you look like you could go ten rounds with a contender."

"I'd take him in three, guaranteed." Teddy laughed and I smiled. We were having coffee at Lefty's. Teddy was now home, honorably discharged after a four-year enlistment. Alive and well. I hoped.

"And the Sun is going to do a story about you?" I asked. The Lowell Sun was the local newspaper. They were going to interview Teddy and wanted pictures, that's why he was wearing his uniform this blustery March morning.

"Yeah, on me and Chris. He re-upped, going to make the Corps his career. He's still out in San Diego but the newspaper guy talked to him by phone so the story will be about the two of us."

"About time the papers write something good. Do you believe all this protest and stuff?"

I mostly tried to ignore the firestorm of anti-war sentiment that was sweeping across the country, but I had to ask Teddy. He's my buddy.

"It's been bad around D.C., blocking traffic, closing buildings. I don't get it, you were there, I was there, I saw a lot of guys doing really good things. We're trying to save that country, aren't we? Doing the right thing?" Teddy looked as confused as he sounded.

"That's what I was trying to do, my unit too. I never saw braver, better people."

"Not what people talk about though," Teddy answered.

"Yeah, like My Lai. What did you think about that?" I asked.

"Can't understand it, the opposite of everything I saw," Teddy answered sadly. "One time I was on this med-cap, two medics, me and three other guys. We went to this villa to give out toothbrushes, soap, give some vaccinations to the kids, you know?"

Med-caps were medical operations where U.S. personnel distributed Red Cross packages, toiletries, medicine and candy to the children and villagers. The men, and sometimes nurses, who went on these missions were all volunteers who understood the danger and chose to go anyway.

"Anyway, we set up in this tiny churchyard. There were maybe twenty kids, their mothers a few papa-sans and the local priest. We were just getting started when two satchel charges went off, killed four little kids and the priest, messed up a bunch of other people. One of my guys was running to help a kid when the second charge went off, blew him in half. These are the guys we're fighting over there; you never hear about stuff like this though."

"At Hue, after Tet, I flew into the Citadel on a med-evac." This was the first time I ever talked about this. "We set down near a graveyard. There were maybe ten dead nuns and a couple of priests in a ditch. They were all kneeling, shot in the back of the head. They had rosary beads in their hands, like they were praying."

Elsewhere in the city there were piles of dead civilians, shot against walls, executed by the VC while they held the place. Over ten thousand according to some barely heard press reports. I never saw much written about that, never heard or read about anything that had to do with the ruthlessness and cruelty of our enemy. Never a word about the bravery, the courage and the sacrifice of our soldiers, men Teddy and I knew well. Only the body count, like some grisly baseball score, day after day.

Teddy and I wouldn't have a lot of conversations like this, but they were there, inside both of us. In my eyes Teddy was a hero, so was his brother, Chris, and so was Woody and Harry and John and Danny and all the guys I served with. You'd never know it by reading the papers or watching the news though. Nobody mentioned it, the press didn't report it, my family didn't ask about it, I didn't tell it. That was never going to work.

"So, you going to work with your Dad down at the garage?" I asked, changing a painful subject.

"Yeah, he's not getting any younger and he's worked hard for years. I couldn't believe how much older he looked when I came home."

"Mine too, I wonder if we look the same to them?"

"You don't look any different to me." Teddy responded.

"I feel a lot different though," Was all I could say in response.

"So, what are you gonna' do now?" Teddy asked.

"Don't know, really. I might give college another try. I've got lots of questions I didn't have three years ago."

"Suck up some of that GI Bill, right?" Teddy laughed.

At the time the Veterans Administration provided a monthly educational benefit to veterans of $175 a month. Ample for that day and age. Also in Massachusetts, tuition at state schools was free to veterans. All of this sounded better than the dryer room at Haartz Auto. Boola-boola, I thought, remembering my earlier misstep at Suffolk University.

"Plus, we get that bonus check," Teddy said.

"What bonus check?" I asked.

"Three hundred bucks, readjustment bonus for veterans. State gives it to ya'"

First, I'd heard of this. I'd been home six months, nobody told me, never thought to ask.

"How do you get it?"

"You've got to go into Boston to sign up for it," Teddy answered. "Didn't you already get yours?"

I hadn't. Teddy and I would take the train to Boston the very next day to correct that and to stumble upon yet another heartbreak in my coming home process.

Kevin, Never Again Butchie's Dream

The polar ice is thick, very, very thick. Nine feet, ten, fifteen feet solid, untold tons and tons of sheet ice, dense ice, pressing down, down, down. Petty Officer Second Class Kevin, not Butchie, Martin feels the pressure crushing his brain, collapsing his lungs, stopping his heart. He tries to fight his way to the surface, smashing himself against the impenetrable ceiling of ice, failing, sinking, dying, feeling nothing but the weight, the pressure, the impossibility of infinite ice.

Kevin, not Butchie, shoots awake in his bunk, covered in sweat, panting. He looks about the squad bay. The other sailors slept on. Butchie tries very hard not to scream. He gasps for breath, chest heaving, trying to forget the dream. And failing.

The USS Skate has been under the Arctic ice for ten days. The mission is to map and gauge the density of the polar cap, to test ultra-secret equipment and to train and familiarize the crew with undersea operations. Kevin, not Butchie, fares well for the first four days. Then the nightmares start, the dread intensifies and within a week his breakdown occurs. Petty Officer Second Class Kevin Martin starts screaming and cannot stop. He is sedated, then confined to the sick bay, heavily tranquilized, semi-comatose, for the remainder of the month-long mission. It would not be surfacing to lessen the mental trauma of one Second Class Petty Officer.

Kevin, never again Butchie, would never be the same again. The tranquilizers took over, the ice in his mind grew thicker, the damage would not be undone.

"Hey! Isn't that...?"

Teddy was pointing across the train platform at Boston's North Station. He and I had just arrived from Lowell on our 'pick up our bonus check' excursion. One platform over a maintenance man pushed a broom along the walkway. He did not see us. We saw him.

"That's Butch!" I proclaimed and Teddy and I hurried over to greet him. As we got closer it was obvious that something was wrong. Very wrong. The guy pushing the broom looked like Butch, was Butch for all we could tell, but something, something critical, was missing. Teddy and I hesitated, watching the guy pushing the broom, push the broom. He didn't look up, he didn't look around, he shuffled along behind the broom like a ghost, lost inside himself. His movements were robotic, almost catatonic. Teddy and I approached.

"Butch! How are you doing?" Teddy asked cheerfully.

The ghost behind the broom barely looked up. He half smiled and kept sweeping. Teddy and I exchanged a worried look and tried again.

"Butch? You okay?"

"Not supposed to talk to people. Supposed to keep sweeping," The ghost that was Kevin, not Butchie, muttered. He didn't look at either of us when he spoke and moved away down the platform. Teddy and I started to follow when another maintenance worker approached.

"Excuse me fella's," he began, "Please don't bother my workers."

"He's our friend," Teddy explained, "We went to school together, trained together. What happened to him?"

"Can't say," the man answered, "he's on a work furlough program from Chelsea Naval Hospital. They send us a couple of guys every week, they work a few hours, gets them off the wards, get a little fresh air."

Kevin, now neither Kevin nor Butchie, shuffled further away, oblivious to our conversation, never looking up from his sweeping. We watched him go, stunned to silence ourselves.

The man, apparently Butchie's supervisor, continued, "All I can tell you guys is your friend gets bussed over here from Chelsea Naval, works four hours, then they pick him up and take him back. We have this program for wounded vets. I don't know how your friend was hurt but we keep a close eye on them and hope being here helps them out."

"His sister, Beth, would know," Teddy remembered as the supervisor walked away.

"You know Butchie's sister?" I asked, quite surprised.

"She wrote to me a couple of times when I was in Nam. We were like pen pals. She's training to be a nurse up at Lowell General Hospital."

"We should definitely talk to her," I agreed.

We should, we did, and this is what she told us two days later.

Beth was wearing her Nurse Whites, a senior in the Nursing program. Teddy and I were seated in the hospital cafeteria. She explained, "Kevin has been home for six and a half months. He received a medical discharge from the Navy, and he's been at Chelsea Naval Hospital all this time. The doctors told me he has an extreme claustrophobic reaction and an anxiety disorder."

Her eyes teared up and her voice became strained as she went on, "I go to see him, and he knows who I am, but he won't look at me and doesn't talk hardly at all. Our mother went with me twice, but she starts crying and that upsets Kevin even more, so she doesn't go anymore."

"What happened to him? How did he get this way?" I asked.

"Kevin was on a submarine. They went on some kind of secret mission and were under the ice cap at the North Pole for a very long time. Kevin had a sort of nervous breakdown and had to be kept in sick bay for weeks. I think they over medicated him to keep him calm and that made him worse."

"Is he going to get better?" Teddy asked.

"They don't say much of anything except that Kevin is in Cognitive Behavioral Therapy and that his recovery will take time and patience."

"Can we go see him?" Teddy asked.

"It would be better if you didn't, not right now anyway. Max went to see him right after he got home, and Kevin didn't react well. Some days he's better than others but most days he's not well."

Teddy and I sat silent. There was nowhere to go with the conversation that wasn't bad. We sat looking at one another until Beth said she had to get back to her duties. She asked us to please stay in touch and she would let us know how Kevin was doing.

Teddy and I left the hospital feeling pretty bad. Within twenty-four hours I would get another call from another hospital and things would get a whole lot worse.

And elsewhere, barely heard, the radio promised,

There must be a light burning brighter,
Somewhere.
Got to be a bird flying higher,
In a sky so blue.

If I can dream of a better land,
Where all my brothers walk hand in hand,
Tell me why? Oh why.
Can't my Dream come true.
Oh Why?

There must be peace and understanding,
Sometime
Strong winds of promise that will blow away.
All the doubt and fear.

If I can dream of a warmer sun,
Where hope keeps shining, on everyone,
Tell me Why? Oh Why?
Won't that Sun appear?
We're lost in a cloud,
With too much rain.
We're trapped in a world
That's troubled with pain.

But as long as a man
Has the strength to dream
He can redeem his soul
And Fly.

Deep in my heart there's a trembling question,
Still, I am sure that the answer will come,
Somehow.

Out there in the dark
There's a beckoning candle,
And while I can talk,
While I can stand,
While I can walk.

Oh, please let my dream
Come True,
Right Now. *

Lyrical Aspiration:

*If I Can Dream, Walter Earl Brown

"Revenge is not always about anger. Sometimes it's about justice."

Chapter Three

Let's Go See Kendall

I see a bad moon rising,
I see trouble on the way,
I see earthquakes and lightinin'
I see hard times on the way.

Don't go out tonight,
Well, it's bound to take your life,
*There's a bad moon on the rise.**

Margaret Mary called me every Sunday night, 7PM, my time. We spoke of our trials and tribulations, her school and my schoolishness, how she was doing, how I was doing and how much we missed each other. This Sunday night the call didn't come. 7:15, no call. 7:30 no call. I called her. Sean answered, troubled, saddened, frightened.

"David, I have unhappy news. Margaret Mary is not here. She is in the hospital. Her suffering is in her mind, a setback I'm afraid, a serious setback. I was about to call you, but I could not find the words."

I felt like ice, head to toe, ice. Silence hung on the phone like thunder until I could croak, "What happened?"

"The boy who attacked her, Kendall, he's here, in Chicago. Margaret Mary saw him."

"What did he do? What happened?" The ice thawed; an inner fire started.

"He did nothing. Apparently, Margaret Mary saw him, but he did not see her. The effect however was grievous. My darling daughter came home a shambles. She would not leave her room, would not eat. Rose and I could hear her crying through the door which she had locked. This went on for two days before we summoned help."

"Help? What help?" I was trying very hard not to yell, not to scream. Why hadn't I been told? What could I do? Where was Kendall now? These were thoughts, not words. I knew in my heart Sean had done all he could, all he thought was best for his daughter as he always had, as he always would.

"She is seeing a counselor, a fine woman named Lois Adams. She came to our home and reasoned with Margaret Mary. They talked for hours in the locked room and when they came out Miss Adams told us my daughter was going to spend a few days in a quiet ward at the hospital. That was four days ago. I hoped she would be home by now, but her suffering continues."

As mine had only begun. Sean went on to tell me that he had not seen his daughter since her hospitalization, that she was sedated and resting and doing much better, but the staff asked that she receive no visitors for at least a few more days. Sean promised to call me as soon as he had any further news and that he would speak to Margaret Mary about my coming to see her. We said goodnight though neither of us would have one. And I had a few phone calls to make.

"Danny H! How are you doing?" This was the first time I had spoken to Danny since we had come home. Anxious as I was to hear his news, I had a bitter agenda to pursue in this conversation.

"I'm walking among the clouds," Danny replied, "How about you?"

"Better lately but not best. How's Brenda?"

"She's the reason I'm in the clouds. Have you heard from anyone else?"

"No, haven't tried really. I'm still trying to get my feet on the ground, you know?"

"You always did overthink things, Dave. It's good to hear your voice though."

Danny and I caught up. He was working in a steel mill making good money but thinking about going to school in the fall. If Brenda wasn't pregnant yet it was not for lack of serious effort on both their parts. I shared my high points with Dan, not that there were that many. Then I got down to business.

"Dan, I've got a favor to ask. Can you find a guy for me? He may be registered over at Loyola."

"If he's got a driver's license, I can find him. My Mom works at the Registry."

"Prescott, Kendall Prescott. Around our age. Please let me know as soon as you find him."

"Serious stuff?"

"Yeah, I'll fill you in when you locate him, all right?"

"Done deal. I'll call you back."

One call down, one more to go. To Teddy, then a visit.

"Just to be clear, we are not going to kill this guy, right?"

Strange as it sounds, this is what Teddy was asking me when I told him of my plan in Lefty's.

"Ted, I can say I want to kill him, but I'm not a murderer and I certainly wouldn't be asking you to be one either. But to be clear I want to put a very serious hurt on this guy."

"You're sure this is the guy who hurt Mags?"

"Raped Margaret Mary, beat Margaret Mary, kidnapped Margaret Mary." I was spitting out the words and as I did murder did not sound like such a bad idea to me once again.

"He walked out of court?"

"Judge said Margaret Mary was asking for it. Apparently, they hate hippies in Colorado."

"Mags isn't a hippie." Teddy sounded surer than I was.

"Whatever she was, or is, she didn't deserve that guy."

"Wait till he gets a load of us." Teddy was in. Danny H knew where Kendall was. We were going to Chicago.

We drove out. Two days on the road. Danny met us in Hammond, Indiana, Kendall's rats nest.

"That's his MG Midget parked over there. He lives on the second floor with some chick named Lucy. She looks about twelve years old, probably older though. I got a good look at her the other day. She's got a black eye."

"Sounds like Kendall's type all right. We'll fix that," I answered.

"He's working at a coffee shop, gets home around 11:30. If he can't park on the street he parks in that little alley. Be a nice place to pick him up."

Danny had done the groundwork. When he called to tell me he found Kendall he asked again what this was about. Initially I told him he was better off not knowing. That wasn't good enough for Danny. I told him who Kendall was and what he had done. Danny said he was in. A snatch is a three-man job.

Teddy and I were staying in a motel nearby. We didn't register under our real names. Tonight, we were going to meet up with Kendall. It was not going to be pleasant.

Danny and I placed six orange traffic cones all along the curb in front of Kendall's apartment. He would pick them up after we snatched Kendall. At 11:36 the MG Midget turned onto the street, cruised the traffic cones and pulled into the alley. Teddy and I were waiting for him.

When Kendall climbed out of the sports car, I stepped out into the full glow of a streetlight. I wanted him to see me clearly. I didn't want him to be alarmed and I didn't want him to see Teddy who was creeping up behind him.

"Excuse me, are you Kendall Prescott?" I asked in as friendly a tone as I could manage. Kendall froze up for a second then relaxed, at least until Teddy smothered his face with a t-shirt full of chloroform and held him until he slumped to the ground. Danny H pulled his white Chevy van into the alley, and we loaded Kendall aboard and we were off to the junkyard.

DeSantis Scrap Metal and Salvage was in a nice quiet industrial area near Kendall's apartment adjacent to some railroad tracks and lots of oil tanks. The yard was securely locked up for the night when we got there. Danny H had the key. We parked in the back behind stacks of rusting automobiles. We unloaded the now groggy Kendall next to a formerly beautiful 1959 Buick Electra 225. Good, solid, heavy car. The driver side front door was swung open. Teddy had pulled the wet t-shirt over Kendall's head after he went down in the alley, and he pulled it off now. Teddy knelt behind Kendall and put him in a very effective United States Marine Corps Arm Bar choke hold. He didn't choke, he just held tight. Kendall woke up. He looked terrified. He was going to look worse.

I knelt in front of Kendall. I wanted him to see me plainly. He couldn't see Teddy behind him or Danny H standing in the shadows.

"Kendall, my name is Dave Ferrier. I'm a friend of Margaret Mary Sullivan. Maybe you've heard of me?"

Kendall didn't answer. His eyes were big as saucers, and he started to struggle a bit in Teddy's grasp. Teddy squeezed his neck and pressed a hard knuckle into the very soft spot just behind Kendall's ear. His eyes got wider, that hurt like hell. Kendall stopped struggling.

"Do you believe in God, Kendall?" I asked trying to suppress my anger. Teddy lightened up a bit on the arm bar. Kendall squeaked a weak and frightened yes. I got right up in Kendall's face. "That's good," I hissed, "because he saved your life tonight, Kendall. I wanted to kill you bad, intended to actually, but you were saved. Wanna' know why?"

Kendall could only nod. He was really scared now. He was probably more scared than I was angry and that was a lot, a whole, whole lot.

"Because I'm better than you, asshole. I don't hurt people for no reason. I don't hurt people who love and trust me. I don't hurt people weaker than me. I don't hurt women and I've never raped anybody. Do you know anybody who's done all that?"

Kendall was too scared to answer now. He was too scared to do much of anything. Teddy had him tight and I was going to hurt Kendall.

"Margaret Mary's in the hospital, Kendall. Did you know that? Probably not, huh? Well, she is, and you are going to be, and I bet she gets out before you do."

Kendall started to struggle again but Teddy applied the knuckle, and a little arm bar pressure and Kendall went limp again. He was staring at me, terrified. I stood up and moved away from him for a moment. I was struggling to keep myself calm, to keep my promise to Teddy, to keep my promise to myself.

I knelt back down in front of Kendall and smacked him across the face, hard, just because I could. It took off a bit of the pressure.

"That guy holding you, Kendall, we're gonna' call him Jesus. You wanna' know why?"

Kendall, I noticed with disgust, had peed his pants. Can't say I blamed him. He didn't answer but I told him anyway.

"We're gonna' call him Jesus because he saved your life tonight too. Just like God. He made me promise I wouldn't kill you. Jesus saves." I was back in Kendall's face, spitting my words.

"There's another guy here too, see him over there in the shadows?"

Teddy let Kendall turn his head a bit, just a bit. From the gloom Danny H waved at Kendall. Kendall whimpered.

"We're gonna' call that guy Sherlock, Kendall. Like Sherlock Holmes. Wanna' know why?" I was pretty sure Kendall wanted to know why.

"Because he can find you Kendall. Just like we did tonight. No matter where you go, Sherlock can find you. And when we are done here tonight you are going somewhere Kendall, somewhere far away. Do you understand me?"

Kendall was nodding his head as hard and as fast as Teddy would let him. That wasn't good enough. I smacked Kendall again. Teddy gave me a dirty look. I was dragging this out too long. Time to get down to business.

"You have one week to get out of town, asshole. Town being anywhere around here, Indiana, Illinois, call it the Midwest. You might try California, lots of scumbags, like you, out there. But be gone Kendall, one week. Sherlock is going to be checking, and one more thing, you're leaving Lucy behind. Tell her you've had a change of heart, tell her any damn thing you want, but you go, she stays. I find out different, I come back, without Jesus."

Kendall nodded some more. He looked like he meant it. "Which hand was it Kendall? The hand you used to beat Margaret Mary with I mean. Are you a dukey? A southpaw?"

I grabbed Kendall's right hand by the wrist and thumb. Took a good hold and twisted a bit. A painful bit. He squirmed but couldn't make much of a sound.

"This it Kendall? This the hand you used?" He knew it was, I knew it was. I pressed his right hand into the door hole of the Buick Electra and slammed it shut as hard as I could. There was a metallic squeal, a shriek and Kendall passed out. The Buick door was closed all the way. Kendall's hand, right up to the wrist was jammed inside. Fuck him.

Teddy let go of Kendall and he slumped to the ground. I took a warm can of beer, shook it up, and sprayed it all over Kendall, most of it in his face. He woke up. I moved in close.

"If you think that fucking hurts now, wait till you open the door, asshole." I felt bad about how good it felt to say those words. Kendall's mouth was opening and closing like a fish on a dock. He was going to slip into shock. I sprayed him with another beer.

"Listen to me assshole," I smacked him a little, "when you go to the emergency room to explain how you accidently slammed a car door on your hand, if my name comes up, if my fucking initials come up, Sherlock will find you, Jesus won't save you and I will fucking kill you. You got that?"

Kendall couldn't speak, but he nodded his head.

"Here," I said, "drink this." I passed him a half pint of cheap vodka. "Drink it all, we want your blood/alcohol levels to be nice and high when you get to the hospital. It might even help with the pain."

Kendall opened his mouth. I poured the vodka in, all of it. What he didn't spit out or choke on he swallowed. I stood up, yanked open the car door. Kendall screamed and fell over in the dirt. You don't want to know what his hand looked like. We left. Fuck him.

The ride home was quiet. Teddy and I were mulling over what we had done. I wasn't sorry, not one bit. Margaret Mary, the one person on the planet I knew who deserved no heartache, no pain, was in a hospital, sedated for her anguish. The Courts, the Law did nothing about it. We did. Fuck him. Almost.

"Thanks for this Ted," I began, "I'm glad we didn't kill the guy."

We were turning onto the Massachusetts Turnpike after sixteen hours of straight driving. Teddy and I were registered at the Sea Latch Motel in York Beach with Donna Delancey and Beth Martin. They were being highly visible in York. We weren't. Alibi.

"We're not murderers, Dave. That guy got what he deserved. You did seem to enjoy it a little too much though." Teddy wasn't kidding and he sounded concerned. Truth was, I did enjoy it. Not the pain part, the vengeance. I couldn't imagine any circumstances where I would have enjoyed meeting Kendall even if he hadn't hurt Margaret Mary, but I was concerned, and newly aware, that there was a part of me I'd have to monitor very closely. When that door slammed on Kendall's hand, I smiled. Smiled.

"I didn't think that car door was going to close all the way," Teddy said, almost matter of factually.

"Clicked shut. Big block Buick, they don't make 'em like that anymore. You should have seen his hand when I opened the door. Strawberry jam."

Teddy squirmed behind the wheel. "Thanks, I don't need the details. Guy deserved it though. Think he'll talk?"

"No, straight pussy. He'll get patched up and leave. Danny will make sure."

Teddy grunted, I smiled (again) and we were quiet the rest of the ride to York Beach as the radio whispered…

Caught between the longing for love

And the struggle for the legal tender,

When the siren's sing,

And the church bells ring,

And the junkman bangs on his fender,

**Where the veteran dreams of the fight,
Fast asleep at the traffic light,
And the children solemnly wait
for the ice cream vendor...**

Say a prayer for The Pretender.**

Hidden secrets, hidden sickness.

Lyrical Aspirations:

*Bad Moon Rising, John Fogerty

**The Pretender, Jackson Browne

Chapter Four

Hospitals

Not Butchie, Not Kevin, awoke before the morning sunrise in the psychiatric ward of Chelsea Naval Hospital. The other patients, five of them, sleep on. He loves these pre-dawn hours, before staff and sleepers stir and he could lay quiet and perfectly still in his bed. Awake but not conscious, alert but not aroused, he cherishes the feel of the crisp, clean sheets which cover him, the silvery moonlight that filters through the high windows and the silence that whispers through the room. It is safe, it is nice.

Soon a kindly nurse will arrive, tell him it is time to shower and dress, tell him what to dress in and where to go to eat his breakfast. That is nice too. Oatmeal he vaguely prefers and toast with lots of butter. That will all be later, as far ahead as he ever allows himself to think. Now he has silence as he lies perfectly still, perfectly safe. He remains frozen in place, thinking of nothing until morning's daylight slowly diminishes the darkness. It is nice. It is safe.

"Promise, promise, promise, you'll come back and see me!" Ten-year-old Anna Koontz would not let go of Margaret Mary, whom she clings to with both love and desperation.

"I will, I promise, real soon." Margaret Mary kneels to come face to face with Anna. "I'll come back with the biggest chocolate chip cookie you have ever seen, and we will eat it together right over there at your favorite table."

Margaret Mary gently unwraps the child's arms from around her legs. The cast from Anna's broken arm, a result of her father's drunken rage, has recently been removed. The arm looks pale white and puffy. Anna is sobbing, softly.

"Come along dear," the ward nurse says, taking Anna by the hand. "It's time for Margaret Mary to go home, just like you will very soon."

"No! No! No!" the child shrieks, "I don't want to go home, not ever!" She pulls away from the nurse and tries even more desperately to hold on to Margaret Mary. Margaret Mary is face to face with the child, "It's going to be alright, Anna, you are safe here and I will come to see you, promise, promise, promise."

Margaret Mary has been on the trauma ward for one week. Little Anna was there when she arrived, bruised, battered, Kendalized. They recovered together, at least partially, and today Margaret Mary is deemed well enough to go home. Anna has no home to go to.

"What will happen to her?" Margaret Mary asks when they are clear of the ward.

"Her mother's sister is coming from Cleveland to care for her. Her father is going to be in jail for a long time."

"And her mother is dead?"

"Two years. Anna will be fine, the sister has been backgrounded, she's married, stable, and willing to take Anna in."

"When?"

"This weekend, three days."

"I'll be back, with the cookie."

Margaret Mary waves goodbye to Anna through the thick glass window. The child has not taken her eyes off Margaret Mary since they had been separated.

Margaret Mary turns to the lobby where Sean and Aunt Rose await. She walks with a replenished sense of confidence and determination. Her night terrors temporarily banished; her fears of Kendall vindicated. What afflicted her now in hand. Practically.

"We must talk daughter," Sean says gently when they leave the hospital. They are in a comfortable booth in Gilligan's, an Irish Pub which serves Margaret Mary's very favorite dish of shepherd's pie, which has been ordered and is on the way.

"The day before yesterday we received a visit from a police inspector by the name of Sanchez. He is looking into an incident where a young man showed up in an emergency room with a smashed hand, received treatment and left before the police arrived. He is traced through his license plates to an address in Hammond. A girl who lived there said he came home, severely frightened and left town the very next day. No forwarding address just vanished. The young man's name is Prescott, Kendall Prescott. Inspector Sanchez wanted to know if we knew anything about it."

Margaret Mary is speechless with fear at first, then curious. "Why would they be asking you about this?"

"Just what I said!" Aunt Rose interjects. "Gave him a piece of my mind I did. I told him we were God fearing people who had no truck with such business and how dare he assume we might."

Sean smiles, remembering Rose's tirade. "Sanchez held his ground though. Said he checked the records and found the Colorado court case. Mr. Prescott has no criminal record, but that case will follow him around for some time. The inspector did some digging and came up with our address. Motive and opportunity he said."

"And didn't I throw him right out in the street!" Rose exclaims.

"Throw, you did not, but the good detective took his leave shortly thereafter. Case closed he said and likely good riddance. People like young Mr. Prescott are likely to make a host of enemies over their lives. Likely we have seen the last of him."

And three steaming hot shepherd's pies arrive as Margaret Mary contemplates the disappearance of Kendall Prescott. With a sigh of relief and a whisper of suspicion she digs into her dinner.

"Buongiorno Padre, come stai oggi?"

"Io sto bene, fratello, e tu?"

Peter answers his early morning visitor. Two months now at the Vatican College and he is becoming as comfortable in Italian as he is in Latin. Peter, now Almost Father Rayburn, is among the rising stars of the Church's latest crop of academics. Quick, insightful, studious and devoted, he rose to the top of his class and set the standard for his classmates. This makes him both popular and disliked. Kind of like the religion he espouses.

"Sono gia arrivati journali Americana?" Even though he had been in Rome almost a year Peter still needs his daily dose of sports updates on the Red Sox, Celtics, Bruins and Patriots. For this he has an overseas subscription to the Boston Globe, delivered one day behind the times, every morning. The staffer proudly waves the newspaper which Peter takes with a smile and gratitude. Liturgy aside, dogma dismissed, Peter turns to the sports page and for the next half hour he will not be Almost Father Rayburn, he will be just another New England sports fanatic keeping pace with the local teams.

"Good morning, Peter, what's the latest from Fenway?"

"Yankees 6, Sox 2, another rung on the ladder to the cellar."

Monsignor Lawrence Specio is Peter's mentor at the Vatican. They have breakfast every morning before the classwork begins. Over the months they have become friends, though the cleric often worries about Peter's occasional maverick thinking.

"I read your paper on civil prosecution of the clergy, Peter. Not exactly in line with the current philosophy."

"The greatest of faults is to be conscious of none," Peter responds in quote.

"Thomas Carlye, an oftimes problematic Scot," Monsignor Specio answers.

"Not unlike myself," Peter grins. Peter sometimes ranges far afield from the established curriculum, it is true, but he has earned the respect of the faculty through his dedication and diligence.

Peter meanwhile is discovering that the Catholic Church is an astoundingly entitled and immune entity, subject to very little civil or criminal oversight outside of its own inner jurisdictions. Even without an intense scrutiny of its finances Peter has come to realize the church is the wealthiest single enterprise on the planet, its worth running into the Billions of dollars, pesos, liras and pounds. The Catholic Church, he discovered, is the largest single landowner in the United States, all properties completely untaxable. Clerics are seldom, if ever, prosecuted for civil or even felonious infractions. The Church's code of silence and temporal immunity is astounding. To Peter it is becoming ominous.

Peter had come under the eye of a newly assigned Archbishop, Paul Marcincus, Secretary to the mysterious Vatican Bank, a position of great power and influence. Archbishop Marcincus would occasionally drop by and discuss the sad state of affairs of the Red Sox and Chicago Cubs. Peter also came to realize that Archbishop Marcincus has very little background in banking but a very streetwise awareness of the power and influence of his position. Archbishop Marcincus often joked, "You can't run a church on Hail Mary's."

As Peter contemplated the extravagance and luxury of his surroundings, he began to wonder why it is necessary for the church to stockpile Billions of dollars in cash and assets while preaching charity for the poor and disadvantaged.

Finance, however, is not Peter's focus at this point. He has immersed himself in the legalities, immunities and privileges of the Church, attempting to understand how these freedoms benefited the congregation rather than the clergy.

So far, he has no legitimate answers.

"David, 7:30, you getting up?" My Father asked as he prepared for work.

I wake up in my childhood bed, my Glenmere Street safe haven, the sanctuary of my childhood, my teenage Bat Cave, my post-military holding cell. Though I feel out of place outside and everywhere else, here I am shielded. Here I am still a child, here I would remain a child. Serenity is becoming my antagonist. I was never going to be an adult living in my parent's home, sleeping in my childhood bed. It is time to leave the nest.

More out of curiosity than intent I applied to the University of Massachusetts several weeks ago. Now I have a letter of acceptance for the fall term. UMass Amherst would admit me as first semester freshman, my blundering through Suffolk University no use at all. Amherst is in the western part of the state, an hour and a half drive from Lowell. Not a commute, a destination. Time to leave the nest.

I had not been back to work, anywhere, since I left Haartz Auto. My Dad understood. My Mother withheld judgment. I procrastinated. Until now.

I swung out of bed and stopped at the bathroom door to watch my Dad shave. Electric razor, like a swarm of bees over the bathroom sink. I'd heard it all my life. I waited until the buzzing stopped.

"I got accepted at UMass, Dad. Out in Amherst." I announced.

"That's good son, if you need any help with money, you know it's there, right?"

"It's not that Dad, I'll have the GI Bill dough and I'll find some kind of work. But I am going to have to live out there." I paused, he paused and let that sink in. "I've only lived two places in my life Dad, at home here and in the Army. It feels strange going looking for another place to live."

My Dad was done shaving now. He turned to face me. "This will always be your home, son. Wherever you go, whenever you need it. Don't forget that."

I wouldn't, never did. But I was going anyway.

"Have you talked to your mother about this?"

"She's still barely speaking to me, Dad. Do you think she's going to be madder?"

"Son, I gave up trying to guess how your mother is going to feel years ago. She does love you; you know that don't you?"

I did. Most of the time.

"I'll talk to her today, Dad. Thanks."

"Thanks for what?" He said, tapping me upside my head as he left the bathroom.

Thanks for everything I replied, just not out loud. Dad left for work. I started looking for another place to live.

"I can't just fix one brake Mrs. Levinson."

Teddy didn't know whether to laugh or cry as he spoke to one of his father's oldest customers at the garage.

"But I can't pay to have them both fixed right now," the sweet old lady pleaded, "My social check doesn't come until next week."

"Don't worry about it, Mrs. Levinson," Teddy's father interrupted, "You can pay next week when your check comes in. Your car will be ready tomorrow morning." Mrs. Levinson left happily, and Teddy sat down to talk with his father in the cluttered and chaotic garage office. The calendar on the wall behind the desk was three years old. Ragged phone books were stacked on the floor. Bills, invoices, newspapers and other assorted paperwork were scattered about. Last week Teddy found a personal check made out to the garage for twenty-five dollars on the floor, under the desk. It was six months old.

"Dad, I checked her account. She still owes you for two tires and a muffler."

"She's good for it Theodorus. In time she will pay."

"Dad, that's what you say about half the accounts in the repair book. Most of the people who come in here owe you money. You can't run a business this way."

"So, what way should I run it?"

"By making a profit, maybe?" Teddy answered, respectfully.

"We make a profit. We eat."

"Dad, you're putting in sixty, sometimes seventy hours a week. You eat here, sometimes you sleep here. This is not good for you."

"And what is good? Work is good, feeding my family is good."

"Dad, Connie and I can feed ourselves. You need to start taking it a little easier."

"That is why you are here, for to help."

"I know Dad, but I've got to talk to you about that. Jimmy McGuire wants to sponsor me for the Lowell Police Department."

Jimmy McGuire was the local beat cop. He had known Teddy since David and Teddy played Little League baseball. Jimmy was a former Marine as well and knew of Teddy's military history. He believed Teddy would be a fine policeman. He was right.

Teddy felt a pang of guilt as he saw the look of concern and uncertainty cross his father's face. For the first time he saw his father as an old man, uncertain of his future, worried.

"What is this 'sponsor'?" He demanded.

"He wants to recommend me to be a police officer, Dad. That's what I want too."

Unexpectedly his father smiled and clasped his hands together on his desktop. "I must tell you something I have not spoken of before." Teddy was surprised. There were lots of things he and his father had not spoken of before.

"Back in old country, in Greece, I was police officer, in my village, Elefsina. I love my village; I love my job. I help people, make them safe. When the war started, the fascists came, Il Duce. They invade our country, we fight them, throw them back into the sea."

Then he shook his head sadly, "Then the Nazi come, monsters. They drop from the sky, thousands. We fight them too. There is much killing. Much. We fight them until we became monsters too."

Nick Gianoulus, garage mechanic, known as the angriest man in Lowell, now has tears in his eyes. "When the Nazis are gone, the communistas came. There is more fighting, more monsters. I send away your mother, Connie too, she is little girl. I send them to America, to my brother who owns this garage. He takes care of them, here, where there are no monsters."

Teddy could not hide his surprise. He waited patiently for his father to continue.

"I love my country, but I too leave, leave my job as policeman and come here. No more police officer for me. When you go to the war to fight the communistas I am very proud, for your brother as well. Now for you to become a policeman I will be very proud also."

Nick stood up and opened his arms to his son. Teddy, also with tears in his eyes, hugs his father. It is the first time he can recall doing so.

Beth Martin sits by her brother's hospital bed. Not Butchie, not Kevin would not look at her. He stares straight ahead, his mind as blank as he could make it. Not nice.

"Kevin, look at me. I'm your sister, Kevin, look at me!" He did not move. Beth did. She rises and stomps to the foot of his bed, into his line of not sight. "You are breaking the hearts of people who love you! My heart, Mom's heart, our whole family's heart. Won't you say something?"

Beth came to the hospital every week, had ever since her brother came home. She came alone, she came with her mother, lately Dave and Teddy had come, twice. Not Butchie, Not Kevin, would not acknowledge them, retreating into himself. He could think only of the miles and tons and layers of ice that smothered him, encased his mind and crushed his spirit. His efforts to not think of the ice led him to not think at all, to shelter in silence, to wait, perhaps until the ice melted.

"He's not getting better, is he?" Beth asks the ward nurse, Karen Lamiere.

"No, he isn't. He's stopped going on work release, barely touches his food, refuses to stand or walk. He will only use a wheelchair now."

Karen and Beth watch him from the nurse's station. Comatose, Beth begins to cry. Nurse Karen suggests, "There is one thing some of the doctors want to try."

"The electric shock?" Beth asks.

"Yes, you should talk to Dr. Neiman. He's convinced it may help Kevin."

"But there are risks," Beth replied.

"He's falling into a stupor, Beth. That has risks as well."

Which led to a last chance conference with Dr. Neiman.

"The treatment I would recommend would be low doses of electrical current under general anesthesia, three times a week for a period of three to four weeks, less if improvements are evident earlier." Dr. Neiman spoke with confidence and clarity. Beth, along with her mother, Gloria, listen carefully, cautiously.

"How long would each treatment last?" Beth asks.

"No more than five to ten minutes. Ten initially, then tapering off. Kevin will be under full anesthesia throughout. He should feel no physical discomfort, no convulsions, no tremors."

"Doctor, will this save my son?" Gloria's response is not a question, it's a prayer.

"I believe it is the best chance we have, Mrs. Martin."

Beth and Gloria look at each other, nod, and Beth says, "Then let's do it."

The following day the shock treatments began. Beth and her mother both attended morning Mass, offering prayers for their lost brother and son.

Whoa, the Games People Play now,
Every night and every day now,
Never meanin' what they say now,
Never sayin' what they mean.
While they while away the hours
In their ivory towers,
Till they're covered up with flowers
In the back of a black limousine.*

The cookie was the size of a car's steering wheel. Wrapped in foil with a red ribbon on top. Margaret Mary sat across from Anna in the hospital dayroom.

"We don't have to eat it all at once," Margaret Mary suggested with a smile.

Anna was speechless, almost. "How did you make this?" She asked in wonderment.

"In a pizza pan, with lots of chocolate chips. Want to try a piece?"

So, they sat next to one another, breaking off cookie chunks between gulps of ice-cold milk.

"My Auntie is coming to pick me up today," Anna announced sadly.

"Your Aunt is here; I spoke to her in the lobby. She seems very nice."

"She is," Anna admitted, "She's not my mother though."

"She is not, but she loves you very much and is going to take good care of you."

"Why can't you take good care of me?" Anna threw her arms around Margaret Mary and held on tight, very tight, as Margaret Mary's heart broke in two.

"You know," Margaret Mary began, "My mother is dead too. I live with my Aunt Rose, and she takes very good care of me. I wouldn't know how to take care of you the way she does for me and the way your Aunt Eileen will take care of you."

"Will you come to see me?" Anna begged.

"Of course, I will, when I can. I've got to finish school and finish getting better myself. We can talk on the phone, and I promise we can visit."

Slowly Anna released her hug and sat up, eyes full of tears but with a smile.

"I'll save some cookie for you," She said.

And Margaret Mary's heart broke once again as a song whispered in her head:

When you're down and troubled,
And you need some loving care,
And nothing, nothing is going right,
Close your eyes and think of me,

And soon I will be there,
To brighten up your darkest night.

You just call out my name,
And you know wherever I am,
I'll come running, to see you again.

Winter, spring, summer or fall,
All you have to do is call,
And I'll be there,
You've got a friend. **

If only.

Lyrical Aspirations:

*Games People Play, Joe South

**You've Got A Friend, Carole King

Chapter Five

Confessions

"I would like to speak to Detective Inspector Sanchez please," Margaret Mary announced at the Hammond, Indiana police stationhouse. The desk sergeant checked his on-duty roster and picked up a phone, mumbled something or other and told Margaret Mary she could find Detective Sanchez in the squad room. He indicated a door and Margaret Mary found Detective Sanchez waiting for her on the other side.

"How can I help you, Miss?" He said politely.

"I am here to ask about Kendall Prescott."

Detective Sanchez motioned her to a chair by his desk.

"May I ask what it is you want to know, and why?"

"Kendall Prescott assaulted me, raped me and held me prisoner for over three months. He was tried for those crimes and found not guilty. He laughed at me when he walked out of the courtroom." Margaret Mary's voice resounded with anger, disappointment and determination."

"You said he was found not guilty?"

"Colorado, which is where this happened, does not like hippies." Margaret Mary's voice now rang with sadness.

"You didn't happen to be told this by a Colorado State Trooper named Girard, were you?"

"How do you know that?" Margaret Mary could not disguise her surprise.

"Because I spoke with him last week. He told me this Prescott character was all bad. Said he should be in prison."

"But he isn't," Margaret Mary replied, "That's why I'm here."

'He's not in prison, Miss, but he's not in Indiana either. I paid a call at his last known address, spoke with a slightly battered young lady named Lucy, who told me Prescott came home from the hospital, packed his bags and took off. She said he was scared, very scared, but didn't tell her anything except she wasn't going with him."

"Going with him where?" Margret Mary wanted to know.

"Hard to say, I ran the plate on his car, and he got a speeding ticket outside Flagstaff, Arizona a couple of days after he took off."

"Do you have any idea what happened to him? Who did it?"

"As far as what happened to him, Not Enough, from what I'm told. Prescott was a low-level drug dealer, marijuana and downers mostly, and he likes to beat up women. People in that line of work generally make enemies on both sides of the law."

"Was he hurt badly?"

"Hospital report says his right hand was smashed up pretty bad. He may not lose it, but he won't be able to use it much either."

"Good!" Margaret Mary blurted out, then corrected herself, "I'm sorry, I shouldn't have said that."

"No worries," Detective Sanchez smiled, "Apparently someone in the state of Indiana doesn't like rapists. My advice, miss, is to let this go. If you are ever bothered by this guy again, if you even think you are, here is my card, call me."

Margaret Mary left the police station feeling better than she had in weeks, months, a long, long time. She couldn't help but wonder who had gotten to Kendall and was mildly alarmed at how glad she was that someone did. Then she recalled a message shared with her by Lois Adams, her life saving counselor, "Do not let this man destroy your future. His harm to you is in the past. Bad things have a way of catching up with bad people."

Margaret Mary knew this, hoped for this, however she knew she would never forget and never forgive Kendall Prescott.

"You're gonna be a cop!"

Teddy made the announcement while we shared Lefty's cup of coffee.

"I start the Academy next month. Twelve weeks," Teddy answered, grinning.

"Good for you! You are going to make a fine policeman; I just know it."

"Thanks," Teddy replied, "How about you? What are you going to do?"

I didn't know how to say it out loud because I was still in mid-drift, no plans, no ideas, no clues. Except one.

"I thought maybe I'd give college another try. UMass accepted me for the fall."

"Where?" Teddy asked.

"Out at Amherst, it's supposed to be nice out there."

"You should talk to this guy who comes in the garage, Bob Baker. He's in Grad school out there. He's a vet, Marine Corps, he was a lieutenant in Nam."

"An officer? What'd he do over there?"

"Trigger puller. He's uh, a little tightly wrapped, but he seems like a pretty good guy."

"I'd like to talk to him. Can you set it up?"

"Can do, will do."

The next day Teddy and I entered the dark and dusty Centerville Tap, a cross-town, townie bar not generally visited by people not living in Centerville. We were greeted by several semi-hostile stares when we came in. Looking around, this place was like the Whipple, only darker and dustier. It was not yet noon and several gloomy locals were glued to their bar stools getting started on another drunken day. I didn't know which one of these mutts was Bob Baker, but I hoped it wasn't the guy with the red bandana headband, jungle fatigue shirt and pants, wearing combat boots and sunglasses perched at the far end of the bar. Of course, it was.

"Semper Fi, Teddy! Gary, three ponies, three Jack backs. We'll be in my office," He shouted to the bartender when he spotted us. Headband and sunglasses headed for the Tap's back room. We followed him to a booth next to a tired looking, fuzzy sounding juke box moaning an Elvis song. We slid into the booth as our drinks arrived.

"Call me LT, got used to it in Nam. What should I call you?"

"Dave will do just fine, got used to it in Nam."

"Teddy says you were in Dustoff," LT said. I nodded; he raised his glass. "Bravo, didn't get any better than Dustoff."

"Or tougher than the Corps," I countered. We clinked glasses. Teddy and I sipped our beers. LT drained his then threw back the shot of Jack Daniels.

"Breakfast of Champions," he announced, considering our full glasses.

"Little early for me," I said, it was still an hour till noon.

"Designated driver," Ted added.

Shrugging his jungle fatigue clad shoulders, LT picked up both our Jack Daniels shots, poured them into his empty beer glass then topped it off with a half pour from each of our beers. Then he drained that glass as well.

"You are both now officially liable for any mayhem which may result from my rapidly developing inebriation." LT grinned like a wolf, sat back and smiled, "So, you're looking at Zoo Mass for the fall?"

"Yeah," I replied, "think so. I'm looking for a place to live out there."

"You have come to the right place my friend. I've got a three-bedroom apartment in Squire Village, just off campus. One of my roommates graduates this semester. I'll have an empty room. Do you know Marty McMahon?"

I didn't.

"He lives with me too. Junior year. He's from here, not a vet though. Nice kid."

"How much?" I asked.

"Hundred bucks a month. Utilities included. You'll have your own bedroom, but you have to bring you own furniture."

"Like what?"

"You know, bed, dresser, shotgun, semi-automatic rifle, pistol, ammo, the essentials." LT is not smiling as he says this.

"I may be a little short on the firepower."

"No problem, as long as you're not short on the hundred bucks."

"So, what is it like out there?" I asked.

"Lots of hippies, entitled little shits running around with mommie and daddie's checkbook, some belligerent frat boys who look really surprised when you knock them on their ass, the usual."

"How about the school?" I figured I ought to be at least half interested.

"Mostly you've got to chart your own course. Some good professors, some assholes. The usual."

I was beginning to get a picture of LT's world view. The usual.

"You should come out this weekend, check the place out. You can stay at my place. The campus is pretty empty during the summer, but we get stuck with a twelve-month lease on the apartment, so I take a course or two in the summer. Marty goes home. He'll be back after Labor Day."

So, we made a plan. I'd drive out to Amherst that weekend and stay at Squire Village. LT would show me around. What could go wrong?

The jukebox sighed on, the fresh lyrics warning…

When I look over my shoulder,

What do you think I see?

Some other cat looking over

His shoulder at me.

And he's strange, sure is strange
He's very strange to me...
Must be the season of the witch.*

I should have listened to the jukebox.

 "Kevin, look at me! I know you can see me. Look at me!" Beth insisted from the foot of her brother's hospital bed. Not Kevin, not Butchie, stirred beneath his sheets, tried to focus on the voice outside his head.

With tremendous effort he whispered, "Beth?"

Who ran to throw her arms around her brother. He remained still, but whispered, "C-c-cold, so cold."

"Karen! Karen! I need a blanket! He's talking, he said something!" Beth shouted across the ward.

Head nurse Karen Lamiere looked up from her desk and hurried onto the ward, carrying a folded wool blanket. She helped Beth spread the warmth over Kevin, who watched them carefully, but watched them after all.

"Kevin, this is Karen your nurse. She has been taking care of you." Beth said.

Now Kevin, almost Butchie looked over at Karen. In a tiny, shaky voice he said, "Thank you."

Karen tucked the blanket under Kevin's chin and smiled. "Welcome back, sailor. You lie still for a moment I need to talk to your sister, and we'll be right back."

Beth reluctantly left her brother's bedside and followed Karen back to the nurse's station.

"I've got to call Dr. Neiman; he left word that he was to be called if Kevin showed any signs of improvement."

Which she did and within minutes Dr. Neiman arrived.

"He recognized his sister and thanked me. His eye contact was good. He said he was cold," Karen reported.

"Excellent, let's go have a word with the young man." Dr. Neiman led Karen and Beth from the nurse's station.

After a brief physical exam Dr. Neiman asked, "How are you feeling sailor? Are you ready to get out of that bed?"

Almost Kevin, almost Butchie, didn't move. His eyes widened with fear. He croaked, "Beth?"

"Here, Kevin," she said as she took his hand, now free from under the blanket.

"Is everybody mad at me?" He whispered.

"Nobody's mad at you, we're all glad you're feeling better." Beth leaned in and hugged her brother, hard. He started to cry.

"I messed up, I didn't do my duty," He moaned.

"You were injured sailor. Not your fault. You didn't let anyone down. It's going to be alright." Dr. Nieman spoke once again with authority and compassion. Kevin listened and understood. Mostly. "Rest now, try to get some sleep. I expect to see you in my office tomorrow afternoon."

"I can't wait to tell Ma," Beth said, "She'll be so happy."

"She's not mad at me?"

Beth kissed her brother on the cheek and told him to get some sleep as well. She promised to be there when he woke up.

"I'm going to stop the electric stimulation treatments. He's had six sessions, and the improvement is evident. Now we must see if he can move forward on his own." Dr. Neiman put Kevin's file aside and said, "I need you to spend some time with him, your mother as well, if he has a few close friends, they could visit also. Short visits, but essential to his recovery."

Beth understood and planned to call Teddy and David as soon as she got home. With a last look in at her sleeping brother she left the ward and returned to Lowell with the good news.

Squire Village was a nice enough place, all student, off-campus housing in the adjoining town of Sunderland. Rural, but close enough to campus to make commuting easy. I spent Friday night getting to know LT. He was born and raised in

Philadelphia, had a bachelor's degree from Temple University and enlisted in the Corps one month after his graduation. He told me all this as he was sprawled on his living room sofa, an overstuffed purple affair rescued from some attic. He sipped from a bottle of Jack Daniels Old Number 7, Tennessee Sour Mash Whiskey as he spoke.

"My Father was a Marine, retired a full bird colonel. He was wounded on Saipan, got a Silver Star. My grandfather was with the Fourth Marine Brigade at Belleau Wood. He was a Major. He died there."

I remained silent. LT wasn't done.

"I didn't really have much choice about what I was going to do when I graduated from Temple. My Monsignor drove me to the recruiter, proud as a peacock. Three weeks later I was at Parris Island, then OCS, then Nam."

"How long you been back?" I asked.

"'Bout a year and a half, right outa' Khe Sanh."

"You were at Khe Sanh?"

"Every day, every night."

"I was up there too. Dustoff."
"Hard Days's Night," he quoted, then went on, "You know, I saw my men getting blown up, sniped, squashed, killed, and there wasn't a damn thing I could do about it. We were surrounded, hemmed in, trapped. All my training, all my caring did no good. Just like the whole damn war."

He then took a long pull from his bottle and passed out. The usual.

Saturday morning LT took me around the campus, showed me the Student Union, the Gym, Admin, the Newman Center and finally The Blue Wall, the on-campus bar where he had another "office."

"You'll like it here," LT suggested as we settled into the Blue Wall. The room was very Joe College, lots of pendants and jock gear on the walls, a small stage for a small band, cute waitresses, two of them.

"What are you studying here LT?" I asked.

"Marine biology," he replied, "Farming the oceans, Dave, the wave of the future. How about you? What are you planning on majoring in?"

"Don't know yet, I signed up for a bunch of general interest courses, Pscyh 101, History, couple of English classes."

"Bunnies," he laughed, "start off slow, pace yourself. The path will emerge for the righteous." He then drained his beer and motioned for two more. While getting half gassed I learned that LT was a very bright guy. He had a bachelor's degree in biology from Temple University, a Cum Laude transcript and a Silver Star and Purple Heart from Nam.

"You kill anybody over there?" He asked, four beers later. "Don't think so, shot at a bunch of them though." This was not a conversation that even started until after the fourth or fifth beer.

"I did, few too many I think," LT said, his voice tinged with sadness. "My job, you know? Platoon commander, search and destroy, sweep and weep, same places, same villages, over and over. Never saw much sense to it."

"Teddy told me you got a Silver Star." I was now half in the bag myself or I never would have asked about that.

"I did," he moaned, "Mostly because I was the guy out front, you know? I never forgot about the guys behind me though. Never enough medals to go around."

"Can I get you guys another round?" Cute waitress number one was at our table. Big smile, big chest, tight t-shirt. Of course, we were having another round. And then another. By the time we left the Blue Wall it was Saturday evening, not afternoon, and we were both more than a little drunk.

"Do you remember where we parked the car?" I asked when the night air hit me.

"We came here in a car?" LT sounded genuinely surprised. It was shaping up to be a long night. Two police cruisers later we were deposited at LT's apartment in Sunderland. First the Campus Police picked us up when LT insisted, we sing the national anthem outside the library. The Campus Police turned us over to the Sunderland police who drove us home while we continued singing the national anthem. Cops were a lot more tolerant in those days.

The next morning, over very strong coffee, LT and I made a handshake deal. I was college bound, had a place to live and another lunatic was about to enter my life.

Peter Rayburn sat penitent in Monsignor Specio's office. As Peter's mentor, his supervisor of sorts in matters of ordination, Monsignor Specio had become aware of Peter's research, his inquiries into Church history and his unrelenting questioning of Church dogma. It was time for a reckoning, hopefully a positive one.

"Peter, it is time we had a talk about your commitment to this vocation." Monsignor Specio sounded grim, with a considerable amount of tolerance.

"I'm here, I'm studying, I'm trying, trying very hard," Peter responded.

"Yes Peter, I see that. But trying very hard at what? Your paper on clerical immunity caused quite a stir, your present research on the actions of the clergy in post-World War II Germany are equally disturbing."

"Three hundred cases!" Peter exclaimed, "Three hundred cases so far of the direct involvement of the Church in aiding top Nazi officials and soldiers to escape Germany after the surrender and escape to South America for asylum."

"These are allegations, Peter. Many fostered by enemies of the Church."

"These are facts, Monsignor. A chain of churches and convents scattered from Germany to Italy to Spain through which these criminals travelled to escape prosecution after the war." Peter was irate. "Not allegations, Monsignor, the proof is right here, in the archives!"

"Archives which I have learned you accessed without permission," Monsignor Specio replied.

"What I did is not the issue here!"

"Yes Peter, it is. You are not here to denigrate the Church or to expose what may have been past mistakes, you are supposedly here to become a member of the clergy, not an enemy to it."

"And telling the truth makes me an enemy?" Peter said, sadly.

"Telling the truth can also make you an instrument of change, change for the better."

"Can the Church change? Will the Church change?" Peter asked.

"It can with the proper leadership. Perhaps you can be one of those leaders."

Monsignor Specio saw the look of skepticism on Peter's face and continued, "Peter, you have a bright, inquisitive, important mind. Your type of thinking is what the Church needs today. Do not let anger or indignation poison you purpose."

Silence descended on the room as Monsignor Specio withdrew a sheaf of papers from his briefcase. Spreading them on his desk top he asked, "Peter, would you be willing to take on a research project for me?"

Peter nodded cautiously. Monsignor Specio continued, indicating the papers on his desk,

"This is a list of what I consider the most significant acts of charity and benevolence the Church has accomplished in the past thirty years, my time as a priest."

He pushed the papers toward Peter.

"Would you be willing to research these, validate these and report on the impact of these deeds as you see them?"

Peter considered the paperwork before him.

"Balance, Peter, equilibrium. Try concentrating on the good as you decide your future, consider both sides, then make up your mind about your vocation."

Peter scooped up the papers, agreeing to the task.

This was going to be interesting.

I wanted to start fresh at UMass in the fall. I wanted a clear mind, a clear conscience, a pure heart. Impossible I know, but it was in the effort to achieve these things that I would find some peace, not in the accomplishment. There was one big thing I had to do to start myself down that path. I had to confess the whole Kendall thing to somebody, preferably someone who wouldn't have me arrested. Someone who, in their eyes, I wouldn't see the disappointment I felt about myself.

Teddy and I never talked about what we did to Kendall. It was like a silent deal we made to put the incident behind us. Like Vietnam. Only it wasn't working for me. I was truly worried about how good it felt to smash Kendall's hand in that door. I also recognized that if he had not peed all over himself and Teddy was not holding him, I could just as easily put his head in that door. Really, I could have.

This is not the way I was raised. This was not the me I was trying to be, the me who would always make my parents proud, make me proud. This was some ice-cold stranger that lived within me and I did not know where he came from. I needed to talk to someone about this. I didn't want to tell my Dad; my Mom would probably tell me to go back and put Kendall's head in the door and I didn't want Margaret Mary to ever know anything about my involvement. But there was one guy, a priest I talked to once. A priest who had been at Anzio and who said I could come back and talk to him anytime. I decided to take him up on the offer. Which led to the most bizarre, unbelievable, eeriest thing that has ever happened to me, or anyone else that I knew of. Yet it happened, it really did.

When I arrived at the rectory of the Immaculate Conception Church and asked for Father Coogan, the nun who answered the door ushered me into a side room and left very quickly without saying a word. I assumed she was going to fetch the priest. I paced the office until Father Scanlon, who was the Pastor of the parish, the man in charge, came in. The room had a large desk with a high-back chair and two upholstered chairs in front of it. He motioned me into one of the chairs as he took his place behind the desk.

"I am Father Scanlon. Pastor here. May I ask your name?"

"David Ferrier, Father. I went to school at the Immaculate, I remember you."

The Pastor nodded, leaned forward onto the desk and clasped his hands together, as if in prayer.

"I am going to ask you a question young man and I want you to be absolutely truthful when you answer me." The somber, very serious sounding Pastor began.

"Yes Father," I answered, feeling twelve years old again.

"Did you seriously expect to come here to talk to Father Coogan today?"

"Yes Father," I answered now feeling ten years old.

"May I ask why?" he asked.

"I was here a few weeks back. I was having a bad day, a number of bad days actually, and I spoke with him briefly in the church. He said I could come back anytime to talk."

Father Scanlon leaned back in his chair and considered me intensely. He rose and said, "Come with me please."

I followed him to a small private chapel in the rectory. As we entered, he dipped his fingers into a font of holy water and made the sign of the cross. Fading faith and all, I did the same. He led me to a niche in the chapel wall fronted by a rack of small red candles and displaying a bronze plaque with the name of Father Paul Coogan, 1917-1944. Under the dates was the Latin phrase, "Requiesce in Pace." Rest in Peace.

In hushed tones Father Scanlon said, "Father Coogan was a priest here at the outbreak of World War II. He was killed on the beach at Anzio in January of 1944."

I felt like someone dumped a bucket of ice water over me. I didn't know what to say. Father Scanlon took a waxen taper from a tray of sand and lit a red candle in front of Father Coogan's plaque. He handed me the taper. I did the same. He turned to leave the chapel and motioned for me to follow. Instead of returning to the small alcove where we talked earlier, he led me to a library room where he took down a dusty photo album, opened it, found a page and a picture and handed me the book.

"Is this who you spoke with in the church?" he asked.

The picture was of a smiling, steel-helmeted, Army chaplain. Under the photo it said, "Father Daniel Coogan, Lowell Massachusetts." The very man I had spoken with, absolutely no doubt about it.

The second bucket of ice felt colder than the first. I stared at the picture, still speechless.

"Did you recently return from military service, David?" Father Scanlon asked.

I nodded and handed him the photo album; not sure my voice was working again.

"You are not the first person I have spoken to who has had this experience," He said.

"Not the first?" was all I could stammer.

"The other was a veteran as well, almost twenty years ago. You are the first in some time."

"I don't know what to say," I stammered once again.

"Nor do I," he said as he replaced the photo album on the shelf. "The other man did not know as well. He has chosen not to speak out about his experience, fearing scorn or hysteria."

This I did understand. There were enough "crazed Vietnam Vet" stories floating around as it was. I did not want to be made part of the narrative. "What should I do Father? Is what happened to me real or am I cracking up?"

"I don't think you are cracking up, David, and I believe what happened to you happened. I am not, however, sure of how to understand the experience. Perhaps if you prayed on it you would know. Would you do me a great favor, David?"

More nodding on my part, my brain was spinning too fast to talk.

"If you do find an answer, would you come here and discuss it with me? I too am baffled and confused by this."

I promised I would and as he escorted me back to the rectory door, I resolved that I would pray and share what I might learn when I did. I left the rectory much more confused than when I got there. The issue with Kendall now smothered by the issue with Father, if there really was a Father Coogan. I mean, things like this don't really happen, do they?

This one did and I had no idea what to do, or say, or think. I needed to talk to Margret Mary, right away.

Chapter Six

Transformations

"This letter arrived today for you my daughter," Sean announced, "it appears to be of some importance."

Margaret Mary took the letter from her father and held it reverently in her hands. The envelope bore the imprint of Oxford University in England. It was a very large envelope, stuffed full of something. Her hands trembled, she stared and hesitated.

"Have you noted the weight of that communication my daughter?" Sean smiled. Margaret Mary looked puzzled.

"Saying "No" only takes one sheet of paper," He whispered.

Margaret Mary carefully opened the letter. It was official. She had been accepted, granted a full two-year scholarship to Oxford University in England. A Rhodes scholarship. One of the most prestigious awards in academia. The scholarship guarantees two years of study and all expenses for a master's program. Thousands apply, few are chosen, Margaret Mary was chosen.

Elation, followed quickly by anxiety, coursed through her. England, Oxford, Europe, lands far away. Home, comfort, family and safety clashed with the prestige and opportunity this honor conveyed. As she saw the smile on her father's face, the pride beaming from her Aunt Rose, she realized this bounty would take her thousands of miles away from those smiles, from her security, from her family. Sean noticed the change of expression on his daughter's face.

"An honor offered, but your decision to make, my daughter. One that will require serious thought on your part no doubt."

"England is so far away," Margaret Mary answered in a low, trembling voice.

"That's true dear," Aunt Rose added, "but it is only far away from here. There are ways and there are ways."

Unknown to Margaret Mary, Rose and Sean had discussed returning to Ireland one day. Sean to teach, perhaps at the University in Dublin, Rose to open her bakery nearby. The topic now could be spoken of openly, as a family matter. Together.

"May I see the letter, daughter?" Sean asked and read after the giving. "It says you have several weeks to reply and consider this offer. Nothing need be decided now, except the considering. Perhaps this is something we could talk about as a family."

"This is not a command my dear," Rose added, "it is an invitation. Yours to accept or decline."

"I left home once before," Margaret Mary whispered, "and made a terrible mess of it."

"That tragedy cannot be laid entirely at your feet my daughter, loving and trusting are part of being human. Your mistake was one of judgment, not of character, and certainly not indicative of the world at large."

"You must trust in the words of a fellow Irishman my dear," Aunt Rose interjected, "it was our own James Joyce himself who said, 'Mistakes are the portals of discovery.'"

"Who then died of an ulcer at a very early age," Margaret Mary answered. You couldn't slip a homily past that girl.

"Perhaps that was from brooding over his mistakes more than the making of them," Sean suggested.

"I would prefer to avoid both," Margaret Mary declared.

"Not likely in this life, my dear, not yours, not mine, not anybody's." Aunt Rose added. "I'll try one last allusion for you and then be done with it. It's from Mr. Mark Twain himself, an Irishman at heart, but born here as you were. He said, 'Good judgment is the result of experience and experience is the result of bad judgment.'"

Which got the most reluctant smile from Margaret Mary who answered,

"I don't know what I need Oxford University for since I have the two of you."

"For experience my daughter, as Mr. Twain suggested." Sean put his arms around her. Aunt Rose put her arms around both of them, the letter from Oxford momentarily forgotten. Margaret Mary relaxed, knowing she was in the bosom of her family now, and always could be. England or no England. Her decision could wait.

'You've got to be sitting down when I tell you this," which echoed a long-ago conversation I had with Margaret Mary on the front porch of her home in long ago Lowell. That time I was telling her that Peter Rayburn was going to be a priest. This time I was going to tell her I had seen a ghost. Or at least I thought I had seen a ghost. A ghost another before me had seen as well. I hoped she wouldn't think I was going crazy. I questioned if I was.

She was in Chicago; I was in Lowell. A long-distance telephone call had to substitute for her front porch, but I could still imagine her settling herself in a chair, folding her hands in her lap and waiting patiently, attentively.

I had not spoken to anyone about the whole Father Coogan experience. I had been over and over it in my mind. I know it happened. I wasn't making this up. I hoped I wasn't cracking up.

After speaking to Father Scanlon, I went to the library and did some research. About one in every five people believe they have at one time in their life, seen a ghost. Two in five, almost forty percent. believe ghosts exist. Most believers attribute their opinion to their religious background. Psychologists and scientists refer to the experience as "sensed presences," hallucinations, delusions, often brought about by heightened stress. A substantial number offer no explanation at all, much like myself and want to keep the incident private.

Nevertheless, as much as I didn't want people to think I was crazy I had to talk to somebody about Father Coogan. I had not been back to see Father Scanlon. Either I was cracking up or I could ask Margaret Mary. She was always a better choice.

When I finished telling her the story there was a long silence. Had it been possible I would have seen her blinking, thinking and wondering. Then she spoke, "David, that is the most wonderful story I have ever been told."

"It's not a story, Margaret Mary, it happened."

"I believe you David, and that is what makes it so wonderful."

'It's either wonderful or I imagined the whole thing."

"Is Father Scanlon imagining it too? Didn't he tell you this has happened before?"

And there was the sticking point.

"You know who I wish we could talk about this with? Peter." Margaret Mary said.

"Rome is a little far off for a conversation," I answered.

"Peter is coming home in June to visit his family. He'll be in Lowell for two weeks," Margaret Mary announced.

"Do you think you could come back while he's there?" I asked.

"I will if you promise to be at my graduation next week."

"Margaret Mary, I was always going to be at your graduation next week. Teddy's coming too and wait till you see who he's bringing with him," I added mysteriously.

"His new girlfriend, right? Who is she? Do I know her?"

"Mystery is the spice of life. You'll have to wait and see."

"You call me to tell me you have seen a ghost and want to tell me about mystery being the spice of life?"

"Some topics are spicier than others. We'll have a lot to talk about when I'm there. I can't wait to see you."

"Come as early as you can. My Aunt Rose wants you all to stay with us. We'll have hours and hours to talk." Margaret Mary sounded as excited as I felt. Then she sounded serious again. "Would you mind if I talked to Sean about Father Coogan?"

"Please talk to Sean, and your Aunt as well. Maybe they can make some sense of it."

"Unless of course sense has nothing to do with what happened," She replied.

Which left me right back where I started on this phone call. We said our goodbyes, hung up and returned to the everyday confusion.

"Just for the weekend, Kevin. Dr. Neiman said it would be good for you. It will be just you and me and Ma. I promise."

Beth pleaded with her brother, knowing how much it terrified him to leave the safety of the hospital.

Kevin, not Butchie, sank back onto his bunk. He stared at the floor and whispered, "I'm so ashamed."

Beth hurried to her brother's side and threw her arms around him as he sobbed. "You have nothing to be ashamed of," Beth said, "Dr. Nieman says you were horribly over-medicated for far too long and that is what injured you."

"I didn't do my duty," He said simply.

"You couldn't do your duty because you were given the wrong medication. That is not your fault." Beth and Kevin had gone down this road before, several times. Kevin did not want to leave the hospital. The staff felt it was time for him to move on but agreed the process should be taken slowly. He had done work release for a short time, then regressed. He refused all visitors except Beth and his mother. Now after three weeks of gentle shock treatments he was recovering. Long walks with his family on the hospital grounds, short drives in Beth's car, a lunch at a nearby café, all were part of his progress. A weekend pass was the recommended next step.

"Just us, you and Ma, you promise?" He whispered.

"Just us, I promise." Beth led her trembling brother from the ward to her car, smiling all the while.

On the road to Lowell Kevin was very quiet. Beth turned on the radio, WMEX, the rock and roll station, in the hopes it would raise Kevin's spirits. A group called Three Dog Night sang about "Joy To The World." After a short while Kevin asked if she would turn the radio off. He wasn't feeling any joy. Beth's concern heightened. Silence threatened in the car.

A few miles passed before Kevin asked, "Does Max still run the gym?"

He could not recall that Max had come to see him in the hospital several weeks ago. Kevin did not recognize Max at first, then broke down and began to cry. The same thing happened when Dave and Teddy came to visit. He had seen no one else since, save Beth and his Mother.

"The building the gym was in was condemned," Beth reported, "Max had to move out. He's still looking for a new location. He asks about you all the time."

Kevin became uneasy, squirming in his seat. "What do you tell him?"

"I tell him you are getting better every day. He says he is glad to hear that."

Kevin returned to his silence, his apprehension growing as they got closer to his home.

"Maybe Max could come over this weekend," He said while staring out the side window. Beth's smile returned, bigger and better than ever.

"Is it true the Church has been offered over $500 Million dollars for the Michelangelo Pieta?" Peter asked Monsignor

Specio as they ate breakfast in the sumptuous Vatican dining hall.

"I believe so," Monsingor Specio answered, "though I am not sure of its actual value. It can of course, never be sold."

"Why not?" Peter asked, stifling his secret, growing indignation.

"The Pieta is more than art, it is history, it belongs not to the Church, but to all Catholics," Specio pronounced.

"Is that true of all the art here?" Peter continued.

"May I ask why this subject appears to be of such importance to you Peter?"

Peter hesitated, unsure of how to go on. He realized he had already acquired the reputation of a dissident, a free thinker who was having difficulty staying within Church boundaries. He did not want to jeopardize his vocation, but he did want to know all he could about the institution to which he was prepared to offer his life.

"I was talking with Father Marcinkus the other day and he told me there is over a Billion dollars worth of art in the Vatican alone and that the total value of the Church worldwide is over fifty Billion dollars."

"Ah yes, the good father is inordinately impressed with the dollars and cents. It is rumored he will be head of the Vatican Bank quite soon. A very powerful position, but I must caution you about becoming too involved with this man."

"Why?" Peter asked, chuckling to himself at the satire of the question he had joined the clergy to stop asking. Due to their long talks together Monsignor Specio too recognized the irony in Peter's question.

"There is the faith of the Church and the business of the Church. One cannot exist without the other. You have told me you have come to embrace the faith of the Church, to live by its principles, to learn through its parables."

So far Peter agreed. He nodded for Monsignor Specio to continue.

"It takes a great deal of money to fund the good works of the Church, to minister to the faithful, to support the clergy, such as ourselves."

This is where Peter's questions began and irritated him most. Cautiously he said, "I look around us here, we live like Princes in a Palace. We have servants, maids, cooks, chauffeurs, valets, bodyguards, the very best of everything, be it food or vestments, wine or travel. We are treated not as clerics but as royalty."

Peter knew he was on shaky ground here. The opulence of the Church, the pampering of the priests, especially the Bishops and Cardinals, was a growing concern among a silent and guarded percentage of Peter's peers. This was a topic Monsigno Specio himself had expressed concern about.

"There are extravagances for certain," Monsignor Specio replied, "and I believe these practices will one day be called into review by the proper authorities. Meanwhile we must concentrate our attention on the saving of souls and the strengthening of our faith. These faults you are becoming aware of may be a test of that faith Peter."

Faith Peter realized could only take one so far in the fiscal workings of the Church. He had come to accept the parables of the Gospels as teaching tools, as much fable as fact. He had studied all the variants of the New Testament, chartered its development and alterations over the centuries and researched earlier religious accounts with much the same content. The faith he was clinging to was being weakened with facts, histories and anomalies he was not able to fully reconcile with faith. Yet he persevered, believing this path would bring him more peace than any other.

"It is not just my faith which is being tested Monsignor. Do you remember Kurt Valden, Father Valden now, who was with us last year?"

"Of course, you and he were good friends, no?"

Peter nodded and produced a letter from his study bag. "I received this letter from Kurt only yesterday. Would you care to read it?" Peter offered Monsignor Specio the letter.

He took it, checked the postmark. "Kurt took a mission, Central Africa I recall, Gabon?"

"Yes, father. He's been there almost a year now. Please read what he wrote."

Monsignor Specio read:

Dear Peter,
I hope this letter finds you well and advancing in your studies. I am in a small village outside of Tchibanga, which is on the Nyanga River in West Gabon. The poverty here is indescribable, the sickness rampant, the future very bleak. What little aid we receive is stolen by the warlords who resell the goods on the black market.

There are virtually no food or medical supplies to be had for miles. The only water is from the river which is foul with waste and the corpses from the ongoing fighting here. The river water must be carried in buckets from the river over a mile from the village. The people here are dying from starvation, from infections and from hopelessness.

I am asking, no, I am begging for your help. For $700 dollars I can buy a water pump and filtration system which will clean the river water and pump it to our village. I have asked the diocese for the money, and they have refused. They say it is a civic project and the Church cannot become involved in civil matters. People are dying here every day from drinking contaminated water, from being attacked by crocodiles and hippopotamuses along the bank of the river, from malnutrition and from neglect. I have no money left, what little I had I spent on medical supplies and bribes to get these supplies delivered. Can you speak to someone there and try to get this money? I pray for this as I pray for you.
Your Friend, Kurt

When Monsignor Specio passed the letter back, Peter said quietly, "Father Marcinkus told me the Vatican is about to be gifted a Van Gogh painting worth 30 to 50 Million dollars. Is that true?"

"I have heard that, yes."

"And we cannot help these people?" Peter refolded the letter.

"I will look into the matter," Monsignor Specio said as he rose from the table.
And the people of Kurt's village will continue to die as you do, thought Peter as he watched his mentor leave.

Chapter Seven

Reunions

All these years later the dining room of the Pewter Pot still looked the same. Dim, electric candles lit the room. Tiny tables for two and an occasional four-seater with red checkered tablecloths filled the room. The enchanting smell of freshly baked blueberry muffins, hot coffee and cinnamon tea filled the air.

Margaret Mary, Teddy, Peter and I filled a four-banger table, comfortable, happy, content in each other's company. We had walked many different roads since our last gathering here, some good, some bad, all behind us as we talked of our futures.

Only three weeks before I watched Margaret Mary walk down the aisle of her Loyola Graduation ceremony and receive the highest academic honors her school could give. Naturally, it was Margaret Mary after all. Tonight, she sat in cheerful radiance and told us about her impending trip to England and how Sean and her Aunt Rose planned to return to Ireland, Sean to teach at the University of Dublin, Rose to open a bakery near the campus, a train ride apart rather than an ocean between them.

Peter was dressed in the stark black attire of his imminent priesthood. His tenure in Rome was almost finished, his ordination scheduled for the fall. He spoke with an insider's knowledge about the grandeur of the Vatican, the wonders of Rome, and his travels around Europe. But there was a hesitation, a reserve in his voice that sounded familiar to us, the bothered, skeptical, questioning Peter we had grown up with, now wrapped in priestly garb. Something was on Peter's mind. There usually was.

Teddy announced he would start his Police Academy training the week after Labor Day. This announcement, however, was outshined by the glittering engagement ring Beth Martin wore when she accompanied Teddy and I to Margaret Mary's graduation. A November wedding was planned.

I contributed my imminent relocation to Amherst to restart college. I was waiting for the chatter to die down a bit before bringing up the topic Margaret Mary and I had already discussed. Earlier Sean and Aunt Rose concluded my experience with Father Coogan was some sort of miracle. I had discussed this with no one else so far. Peter and Teddy were next.

"You guys don't think I'm nuts, right?" Was how I chose to begin.

"I never said I didn't think you were nuts," Teddy replied.

"For the most part," Peter added, "though we haven't spoken much of late." Peter smiled his good old wolf grin. Margaret Mary took my hand.

"I have a story to tell you. I don't want you to laugh at me." Truly I never thought they would, but perhaps I thought somebody ought to. Margaret Mary squeezed my hand. Teddy and Peter gave me their full attention. I began…

"A couple of months ago I was down at the Immaculate Conception Church. It was in the middle of the week, an afternoon. I quit my job earlier that day and I was driving around in my car, not really knowing what to do or where I was going. I don't know why I stopped at the church. I went inside. I just wanted to be someplace quiet where I could get my thoughts together. There was nobody in the church when I went in. I'm sure of it. I looked around."

So far, so good.

"A lot of things were running through my mind as I sat there and I kind of lost it for a minute and shouted out loud. Something about where was God when everybody was getting messed up in Vietnam. Why didn't he put a stop to it? I didn't mean to yell; it just came out. I was angry, you know? But I figured nobody was around and nobody heard me. The next thing I know this priest comes over to where I was sitting. He asked me if I was alright and what was bothering me. We talked for a few minutes. He reminded me that men made wars, not God. He told me he had served too. At Anzio, WWII, invasion of Italy. He was a chaplain. He told me his name was Coogan, Daniel Coogan."

Now it was going to get weird.

"After we talked, he left. I felt better. Father Coogan said I could come back anytime if I needed to talk. So, I did, a week or so later. I went to the rectory and asked for him. I ended up speaking to Father Scanlon."

"I know Father Scanlon, he's a good man," Peter commented.

"Father Scanlon showed me a book that had a lot of pictures of priests who had been at the Immaculate, like a yearbook for priests."

"The parish register," Peter said.

"Yeah, only this was an old one, from the Forties. There was a picture of a Father Coogan in it. He was wearing an Army helmet and fatigues. The caption under the picture said Chaplain Daniel Coogan, killed at Anzio in 1944. It was the guy I talked to in the church." Suddenly it felt like the whole dining room got very quiet. Peter said nothing, Margaret Mary held onto my hand.

Teddy whispered, "**Daimones**".

We all looked at Teddy who explained, "**Daimones**' is the Greek word for ghosts. My mother used to tell me about them when I was small. Chris used to tell me they were under my bed."

"*Taibhse,*" Margaret Mary added.

"Tie what?" Teddy asked.

"'*Tie-v-sheh*', it's Irish for ghost, like '**Daimones,**'" Margaret Mary pronounced.

"Spirits, specters, apparitions, phantoms, banshees, poltergeists," Peter recited, "every religion, every culture around the world has its ghost stories. The resurrection of Christ could be considered a ghost story, Lazarus brought back from the dead is another, then there's Fatima, Lourdes, Guadalupe in Mexico, more and more and more. We are surrounded by such tales."

"Yes, but do you believe them?" Margaret Mary asked.

"I'm supposed to," Peter replied, "those related to the church anyway. Dave, what day did this happen?"

"I don't remember the date. It was a Monday, in February. Is that important?" I answered.

"I don't know. What did Father Scanlon say about this?"

The weird part wasn't over yet. "He said this has happened before."

Now Peter was on full alert. Leaning forward on the table, earnest. "At the Immaculate? How many times before?" He asked.

"Once that he knew of," I answered. "Twenty years ago, just after World War II. Another veteran, who asked him to tell no one about it."

"Do you know whether Father Scanlon reported these occurrences to his superiors?" Peter asked.

"He said he didn't. He told me he would keep my story between the two of us unless I told him otherwise. I haven't told him otherwise."

"Is it the policy of the church not to talk about such matters?" Margaret Mary asked.

"It's the policy of the church to be very skeptical of such matters," Peter replied.

"Don't they teach you guys to talk about this stuff in priest school?" Teddy added.

"Mostly they teach us how not to talk about this stuff in priest school," Peter responded. "The church gets literally hundreds of accounts like this every year. Most turn out to be from hysterics, delusional people, fakers, but some, <u>some</u>, are unexplained. All have the potential to be ridiculed by skeptics, causing harm not only to the church but to the people who report them. Dave," he continued, "I believe every word you said. I don't know if this apparition is spiritual or paranormal or what, but I know you, and I don't think you are crazy or lying. Would you mind if I spoke of this to Father Scanlon?"

"I wish you would. I don't know what to say to him."

"Did you ever go back to see if this guy was still there?" Teddy asked.

"Twice," I admitted. "I sort of snuck in, late afternoon. He never came back."

Which pretty much put a capper on our night. Unresolved, but no longer secret, I felt better about the whole Father Coogan thing, and I felt supported by the people I was closest to in the world. I still did not want to share this with my family, I can't explain why but Margaret Mary agreed that, just for now, we would keep it between us.

We said our goodnights outside the Pewter Pot. Margaret Mary was staying with me at Glenmere Street, separate bedrooms of course. Peter was returning to Rome in four days and Teddy was helping his father close down the garage. A representative from Shell Oil company wanted to turn the garage into a Shell station and made a generous offer to buy Teddy's Dad out.

Life was changing all around us, we were marching in different directions and realizing gatherings such as tonight would be rare. Margaret Mary and I returned to Glenmere Street to find that my Mom and Dad were already in bed. John and Bob as well. It was well past midnight, but sleep was not on our minds.

We sat in lawn chairs beneath The Big Oak in the back yard under the summer stars. Quietly at first, comfortably until…

"I'm going to be very far away for the next two years, David," Margaret Mary said softly.

"We are all going to be far away, one way or another, from now on," I answered regretfully.

"We can write to each other, just like when you were in Vietnam," She said.

"I really hope your trip to England is nothing like my trip to Vietnam." I was trying to be funny. Margaret Mary didn't think so.

"You have never really told me what your time in Vietnam was like," She said softly.

"It wasn't like anything!" As much as I tried not to, my words came out angry. Margaret Mary stiffened, I apologized. "I'm sorry. I didn't mean it to sound like that."

"What did you mean it to sound like?" Good question.

"It was hard Mags, day in and day out hard. Even writing letters was hard."

"I don't understand." She said, taking my hand once again. Margaret Mary did that a lot.

"Writing home, or writing to you, I had to make a lot of stuff up. I was fine, don't worry about me. The fighting is all far away. I'm safe. I learned to hide the truth. I learned how to not say what I really felt. I learned how to lie to people I loved."

"Because you didn't want us to worry about you?" She asked.

"Because I didn't want you to know how terrified I was," I admitted. "I was scared all the time, Mags. People were getting killed every day, every hour, everywhere. If you didn't see it, you heard about it. I learned to stuff the fear way down inside me, to not let my buddies see how scared I was or how scared they were. I just got numb, it was better not to feel anything than to feel the fear. Now I don't know how to not feel numb."

"Do you remember Kendall Prescott?" Margaret Mary asked as a chill ran through me.

"Yeah," I answered cautiously.

"Somebody beat him up recently, the police said his hand was smashed and he had to go to the hospital."

"You talked to the police about Kendall Prescott?"

"They came to my house when I was in the hospital. When I got out, I went to see them. They knew about the trial in Colorado and thought maybe my family had something to do with the beating."

"What happened?" Now I was really worried.

"My Aunt Rose threw the detective out of our house. She told them we were good people who did not do such things. The detective I talked to told me people like Kendall make a lot of enemies and that he probably got what he deserved."

"Do you know where Kendall is now?"

"The detective said he left town right after he left the hospital. He got a speeding ticket in Arizona somewhere."

I stayed quiet. Best way to keep a secret.

"The reason I'm telling you this is that when I found out Kendall had been hurt, I was glad, really glad. The gladder I was that he had been hurt the worse I felt about myself."

"I'm kinda' glad he got beat up myself," I answered as cryptically as possible. "Does that make us bad people?"

"It makes us people, people," She replied. "a mixture of bad and good. I try to be better more often than bad, and I know you do too."

But I knew something Margaret Mary didn't know about Kendall. Fuck him.

"Remember when we couldn't wait to be grown up?" She asked.

"Not as much fun as we thought it would be after all," I answered.

"Do you remember the night on the ski trip when we slept together for the first time?" Margaret Mary asked softly.

"Slept being the key word there," I answered snarkily and earned an affectionate punch on the arm from herself.

"I thought that someday when we were grown up, we would get married and sleep together every night," She sighed.

"Sleep no longer being the key word," I snarked again, never knowing when enough was enough.

"I have to tell you something, David, something I haven't told anyone else," Margaret Mary whispered, not looking at me. I knew this was going to be important.

"After what Kendall did to me, after he raped me and raped me, I don't think I could ever, you know, have sex again. I know I don't want to." She wasn't finished, the worst was yet to come, "And I don't think I will ever get married."

"Ever, never?" I asked as another dream of my childhood fell apart.

Margaret Mary took my hand as she so often did at just the right time.

"I don't think so," she replied, and her voice cracked, and tears ran down her cheeks as she continued, "But if I ever do I hope I marry you."

And then my eyes filled with tears, and I couldn't find a reply.

"I'm going to miss you," Margaret Mary said softly.

"Me too," I replied, through that familiar, gigantic lump in my throat.

And the summer night passed on, as did we, on the journey Onward.

And a poet named Carole, who was also a King, sang…

So far away.
Doesn't anybody stay in one place anymore?
It would be so fine to see your face at my door.
Doesn't help to know,
You're just time away,
long ago I reached for you
And there you stood,
Holding you again would only do me good.
How I wish I could,
But you're so far Away. *

This your new gym?" Kevin, not Butchie, asked as he and Max entered the YMCA gymnasium. Kevin was walking on eggshells, cautiously re-entering the outside world after several in-home, weekend visits with his mother and sister. This was not safe, he knew. He also knew it was necessary. The fog on his mind was lifting, the fear in his heart and head getting smaller each day, but still there, powerful when aroused. As it was now.

"City's letting me set up here, start a boxing program for kids. Don't pay much but the rent's free," Max responded.

"How you gonna' live, it don't pay much?"

"I got my Navy pension, it's enough."

Kevin wandered around the large, open room. There were a couple of speed bags along the wall, two heavy bags on chains draped from the ceiling, several exercise mats spread on the floor and a roped ring centered on the room. Large windows allowed a lot of light and there was heat, a major upgrade from the old gym.

"Lockers are back here. We even got showers," Max said.

Kevin wandered around the room, baby steps, cautious. Max watched as Kevin nudged a heavy bag, jumping back as it swung toward him.

"You wanna' tape up? Work out a little?" He asked.

Kevin didn't answer, touching a speed bag like a light bulb that didn't work. He scuffed his feet on the floor, took several deep breaths and said, "Yeah, maybe a little bit."

Kevin was on the verge of being discharged from Chelsea Naval Hospital. He had been granted a medical discharge from the Navy with service-connected disability and was ready to go home. Almost.

The shock treatments, the individual counseling, the love of his mother and sister had alleviated the night terrors of the ice and the anxiety that overshadowed his thinking. Yet the uncertainty was still in him, the ongoing caution, along with a secret shame, the self-perceived shame of failed manhood. He always felt it was there, his Scarlet Letter, pinned to his chest for all the world to see.

"Teddy Gianoulous is gonna' help out too," Max said. "He's startin' the police academy in a few weeks but after that he'll help out here."

Kevin struggled to remember Teddy, who visited him twice at Chelsea Naval Hospital.

"He the dukey?" Kevin asked.

"Yeah, hits like a mule kicks. Good fighter," Max answered.

"Him and his buddy, Dave something, they used to come to the gym?"

"They did, and they do. You gonna' tape up?"

Kevin nodded and went into the locker room. Max watched the formerly toughest guy in Lowell shuffle past, head down, the fire gone from his eyes, the bounce gone from his steps. Max had spent a lot of time with Kevin over the past few weeks, watching as the drugs drained from his system, as his memory returned, as his sense of shame increased. Eventually, along with Beth, they had coaxed him off the hospital ward, back to Lowell, out for short walks and now to the gym, where he had been Butchie once, and perhaps could become Butchie again.

Familiar faces, familiar places, lots of special handling, encouragement and support was Kevin's new therapy. "He's still in there, inside himself," Doctor Neiman said, "It's just going to take some time to get him to come back out."

When Kevin, not Butchie, came out of the locker room he tugged on a pair of bag gloves and started working a heavy bag, tapping it actually, then jumping back like he thought the bag would punch back. He would poke the bag, stop, sigh, and poke it once again. Max watched until Kevin dropped his arms and stood staring at the bag. Max turned away, unable to watch anymore. As he walked toward his cubby-hole office he heard two claps of thunder, two booms that filled the room, then two more. He turned and saw the heavy bag bouncing and spinning on its chains. Max saw Butchie, not Kevin, pound the bag more three times, left, right, left, and the bag nearly rattled off its chains. Max also saw, for the first time in many months, that Kevin, now Butchie, was smiling.

High over the Atlantic Ocean Peter Rayburn luxuriated in his First-Class seat four hours out of Rome. He had spent much of the flight pondering his conversation with Father Scanlon at the Immaculate Conception church rectory two days earlier.

Some mysteries, they decided, are best left as mysteries, apart from the hysteria and skepticism that often accompany such instances. Peter had shared David's preference not to go public with his experience and Father Scanlon agreed.

"Perhaps certain experiences are best judged by the soul," Father Scanlon offered. "Public attention and public opinion, may not serve him best here."

"Is that what happened with the previous occurrences?" Peter asked.

"As far as I know, yes. All were veterans recently returned from their war. All apparently benefited from the encounter. Each wished to keep the encounter undisclosed."

"Is that what we are going to call it? An encounter?" Peter asked.

"Rather than miracle, Brother? Yes, I believe that is best. Miracles shine a very bright light, not all of it beneficial. Skeptics abound, believers are ridiculed, and everyone is left with the same questions they began with."

"Faith over doubt?" Peter responded.

"Faith or the lack thereof, sadly," Father Scanlon concluded.

His conversation with Father Scanlon left Peter in a haze of confusion. He entered the priesthood looking for peace through faith. So far, he had learned that while faith smoothed the inconsistencies of reason, peace was proving far more elusive. He reflected on the grandeur of the Vatican, the immense wealth of the worldwide Catholic church, the horrific historical alliances, and even his first-class accommodations. Then he recalled the sprawling slums of back street Rome, electrical cords strung out of apartment windows to bring light to powerless rooms, buildings without heat, plumbing without water, people without hope. Run down neighborhoods centered around huge, ornate churches, where well fed clergy ministered to undernourished children, mission villages in far away Africa where the church brought prayer, but not progress.

David's encounter with Father Coogan had re-enforced Peter's faith in the spiritual but done nothing for his growing sense of skepticism over how the Catholic church was run. He recalled a conversation with Monsignor Marcinkus shortly before he left on this trip.

"You can't run a church on Hail Mary's." He said, a Rolex watch peeking out from under his shirt sleeve.

"You can either be part of the solution or part of the problem," Father Scanlon counseled when Peter broached this subject to him.

"Is the Church looking for solutions, Father?" Peter asked.

"I have to believe so," Father Scanlon replied, "I behave as if it does, and I do my best to create positive change. Perhaps you can do so yourself."

Peter sighed, remembering the conversation. The airplane soared on. Peter mulled over his, actually Dave's, Ghost Story. Real or imagined? Miraculous or paranormal? Spiritual for sure, but spiritual how? A matter to discuss with Monsignor Specio? A mystery that either reinforced faith or deepened uncertainty.

"More champagne, Father?" The attractive, attentive stewardess asked.

Peter had a funny thought before answering. "When in Rome do as the Romans do." He held out his glass for a refill.

Lyrical Aspiration:

*So Far Away, Carole King

Chapter Eight

Beginnings

My experiences in Amherst during the first weeks of the fall semester were the closest I had ever been in my life to spending the rest of my life in prison (for homicide).

LT had arranged for me to become a school bus driver, as he was, for the Northampton School District. In a community flooded with thousands of college students, part-time jobs were scarce and underpaid. Minimum wage was the standard, and the standard wasn't very high. School bus drivers on the other hand made a cool six bucks an hour and after some falderal with a Class II license I was behind the wheel. Apparently, there was no "Don't let the kid drive the truck" rule in Amherst.

"If you can start it, I can drive it," I told the examiner from the Registry of Motor Vehicles, stealing an old helicopter pilot boast. And after a quick spin around a stadium parking lot, I was certified. They should have checked a little further. I should have checked a lot further.

"Sit down and shut up or I'm gonna' drive this goddamn thing off a cliff!" I shouted for the fourth time that day and the twentieth time that week. Meanwhile thirty or so grade school monsters jumped on their seats, chased each other in the aisles and hung out the windows of the bus. Their screaming was non-stop, high pitched and constant. My screaming was largely unheard and unheeded.

I had a four-hour shift Monday, Wednesday and Friday afternoons from two till six. Two hours of that was chauffeuring these little bastards from the elementary school to their bus stops. One hour was prepping the bus, the final hour was drinking heavily at Mikes Tavern, next to the bus yard.

"Ya gotta look at the bright side," LT said as we gulped boilermakers at Mike's. "You just made twenty-five bucks."

"I'm going to spend half of that for my bar tab today," I answered.

"Like I said, the bright side." LT laughed.

"I'll tell you one thing," I said as I drained my glass and signaled for a refill, "I'm never having kids."

"Yeah," LT agreed, "Driving a school bus is the best form of birth control you could ever have."

"I'm serious, I've got to get away from those little bastards, before I end up in prison for manslaughter."

"Didja' give any thought to what I said about Alaska?" LT asked.

Lately LT had been talking about quitting school and going to Alaska. Freedom, he said, and something called Serenity, a thing I barely recalled ever having. We could get jobs on the fishing fleets, he said. Maybe start a farm, a salmon farm. No kids, no school buses, no war protests, no demonstrations, sweet dreams he envisioned.

"Cold up there though," I answered. "I think I'm more of a tropical guy."

"South Africa then," he countered, "They give ya' a 200-acre farm and citizenship if you immigrate and join the militia."

I shook my head and ordered another beer. I had to look for another line of work.

There was this song they played in Nam at the end of every USO show that came through. The band played it, we shouted it. It went like this…

"We gotta' get out of this place. If it's the last thing we ever do, We gotta' get outta' this place, Girl, there's a better life for me and you."

I was starting to hear it in my head every day.

Then there were my fellow students. As advertised, many of them were entitled little shits riding on their Mommy and Daddy's dime who were sure they knew how to run the world better than their parents. Apparently, this involved smoking a lot of dope, listening to a lot of very loud music and abandoning all the basic forms of personal hygiene. Those were the enlightened ones, the hippies. Their music came from Jefferson Airplane, Buffalo Springfield, Jimi Hendrix, Janis Joplin and the Doors.

There were also the frat boys and sorority sisters, Nixon worshippers with life insurance policies and sparkling resumes. They motored around campus in tiny, two-seater sports cars wondering why poor people didn't drive convertibles. No getting high for them, they were apprenticing alcoholism, just like their parents. They listened to the Kingston Trio, Joan Baez, Peter, Paul and Mary and the New Christy Minstrels.

On the fringes of this herd were the vets, like myself. We were sullen, separate and heavily armed. I had been carrying a .25 MM Beretta since I got here and assumed everybody who wasn't an asshole was packing too. LT had a 1911A, Colt .45 hand cannon he inherited from his father. He wore it in a not-so-subtle shoulder holster he thought girls found attractive. Vets, like me, were a very small minority on campus and we didn't talk or fraternize much. I could always recognize one though, alert, apprehensive, apart. I still listened to early Elvis, Roy Orbison, The Everly Brothers, Patsy Cline, The Supremes and the Ventures. I assumed the other vets did too.

Mostly I ghosted through that first semester. I was a stranger on a stranger planet, still apart, but among them. I drove my school bus, attended classes and sat as far apart from my classmates as I could. I kept silent in class but took lots of notes. I culled decent grades on generic topics. On weekends I got drunk with LT, or tried to. Often, I became his caretaker after he went off the deep end. His drinking was more earnest than mine, more desperate than social.

An occasional cutie caught my eye, or hers mine, but I stayed clear. They all seemed so wide-eyed, so childlike, sporting a false sophistication that barely covered the naiveté. Even when they were interested, hitting on them felt strangely like robbing the cradle. Two trips to Bangkok on R&R from Nam will do that to a guy.

My college education was off to a mundane, unpromising start when I got the biggest surprise of the fall when LT took me to a Chinese restaurant.

"You're gonna' love this place. Trust me." Trusting LT was always an adventure, so off we went to the China Rose, an off-campus Chinese restaurant, bar, motel and much, much more.

The bar, generously referred to as a Cocktail Lounge, was in the basement of the motel lobby. Deep, dark, dank and dingy, the room was sparsely illuminated by fading red light bulbs set in the walls and a brightly lit Wurlitzer Juke box pulsating from a corner. A bamboo bar fronted the longest wall backed by a mirror which reflected only darkness. There were six booths scattered about and several small round tables clustered around the edge of a tiny, empty dance floor. When LT and I entered the population increased to three, the bartender, LT and me. And that is when the amazement started.

He saw me, I saw him, and before I could express my surprise the shockingly familiar bartender signaled me to stifle myself, play it dumb. I could hardly believe my eyes. The bartender was Eddie, Eddie Legrand, my old Suffolk University, nine ball hustling, gambling and rambling, draft dodging buddy. His hair was a lot longer; he was dressed like a Hawaiian beach boy and had a black, piratey looking eye patch over one eye, the left. And he didn't want me to say I knew him. Interesting.

"Mahalo Marcus!" LT announced to the empty room. I assumed Eddie was now Marcus, this was going to be intriguing.

"This is my buddy, Dave Ferrier," LT said as we took seats at the empty bar. "He's new to the school but a recent graduate of the University of the South Vietnam School of Warfare, much like ourselves."

Marcus/Eddie was apparently passing himself off as a Vietnam veteran, which might explain the eye patch. The reason I could guess for myself. Eddie was a long way from Montreal and had, I knew, Federal warrants out for his arrest for not being a veteran of any kind.

Marcus held out his hand for me to shake with a 'We'll talk later look'. I could hardly wait. "Welcome home bro. Glad to see you made it." I could tell without doubt that Eddie meant it.

"Mai Tai's for two," LT said, breaking the spell. "Looks a little dead in here."

"Crowd comes in after six LT, the action upstairs is alright though," Marcus answered while he poured something red into two tall glasses, put a tiny umbrella in each glass and placed the concoctions in front of us. "On the house," he announced as he winked at me. LT didn't notice, he plucked out the umbrella and drained the glass.

"So, what's upstairs?" I asked.

"LT will give you the tour, how's your drink?"

"Little sweet for me, can I get a beer?"

Eddie switched drinks. LT claimed my Mai Tai.

"You still lookin' for a guy?" LT asked.

"Could be," Marcus answered as two couples entered the lounge. They seated themselves in a far booth and Marcus excused himself to go wait on them.

"So, what's the story with this place? What's to love?" I asked.

"Finish your beer, I'll show you." Eddie grinned, I guzzled, and we went upstairs. Upstairs meant through the restaurant, back into the parking lot and across to the motel which sat on the border of the property. The motel was a two story, L-shaped structure. Eight rooms below with eight above plus an additional four rooms on the short leg of the L, which is where we headed.

This section of the motel, interestingly, had a low gate across the walkway and a doorman, a large Samoan looking guy who didn't smile but recognized LT and waved us past. We entered the first door, which turned out to be the only door accessing one very large room filled from wall to wall with slot machines, card and craps tables, a roulette wheel and hostesses, all Asian, all very pretty and all wearing very little. Patrons, many of them Asian, filled the tables and slot machine chairs. In addition to the standard games there was Pai Gow, Mah Jong, Baccarat and Pachinko.

LT immediately attracted the attention of a very pretty lady wearing a black hardly anything and, as they wandered off Eddie said, "Mingle, make friends, I'll be back in a while."

Interested as I was in the goings on, I went back downstairs. I needed to talk to Eddie.

"I run the whole joint," Eddie explained, "Restaurant, bar, game room and off-site activities as well."

"Off site activities?" I asked.

"Yeah, sports book, football cards, ponies, this place is a gold mine I tell ya'."

"You own it?"

"Nah, I'm the manager. You don't want to know who owns it."

I didn't. "What are you doing here, Eddie? I talked to your Mom not long ago. The Feds are still sniffing around after you."

"Yeah, I know. I got papers though, Marcus Hawkins, joint Canadian American citizen. Also, an honorably discharged Vietnam veteran, no offense."

"The eye thing real?"

"Nah, itches like hell though."

"LT know about this?"

"Hell no. No offense once again, but your friend is a little volatile, you know?"

I knew. As we talked several girls from upstairs entered. They were wearing slightly more than before, but only slightly.

"Working girls?" I asked.

"Sometimes. They waitress too."

The bar started to fill up. Older guys mostly, not the college crowd. A second bartender arrived. Eddie and I took a booth.

"Dave, I'm clearing ten grand a month here. It's legit, the games are straight up, the house advantage is all I need. The bar, the restaurant, they make money. It's the off-site stuff I need help with."

"Booking bets?"

"Yeah, these college kids are mostly stiffs but they love the football cards. I need somebody on campus, somebody I can trust. Somebody like you. You want in?"

"What about the cops?

"Some of them are my best customers. Nobody much cares about the football cards, under the radar, you know?"

"What about the hookers?"

"Free agents, they do or they don't. There's a house cut but I don't take a dime. Not my line of work."

"Just the football cards?"

"Just the cards."

"Look, Eddie, I appreciate the offer, but I'm not exactly wired in on the campus. I'm just there, you know? I don't know who I spread the cards out to."

"That would be the least of your problems, Dave. Word gets around, you know?"

"Let me think about?" I asked.

"Not too long, my friend, time is money."

At that point one of the newly arrived waitresses gave me a big smile. I gave her my full attention. Two trips to Bangkok on R&R from Nam will do that to a guy.

I could sense my time as a school bus driver was coming to an end.

"Where did you learn to shoot like that Cadet Gianoulas?"

"United States Marine Corps, Sergeant. Semper Fi," Teddy answered. He was in week four of the police academy near the top of his class and they hadn't even started their boxing lessons yet.

"Outstanding recruit. How are you with the rifle?"

"Better than with the pistol," Teddy answered confidently. Teddy may have struggled with academics during high school, but police work, tactics and protocols came easy to him. He knew, without question, he was in the right place, doing the right thing and doing it well.

"Boston Metro is forming a Special Weapons and Tactics squad. They are looking for candidates. I think you are exactly what they are looking for. Would you be interested?"

Teddy considered his instructor's question, but only for a moment. "Thanks for asking sir, but I don't want to leave Lowell. Lowell is my hometown, my fiancé, Beth Martin is a nurse at Lowell General, our families are there and that is where I want to raise my family." Teddy paused, then added, "And besides, I had enough of special weapons and tactics in the Marine Corps. I just want to be a good cop."

"Well, good for you candidate. I believe you will be. Now let's take a look at how you handle the rifle."

True to his word Teddy handled the rifle better than the pistol. The rest of the Academy went just as well for him and on a cold and wintry morning, December 12th, 1970, Teddy graduated sixth in a class of forty-two from the Academy and became a Lowell Police officer. One hour after the ceremony, Teddy, in full Lowell PD uniform, married Beth Nelson in the chapel of the Academy. I was best man along with Kevin, not Butchie, who was becoming a better man every day.

"Where do you want me to stand?" Kevin, almost Butchie, asked.

"Right next to me Butch," I answered. "Just take deep breaths, do what I do, watch how happy and proud your mother looks and think about how much Beth appreciates your doing this."

Kevin and I were in the Police Academy chapel, stuffed into matching tuxedos, waiting for the ceremony to begin. Teddy was in a last-minute conference with the chaplain. Teddy's brother, Chris, who had flown in from San Diego for the ceremony, was fussing with his father's tuxedo while family members and fifty police candidates and staff filled the chapel waiting for us.

Kevin was visibly shaking. This was a huge step up for him. While he had ventured out of his family home to help Max at the gym, he had not socialized anywhere else with anybody. Teddy and I had gone over to his house several times to try and coax him out for a drink or a drive and been turned away each time. Initially he wouldn't come out of his room, eventually he would sit with us in the living room but never came with us when we left. It was like watching a ghost of who Butchie was, and it was heartbreaking.

"What if I mess something up?" Kevin asked in a shaky, tentative voice.

"Kev, you hand me the ring, I hand Teddy the ring, Teddy puts the ring on Beth's finger then we go eat a lot of cake. What could go wrong?"

More than we ever could imagine actually.

"Has anybody seen Kevin?" Beth asked after the cutting of the cake.

I was all wrapped up in negotiations with a bridesmaid. Chris was catching up on old times with Max. Teddy and Beth were, you know, newlyweds. Nobody had seen Kevin for a while. A quick search revealed that he was gone. Nobody knew where.

Beth was the first to panic. This is not pleasant for a bride on her wedding day, and we all knew it. Kevin's mom suggested we call the police. We were at the police academy. A "Be On The Lookout" call went out. Teddy and I got in my car, Chris and Max in his and we went looking. The police academy campus was fairly large and was being searched by the forty or so newly minted officers. We took to the surrounding area. Teddy saw him first. He was standing stock still in the middle of a frozen field staring up at the sky. He wasn't wearing his tuxedo jacket. He looked cold.

When Teddy and I walked up to him he did not acknowledge us. He was ice sheet white, and his lips were turning blue.

"Kevin, you alright?" Stupid question, by me of course.

Kevin slowly focused and looked at Teddy and me.

"I shouldn't be here," He whispered.

"If you mean in the middle of this field freezing your ass off, I agree," I answered. "C'mon we can talk about this in the car."

He let us lead him away. He was cold, ice cold. When we were back in the car, the warm car, with the heater going full blast, Teddy said, "Beth and your Mom are scared, Kev. You shouldn't wander off like this."

"What should I do, Ted? I don't belong here; I don't belong anywhere. I'm ashamed of myself all the time. I'm embarrassed to be around people."

"Kev, you've got nothing to be ashamed of. What happened to you was medical, man. The medics did you wrong. They thought they were helping but they bombed you." I began, "I know a little about this medic business, Kev, it wasn't your fault."

"Then whose fault was it?' He begged, "I'm the one that let everybody down. I let myself down."

"The Navy let you down, Kev," Teddy added. "Seems we all got let down a little bit."

For the past six months we all were struggling to keep our feet under us. Turmoil and unrest ripped the country, things appeared to be getting worse, not better. In April President Nixon announced we were invading Cambodia, widening the war, increasing the casualties enhancing the deceit. In May four college students were gunned down, killed, on the Kent State campus for protesting the war. Summer brought riots in the inner cities; another six thousand US troops were killed in Vietnam in this year alone. And the chaos and the confusion went on.

Kevin was shivering now, shaking hard. Teddy and I took off our tuxedo coats and draped them around his shoulders. Kevin sunk beneath the jackets, hiding his face.

"I looked around in there," he said peeking out from under our jackets. "I saw how happy everybody is, how nice Beth and my Mom look. I saw you dancing with the bridesmaid, Max grinning with Chris, and I knew, knew, I will never be able to do any of that. I don't deserve it."

"Just because of what happened to you?" Teddy asked, "You had an accident, the Navy made it worse by giving you the wrong medication. I saw lots of guys get messed up worse than you. It wasn't their fault either."

"You guys were in a war," Kevin added, "I was in a submarine."

"In a submarine under a mile of ice. I wouldn't have lasted five minutes doing that," I said.

"Me neither," Teddy declared.

"I broke down, I chickened out." Kevin hung his head in shame.

"I saw lots of guys break down, Kev. Marines, like me. I was close myself, sometimes. I hung on, bounced back, you know? Maybe you would have to if they hadn't pumped so much bad medicine into you."

Kevin was listening to Teddy. When he spoke, there was a ring of truth.

"Beth told me your doctors said that the damage done to you happened after you were in the hospital. Too many meds for too long messed you up. Not your fault."

"So, what do I do now?" Kevin implored.

"You keep punchin'," Teddy declared, "Just like you told me and Dave to do when we first came to the gym."

"Then you forgive yourself if that's what you feel like you need to do," I added.

"I don't feel like I deserve forgiveness."

"I read about a prayer once," I said. "The British soldiers used to say it during the Zulu wars. It went like this, 'God protect us from what we deserve.'"

Kevin looked confused. Teddy rolled his eyes. I sputtered on. "I just meant that things aren't always as bad as we think they are. Kev, if what happened to you happened to Teddy, or to me, do you think it would have been our fault?"

Kevin looked at Teddy, then at me. "Maybe not if it was Teddy," He replied with the slightest ghost of a grin.

The tension broke in the car. Kevin stopped shivering. He gave Teddy and I our jackets back. "Thanks guys," he said, "I feel better now. Warmer too."

"Can we go back to my wedding now?" Teddy asked.

"Yeah," I added, "I've got an usher to interrupt."

"You interrupt the bridesmaid; I'll interrupt the usher," Kevin offered, again with the ghost of his old smile.

December in London was cold, rainy, foggy and wonderful. Margaret Mary stood at the arrival gate at Heathrow Airport waiting for Sean and Rose to clear customs. Their smiles stretched across the barriers and increased as the distance between them decreased. Rushing into her father's arms Margaret Mary exclaimed, "Oh Father I am so glad you are here!"

Aunt Rose stood benevolently to the side until Margaret Mary embraced her as well, eyes now full of tears of joy. All three of them.

"I've got so much to tell you! So much to show you!" Margaret Mary could barely contain herself as they reached the shuttle to the Tube, the in-crowd Londoner's name for the subway.

Margaret Mary was showing off her familiarity with the local currency, the fares, the routes, and the local lingo. Sean and Rose were gleefully amused at her demonstration of how well she had acclimated to her new surroundings.

"Hurry along mates," she said in her best almost Cockney accent as they boarded the tram from the airport.

"Have you met the Queen herself yet, daughter?" Sean asked. Rose chuckled.

"I thought we would wait, and all meet her together," Margaret Mary answered. You couldn't slip a wisecrack past that girl.

"Our stop is Amersham. Your hotel is right there. You can unpack and we can go to lunch," Margaret Mary announced as they found seats on the Tube.

Ten weeks into her graduate studies Margaret Mary was already noticed as a "comer," a top student. Tuloc Meadows and Kendall Prescott were an ocean away and the trauma of those episodes receded with her newfound friends and aspirations.

They exchanged news and stories and hopes and dreams as the afternoon turned to evening. Then the jet lag hit and Sean and Rose succumbed to giant yawns and weary bones.

"We are to our rest, daughter. You should prepare yourself for your testing and we shall breakfast tomorrow," Sean said.

"A late breakfast or an early lunch, I'm thinking," Rose added.

"Tomorrow, I want you to meet my roommate, Gianna. She is from Palermo and is studying the classics as well. I know you are going to like her."

"Meet her we shall then. Slan leat my daughter."

Final hugs, fond goodnights, and "sleep tights" as Margaret Mary returned to her dormitory with the biggest revelation of her new life yet spoken.

Chapter Nine

Crossroads

"LT, please put the gun down."

We were in our Squire Village living room. It was four o'clock in the morning. I had to get up for classes in three hours. LT had been at the Jack Daniels most of the day and all of the night. More than quite drunk, he considered the Military Issue .45 in his hand.

"They should know, Dave. They should know what it feels like to have a loaded gun pointed at them by someone who intends to use it. You know, I know, they don't know."

LT continued to wave the pistol. I needed him to put it down before something really bad happened. To him or to me. Marty McMahon, our third roommate, was bunkered down in his room, fearing LT's increasingly erratic, and drunken behavior.

"You're absolutely right LT, but please put the gun down on the table. We'll talk about it."

LT considered the weapon, then me. "If they knew Dave, if they knew what it felt like, maybe they'd have some respect for guys, like my guys, like you and me, who had guns pointed at us every day."

LT was looking more bewildered than angry, more lost than found. Finally, he dropped the gun onto the coffee table and leaned back into the sofa, staring up at the ceiling, seeing nothing at all. He took a couple of deep breaths, leaned forward and took a couple of big swallows of Jack Daniels.

"I put heads on stakes Dave. Two of them. Cut them off myself with a bush machete. Two wacks each." He half whispered this, sounding like he was talking about somebody else, something else. But he wasn't.

"We caught two gooks running away from a ville we just lit up. We killed four in the ville, they all had weapons, AK's. These two took off then stopped and knelt in the road like they were surrendering. I held my men back and approached them myself. I put them both face down in the road real quick, tied their hands tight behind their backs, cowboy style, like you see in the rodeo. When I cut off their clothes one guy had two grenades up under his arms with a pull string to detonate them. Couldn't move his arms though. I shot him right behind the ear, took most of his head off. Then I shot the other one twice in the back. He knew about the grenades."

LT looked around the room, seeing what he could not stop remembering.

"I called my men up and took the machete from the point man. I cut off their heads and told my men to put 'em up outside the ville. Put an Ace of Spades in each mouth, let Charlie know what will happen if they mess with 3rd Mar Div."

I was stone cold silent. I knew of such things, heard of them, even accepted them back there, back then. But this was

Amherst, two years later. Here I realized the horror. There it was a message.

"You know what my CO said when he found out what I did? He said, "Outstanding Marine, I'll send an ARVN unit down their tomorrow, give them the heads, you get credit for the ones in the ville. Better PR that way."

"Outstanding, He said. Who the fuck tells a guy cutting heads off is outstanding?" LT took another big pull on his whiskey. Bewildered and drunk, trapped in his memories, LT waited for an answer I did not have.

I gently picked up the gun, unloaded it. I put it on the floor at my feet and when I looked up LT had passed out on the sofa.

Semper Fi.

Events had been going well and not so well my first semester at UMass. I kept to myself, mostly, had a few semi-interesting courses, and hadn't driven the school bus off the cliff, yet. I was getting by, by getting along, keeping my head down and my feet moving forward. I wasn't sure to where yet, but at least I was moving.

On campus I endured student protests against the war, spontaneous and not so spontaneous, noisy demonstrations orchestrated by student radicals and egghead faculty, cancelled classes and closed buildings. An occasional flag burning, or sit-in contributed to the chaos, as well as my own bewilderment. I was as confused inside as the world seemed outside. I took invisible comfort in the fact that nobody was shooting at me, and I hadn't seen anything explode in almost enough time for me to start to relax. A bit.

But still there was my roommate and friend, LT, falling apart. He got worse as the semester went on. His increased drinking didn't help either. There was no name for what LT was going through, not yet. There was a post-military legacy variously called "combat fatigue" or "the thousand-yard stare", "shell shock", even "Vietnam syndrome," but these were terms applied to soldiers still in combat zones. Those of us who came home from war suffered in a different way perhaps best explained by the French expression, "les couers des soldats" or "soldier's heart." A burden hard to explain, harder to live with.

LT was crumbling under the weight of soldier's heart. We had been living together for three months now. He was a brilliant student, top of his graduate studies class, half student, half faculty. I monitored a lecture or two he gave and the parts I understood were fascinating. His visions of farming the oceans, breeding fish and shellfish in controlled conditions were far ahead of the times, far ahead of his aspirations. LT had a dream, two dreams really, only one of them was a nightmare.

A boots-on-the-ground combat soldier in Nam, he was in the middle of the "kill more of them then they kill us" mindset and he was good, if that is the proper expression, at his job. Through long, whiskey fueled talks I had learned that LT was a natural born leader, following the wrong orders. He did what he did because he was ordered to, and in that time and place that was Vietnam, in the jungle, killing more of them than they did us made sense in a twisted, barbaric way. "Outstanding," to some. I was blessed to never be part of the slaughter. Dustoff saved lives so that more lives could be taken. How's that for an anomaly? Hence LT's heart was heavy, mine felt broken. Neither of us felt blameless.

I spread a blanket over LT, clicked off the living room lights and passed out on the sofa. This was not going in the right direction, and I had no idea what the right direction might be.

"I'm afraid you are going to lose that arm young man."

Kendall Prescott sat in the storefront office of the Haight-Ashbury free clinic on Oak Street in San Francisco. Dr. Daniel Arnett volunteered there three days a week treating street kids, free spirits, addicts and outlaws. Like Kendall Prescott.

Kendall had been self-medicating the injury for weeks. Not strong enough antibiotics, a host of pain killers and lots of marijuana had not turned the trick. Infection had turned to gangrene, gangrene necessitated amputation.

"I'm afraid I'll have to take it from the elbow down. If you wait any longer you could lose it from the shoulder, or you could die." Dr. Arnett had come to learn that straight talk worked best with these patients. "How did this injury happen?"

"I had an accident," Kendall muttered through gritted teeth.

"Some accident, looks like an elephant stepped on it," Dr. Arnett replied.

An elephant named Dave Ferrier, Kendall thought. And one day I am going to step on him and he'll lose a lot more than an arm. And that's nothing compared to what I'm going to do to that little bitch Margaret Mary everybody seems to love. She'll wish all I did was take her arm. I'm going to take her whole fucking life. Kendall swam in his hate, relished it, nurtured it, let it grow and grow. He'd get even. More than even.

"You gotta' do what you gotta' do, Doc." Kendal proclaimed. "When do we do this?"

"Immediately if not sooner. I will arrange the surgery, be back here tomorrow. You will be in the hospital for several days."

"From the elbow down?" Kendall asked.

Dr. Arnett nodded.

Small enough price to pay for what I'm going to do to "Mags" and that Ferrier asshole when I get healed up, Kendall ruminated. They'll wish all they lost was an arm.

"Nullaig Shona Duit!"

Aunt Rose heralded as Margaret Mary stepped off the train in Dublin.

"That's "Merry Christmas" in our own Gaelic tongue," She explained as she threw her arms around her favorite and only niece.

"Null-ig-hun-a-dit," Margaret Mary responded phonetically. "Where is himself, my Father?" She asked while they gathered bags and moved off the arrival platform.

"Isn't he dashing about from the butcher to the baker to the candle shop preparing all for your arrival, lass."

"Mince pies and roasted turkey?" Margaret Mary proclaimed as they climbed aboard a festive red bus.

"Indeed, and much more. He cannot stop himself from singing of your arrival my dear."

"And me of my being here," Margaret Mary answered as she watched the streets of Dublin roll past. Christmas trees and holly were all about, a perfect dusting of snow blanketed the city and brilliantly colored lights decorated the shops and windows and doorways of the city.

Margaret Mary could barely contain her joy, a feeling she had not been able to conjure for a long, long time. And the happiness shone from her, around her and from within her.

"And your schooling? It went fine?" Rose asked.

"More than fine, Antaidh."

"Aunt, or Aunty will do fine, my love, lest we lose our native tongue altogether," Rose replied.

"Gaelic is our native tongue," Margaret Mary responded cheerfully, "At least for you and Da. I'm working on it for me."

"Work on it you will then. How long will you be staying with us lass?"

"Three weeks!" Margaret Mary responded joyously. "Three whole weeks before I must return to my studies."

"And isn't that your Father, waiting for us at the bus station?"

As Margaret Mary's joy grew larger than the season.

In Rome, Peter leaned into the Church's holiest time of the year, both festive and reverential. Putting aside his growing skepticism, he rejoiced with the faithful, prayed with the worshipful and sang with the joyous. He felt in his heart the uplifting, rapture of the season. He noted the gratification these ceremonies brought to the masses, the ecstasy of pomp and circumstance brought to the faithful. Peter was coming to understand the contribution of the pageantry, the value of the Church's rituals, traditions and teachings in providing a framework for faith, conscience and salvation. "What the eye can see, the heart will feel." Peter recalled reading somewhere, giving him pause in his studies and temperance to his doubts.

"If indeed the Gospels are parables, are they not beneficial parables?" Father Specio asked in one of his many instructional talks with Peter.

"Beneficial being more prized than truthful? Peter would respond.

"Peter," Monsignor Specio would advise, "My years as a cleric have taught me to value consequences above actualities when those consequences are more beneficial to mankind."

"Are you saying that the Gospels then are not the actual word of God?" Peter asked indignantly.

"The Gospels were written by man, many of them long years after the death of Christ and no doubt amended, embellished and somewhat fictionalized to convey God's message," Father Specio responded, frankly and off the record. "You must learn to see beyond the dogma to the benefit of these parables. What they provide are guidelines, moral truths and profound examples. Combined then with faith and goodwill they form the basis for positive morality and conscience. It is how the Gospels make you feel rather than what they report that is important."

Peter recalled all this while considering the splendor of the Christmas Vatican. Mangers, angels, magi on life size camels, choirs a hundred voices strong, glowing neon babes in swaddling clothes and bright Christmas stars abounded throughout the Basilica. The evening past thousands of worshippers had come to sing and pray in the Rotunda. At noon this day Pope Paul VI would address thousands more in Saint Peter's Square bringing a message of hope and deliverance to the crowd. All this spectacle, Peter realized, was essential to the essence of Christendom, the framework of tradition providing the conduit for devotion.

Oh Come all Ye Faithful
Joyful and triumphant
Oh Come Ye, Oh Come Ye
To Bethlehem.
Oh come and adore Him,
Born the King of Angels.

Oh come let us adore him,
Oh come let us adore him,
Oh come let us adore him,
Christ the Lord.

And the words echoed in Peter's aching heart.

My first semester at UMass ended with a flurry of final exams, rote repetitions, and course summations. I breezed through them all, not really caring about the difference between an "A", "B", or "C" grade. I passed all my tests, a proclamation I remembered making many years ago at Keith Academy, to no avail.

At semester's end our nearly invisible third roommate, Marty McMahon, announced he would not be back for second semester, leaving LT and I with an increase in overhead and a shortage of a roommate. Before leaving Marty confided in me that he had become increasingly wary of LT's drinking and ranting, not to mention that he thought there were a few too many firearms about the apartment. LT actually had a small arsenal, the wrong guy with the wrong weapons.

LT announced he was going to Philadelphia for the holidays to see his parents. Apparently, his relations with them had become somewhat strained in the past year or so and he was off on a peacekeeping mission. He hoped. Our apartment would be empty for a week or so, then I had to be back to drive that goddamn school bus that was eventually going to get me arrested.

I was going to Lowell and looking forward to spending some time with my family. I had seen little of them since school started, spending most weekends in Amherst and often lacking the funds for the round-trip gasoline. I wanted, needed, very much to reconnect with my family. My brothers, Bob and John, were becoming strangers to me with separate lives I could not fathom. Bob was an apprentice electrician, still living at home but making decent money. John, just out of high school was adrift, not unlike myself, but engulfed in a frequent haze of marijuana, unemployment and recreational drugs. Nothing serious so far, I hoped, but a slippery slope.

Mom and Dad were supportive of my educational efforts, tolerant of the behavior of their no longer children, children, and content in their passing years. I had Christmas gifts for all, hoping to recreate the magic of long-ago Christmas mornings. For my Dad I purchased "Diving For Sunken Treasure," from the Undersea World of Jacques Cousteau collection. I had old reliable, "White Shoulders" perfume for my Mom and a couple of nifty four blade jackknives for my brothers. I would treat myself to a lengthy cross-Atlantic phone call to Margaret Mary in Dublin and a shiny black leather badge case and wallet combo for Officer Gianoulous, Teddy. He's, my buddy.

As I locked up the apartment for the week in Lowell, I repeated the mantra I had been whispering to myself a lot lately. *So far, so good.* Fragile but functional.

Ho, Ho, Ho, at least for now.

Chapter Ten

Yuletide

The streets of Lowell looked even smaller when I returned home for the Christmas holidays. They looked dingy and drab, festooned with fading holiday colors, dim Christmas lights, and potholes. Christmas Eve looked like Christmas long past.

When I arrived on Glenmere Street, the house was sparkling in colored lights, the porch railing wrapped in holly and a flickering plastic candle in every window. In the living room a festive tree with mysteriously wrapped presents nestled around the base filled a corner with joys to come. I added my treasures to the pile and sat to have tea with my mother. Bob and John were out and about, and my Dad was not yet home from work. Quality time with Mom, this could go right or wrong in a heartbeat.

"What are you studying out at school?" She asked as we sat at the kitchen table. She looked more tired than sad, a good sign, and seemed genuinely interested.

"General subjects, Mom, Introduction to this and that. I took a Psychology Course, Freshman Literature, Basic French, I'm just sorta' getting my feet on the ground."

"Do you like it?"

"It beats the dryer room at Haartz Auto and making burgers at Lefty's." So far so good. "How about you, Mom? How are you feeling?"

"Fine," she lied. "I'm just a little tired." Which is as deep as it ever got with my Mom.

She asked if I had heard from Margaret Mary and how Teddy liked being a policeman. I told her Margaret Mary was very happy in her school and that Sean and Rose had moved to Ireland to be near her. I said Teddy and Beth were living in an apartment over on Boylston Street and I was going to stop over later that day.

After several minutes, as silence was starting to thunder, my Mom said, in a very low voice, "David, I'm sorry I gave all your things away while you were in the Army."

She stared at the kitchen tabletop as she said this and did not look up at me as she continued, "I was so angry that you were going back to Vietnam when you didn't have to. I was worried sick about you every day and prayed you would get home alright. When you did and then told us you had volunteered to go back, I thought I'd never see you again. I threw everything of yours out so I wouldn't have to think about it." Then she did something I had never before seen my mother do, she started crying.

I was stunned silent. I couldn't find words. I took her hand and squeezed gently. We were both quiet for a while until my brother John came home, saw us, noticed our Mother was crying and high-tailed it down the hall to his bedroom.

"I was with Men of Honor, Mom. They, we, were doing good, saving lives. I didn't want to stop doing that. I didn't think my going back would hurt you."

"Then we were both wrong, weren't we?" She said, withdrawing her hand. With that she stood up, went down the hall and closed her bedroom door behind her. I sat in silence, still stunned, until John crept up the hall, poked his head into the kitchen and said, "Is Ma all right?"

"I hope so," Was all I could mutter. John took a seat at the table.

"What was that all about anyway?"

"I was telling her why I went back to Nam."

"Boy, was she pissed," John recalled. "She got rid of all your stuff after Ricky Burke's funeral. What she didn't throw away she gave to the Church, you know, the thrift store. I tried to save some of your stuff, but she caught me and said she didn't want any of that in the house."

I thought about that for a moment. "Thanks for trying," was all I could think of to say.

"You know what she said on the way home from the cemetery after Ricky's funeral?"

I wasn't sure I wanted to hear this. "You know the part where they fold up a flag and give it to the family?" I nodded; John continued. "She said if they ever gave one of those to her, she'd throw it back in their face."

"That sounds like Ma," I said.

Christmas was off to a flying start.

"You're sure about this? It's for real?" Teddy asked as Beth smiled a Christmas smile. She nodded her head as Teddy swept her up in his arms. "So, for Christmas I'm getting a baby?" Teddy rejoiced.

"That's what Dr. Repucci said," Beth squealed as Teddy squeezed. "And he's never been wrong so far."

They were sharing a quiet, intimate Christmas morning in their soon-to-be, no longer large enough one bedroom apartment. Noon would find them on Glenmere Street where Connie was cooking a turkey with help from Beth's mom and a guy learning to think of himself as Kevin, and Butchie, once again. 4PM would find Teddy in a patrol car, cruising Centerville. Rookies work holidays.

"Does anybody else know?" Teddy asked.

"Nobody, just you and me," Beth replied.

"Can we tell them today?"

"I can't think of a better day to tell them," Beth smiled, Teddy squeezed her again.

LT woke up Christmas morning hung over with a black eye and a swollen jaw. He vaguely remembered arguing with his father, his mother crying and, even more vaguely, blows being exchanged. He could not recall what the argument was about.

He dressed as quietly as he could in his room and tiptoed to the kitchen where he hoped to find coffee. He found his mother.

"Your father wants you out of the house before he comes down here this morning," His mother said, saddened and furious at both of them.

"Merry Christmas to you too, Mom," LT replied through the hurt and confusion.

"Don't Merry Christmas me! You ought to be ashamed of yourself as your father will not be. I'm sick of the two of you!"

LT moved to try and hug his mother. She squirmed away. "You should leave. You struck your father!"

"I seem to recall him striking me a few times as well, Mom."

"You were both drunk! Drunk and fighting on Christmas Eve and about what? A war neither of you understand!"

It was all coming back to him now. His father was defending President Nixon, saying what we needed in Vietnam was more soldiers trying to win the war than protesting it. LT recalled saying his father didn't know what the hell he was talking about, and that Nixon would drag the damn war out so that he could be reelected. Sometime around there the punching started.

"Can I get a cup of coffee first?" LT asked.

"Just don't wake your father, then you should leave," His mother answered sadly.

LT took the coffee to go. He started back to Amherst. He had nowhere else to go. On the lonely ride back, LT took stock. A couple of friends, Dave, his roommate, and Marcus, down at the China Rose, his bartender. He was dating a hooker at fifty bucks a date, majoring in a science nobody really gave a shit about and doing his daily best not to shoot the hippies swamping the campus with anti-war protests. In the few moments he was not boiling with anger and could take reasonable stock of himself he realized he was going nowhere fast and in a big hurry.

He missed and needed the structure and discipline of the Marine Corps and wished he had the chance to use the training and skills he learned there in a cause more worthy than he found in the jungles of Vietnam. The war haunted his days and tortured his nights. More than honored memories he harbored deep regrets and heartfelt remorse, smothered pride and unmerited shame. And that was on his good days.

As he drove through the nearly abandoned campus, past the dangling Styrofoam candy canes and plastic reindeer, he passed a lonely looking manger scene, noticed someone had stolen the Baby Jesus from the crib and chuckled to himself. "Lost as the Lord, that's me, only nobody will notice I'm gone."

By the time he turned the key to let himself into the Squire Village apartment LT had decided what to do. It wasn't going to make many people very happy, and it was kinda' going to screw Dave over a bit but he had made up his mind. School was out and it was going to stay that way.

Not quite yet Father Peter Rayburn stood in the doorway of Saint Peter's Basilica handing out Mass cards to the faithful on this beautiful, clear Christmas morning in the Eternal City. He could not help but notice the joy, the rapture, the anticipation on the faces of the faithful as they filtered into the cathedral for the Nativity Morning Mass.

Peter listened to a chorus of "Buon Natale's," "Joyeaux Noel's," "Feliz Navidiad's," and several "Merry Christmas, Father's" as he handed out the precious cards.

"Felicem Natalem Christi," he replied in the Church's Latin, feeling the pride of belonging and of sharing the happiness of the devoted. In the background the Basilica reverberated with the sounds of the ancient pipe organ gifting holiday hymns to the gathering congregation.

Awash in the smiles and joy of the congregation, Peter's vocational misgivings receded, and his doubts diminished. Dressed in the brightest and whitest of Christmas Day cassocks and surplus, he realized the unique and essential gift of the Church to the churchgoers. Hope of salvation, belief in a loving god, life after death, forgiveness for their sins, all heralded on this day by the birth of their Saviour. He recalled the comfort of the Christmas carols of his youth, "O Come All Ye Faithful," "Silent Night, Holy Night," O Little town of Bethlehem," sung "en choir" in the comforting cathedral of Lowell's far away Immaculate Conception church.

For this morning only Peter would rejoice in the promise of the Church, the sanctity of its rituals, the richness of its message. He chose to concentrate on the joyful tidings of the Church and not the machine that ran it as he exchanged Christmas greetings with the happy faces around him.

"It's a Crock Pot, Mom," My brother Bob explained. "You make stew and soup and things like that in it." My mother eyed Bob's gift skeptically. "New Fangled," unfamiliar and destined to be underused, she thanked him for the present.

"This one's from me, Mom," John proudly announced passing her an atrociously packaged bundle of mangled holiday wrapping paper. As she un-mangled her gift the slightest hint of a smile crossed her face. Letting the green and red paper fall to the floor she considered the brightly colored knitted hat and gloves best worn by teenage girls and thanked John for them.

A smile of any kind from our often-saddened mother was a holiday gift of its own and she tried hard, to be at her sunniest on this Christmas morning.

"You get this one, Dad," Bob announced passing my Dad a hefty square package wrapped in more of John's discarded green and red paper.

"We chipped in together for it," John added as my Dad revealed a "Ted Williams Fish Finder" from Sears & Roebuck. Designed to dangle under our boat it promised to locate fish for the catching. Dad grinned like Sunshine, as he always did and thanked me and my brothers.

There were more gifts of course, do-dads and trinkets, garments and games, evenly distributed about the room. Around the Christmas tree old wounds were healed, old memories reawakened, new affections were formed. Mom kissed me on the cheek and thanked me for the White Shoulders perfume. Dad scanned his Jacques Cousteau book with a great smile, while wearing a battered yellow baseball cap with a blue fish upon it. Bob and John clicked through their jackknife blades. I stacked my collection of woolen scarves, knitted gloves, sweaters and underwear next to the latest Everly Brothers album (from my brothers) and took in the room. For today, for this quiet comfortable Christmas morning we were a family again. The delicious aroma of an overnight baking turkey with stuffing filled the house. English muffins, coffee and orange juice would hold us to the holiday meal. We gave to one another not just our gifts but our love, our attention, just for now apart from the everyday, week to week trials and troubles and distractions of daily life. Tomorrow would bring back the distance, the drifting apart all such unions must suffer, but for just that moment, that single instant in time all was well, the Christmas magic was working.

Somewhere an angel sang…

***Have yourself a Merry Little Christmas,
Let your heart be light.
From now on your troubles
Will be out of sight.***

Have yourself a Merry Little Christmas,
Make the Yuletide gay,
From now on your troubles
Will be far away.

Here we are as in olden days,
Happy Golden Days of yore,
Faithful friends who are dear to us
Together near to us once more.

Through the years we all will be together,
If the Fates allow,
Hang a shining star upon the highest
bow,

And have yourself a
Merry Little Christmas now. *

If only.

Lyrical Aspiration:

*Have yourself a Merry Little Christmas, Ralph Blaine and
Hugh Martin.

Chapter Eleven

Salvation and Other Occurrences

When I got back to Amherst after Christmas, I found LT's car outside the apartment but no LT inside the apartment. Then I saw the note and the gunny sack on the kitchen table. The note read:

Dave,

I have taken off for the tall and uncut. Alaska beckons. Maybe I can find some peace there. I left the pink slip for my car. Sell it, make my share of the rent with it, throw a party, buy yourself a toy. Whatever.

The rest of the stuff in the bag is better off with you than with me. If it's not too much trouble maybe you could save what's in there for me. The rest of my junk is yours. I'm sorry for the hassle but I have to get away before I hurt somebody, or myself.

See you down the road,

LT.

I looked in the bag. His 1911 Colt .45, holster and lots of ammo. An envelope of papers I did not open or read. A pair of silver First Lieutenant bars, the Vietnam campaign bar, a Silver Star ribbon and two Purple Hearts. Not much to leave behind, unless you knew how much they represented. I was down to no roommates, a three hundred dollar a month apartment, LT's ex-car, and five rooms of thrift store furniture. Then things really started to suck.

Also on the table was my second semester pre-registration packet which I had forgotten to mail before I went home for the holidays. This meant I would have to register on cattle call day when a couple thousand more forgetters like me would fight to get into classes that were already filled during pre-registration. This fiasco happened on Saturday morning at Boyden Gym on campus. Hundreds of tables, thousands of students, lots of confusion, and me. Not Yippee.

After digesting that bit of information, I called the bus company to see when they wanted me back to work. I was told they had re-routed some buses and combined routes so they would not be needing me this semester, or this year. They also asked me to let LT know he was not needed as well. Also, Not Yippee.

No classes, no job, no roommates, little money, I was out of ideas for what to do next.

It was time for an emergency call to Margaret Mary.

"Please, please, please, give it one more semester, Please! For me. One more."

I have all my life found it very hard to say no to Margaret Mary but here I was at wit's end. My wits, my end. Margaret Mary's voice rang with concern and care all across the ocean, the miles and miles between us. I called to tell her I was quitting school, maybe following LT to Alaska, or heading South, all the way to a magical place called Key West I had read about and yearned to see. College had become an upside down, convoluted hassle for me with no upside in sight.

The GI bill gave me $175 a month. I had no job and a $300 tab for the apartment. Even if I sold LT's car, a shiny, turquoise green 1966 Thunderbird, the money wouldn't last long enough to get me through the year. Jobs were scarce, paid peanuts and demanded a lot of patience, time, and tolerance, three things I did not have a lot of.

"Didn't you learn anything from the last time you quit school?" Margaret Mary scolded.

"I learned how to shoot a machine gun," I answered with inappropriate and unfunny wit.

Our phone connection was excellent, I could hear her snort in frustration plain as day.

"David, be serious. Do you want to end up back at Lefty's or at that factory where your father works?"

Haartz Auto, the dryer room. Playing the ponies. Playing dead.

One thing I had learned the last time I quit school, the guys with an education got ahead. The rest of us filled sandbags, dug ditches or stopped bullets. I knew this to be true. Often during my first, unhappy semester at UMass I heard the voice of my hooch mate Army buddy Don Avila, himself a college graduate say, "You don't want to burn shit and fill sandbags the rest of your life? Get an education."

So that is what I set out to do and hadn't done so far.

"David you are far too intelligent to do something this stupid. Alaska? Do you seriously think your friend is going to solve his problems by going to Alaska?" Margaret Mary's exasperation was intensified by her sincerity. And I knew LT wasn't going to find peace in the fiftieth state. They sold Jack Daniels in Alaska.

"You are smart, you will find a way through this," Margaret Mary implored, "Don't become a quitter, David. Don't give up."

"You're right, I know you're right. I'll give it one more try." Thanks to Margaret Mary I re-made up my mind, sort of. One more semester, somehow.

"Father Valden should have received the funds he requested for the water pump and filters by now," Monsignor Specio announced as he sat with Peter in the Vatican library. This would be the one quiet period of the day which would soon be filled with classes, lectures, ceremonies, prayer and meditation.

"That is a wonderful thing," Peter replied, thankful for his help, bothered by its necessity.

"The Church can and does perform good works throughout the world every day, Peter. Perhaps that is where your focus should be." The Monsignor dropped a sheaf of papers in front of Peter, his latest research project.

Peter had just submitted the paper for review on the historical origins of the celibate clergy, much to the discomfort of his superiors. He was rapidly gaining on, even outdistancing, many of the church's toughest critics. Clamoring for change among multiple antiquated church policies was viewed as positively progressive by some, as dangerously radical by others. Unfortunately for Peter there were more "others" than "somes" in the present church hierarchy.

"Your thesis on celibacy among the clergy was not well received, Peter. The feeling is your efforts should be focused on more constructive efforts."

"I thought perhaps Christmas and the birth of Jesus might have been a good time to discuss the benefit of holy matrimony," Peter replied with more than a little sarcasm.

Monsignor Specio frowned, his patience with his brightest, yet most controversial, acolyte starting to run thin. "You have six short months until your ordination Peter. Your attitude is being called into question."

"As is my vocation?" Peter asked.

"Along with your unwillingness to concentrate on the good the church does rather than the inconsistencies within our structure."

"Sixty-three billion dollars in assets is more than just an inconsistency," Peter replied.

"An arbitrary figure at best, Peter. One you should perhaps not spend so much time focused on." Peter heard the sternness in Monsignor Specio's voice. The first of the official warning bells.

"Archbishop Marcinkus seems to think it's a minimum figure," Peter replied defiantly.

"Another influence you would be well advised to spend less time with."

Archbishop Paul Marcinkus was born in Cicero, Illinois in 1922. He sat out World War II in a couple of seminary schools before being ordained in 1947. He rose through the Church's byzantine ranks eventually becoming a confidant and advisor to Popes John XXIII and Paul VI. Nicknamed "The Gorilla" he became an informal bodyguard to both Popes accompanying them on any and all overseas excursions.

In 1968, despite having no prior training or background in banking, he was named secretary of the Vatican Bank. Subsequently he came under the scrutiny of the Racketeering Section of the United States Department of Justice regarding a number of questionable financial practices. Despite this his star, and his power, within the Church was rising.

"Archbishop Marcinkus is becoming a powerful man here," Monsignor Specio continued, "In all confidence Peter I am not sure he is not part of the problem you are so concerned about. You would be well advised to be wary of the man."

As Monsignor Specio left Peter with his doubts and his discoveries about the Catholic church, he struggled with similar misgivings about his future as a clergyman. Aside from an uncountable stockpile of immense wealth, a clerical lifestyle as privileged as princes, real estate holdings throughout the world with a land mass larger than many countries and a profusion of immense, ornate, half empty cathedrals in every major city in the western world there was the disgraceful legacy of history from pacts with Nazis to present day tribal genocides in Africa.

Peter realized the Church funded many charities, but an accounting of monies received, and monies distributed was hard, very, very hard to determine. Faith may bring comfort to many on Christmassy mornings, but fiscal facts and tarnished history troubled, troubled deeply, almost Father Peter Rayburn.

"Marcus, did you have a Merry Christmas?" I asked, taking a seat in the China Rose cocktail lounge.

"Snuck into town, saw my Ma, snuck out of town, 'in a one-horse open sleigh.'" He answered partly in song.

"No Rudolph?" I countered.

"No FBI either. How about you? You hangin' in there?"

"LT took off. Alaska, he said. Lookin' to solve a personal problem geographically."

"I tried that; it'll never work. Beer?" Marcus drew me a draft before I could answer.

"Eddie, I've got a problem," I whispered leaning across the bar. Eddie scanned the mostly empty room. One table, two couples waiting to have dinner. Two plain clothes cops at the other end of the bar, drinking on the house. One pretty waitress with very little to do.

"Angel," Marcus called, the waitress looked up, "Watch the bar a minute, will you?" Then to me, "Step into my office, problems get solved in there."

Eddie's office was dim, dingy and full of taped shut cardboard boxes. I didn't ask. Eddie sat behind a battered desk. Two worn green office chairs sat in front. I chose the cleanest.

"What's up?" Eddie asked.

"I need a job. That card thing still open?"

"Card thing ain't happening now my friend. I don't handle basketball, hockey, that shit. Now football, you got college games on Saturday, the pros on Sunday, then this new Monday Night Game, easy. Basketball, hockey, every other night, five, six games a week, different nights, the bookkeeping is a nightmare. Who's got the time? I'm sorry Dave, I'm pretty shut down on that stuff till fall."

This is not good news. My ace in the hole, wasn't.

"Look, Dave, you stuck for cash? I can front you some dough," Eddie offered.

"No thanks, Eddie. I couldn't afford the vig."

"Hey! No vig! Friend loan. I know you checked in with my mother a coupla' times when I was on the lam, told her you were sure I was alright. Made her feel good. Look, I got a bar back, a relief bartender, maybe I can put you on a couple nights a week, you know, clean up, stock the bar."

"Thanks Eddie, that's not a job, that's charity. I appreciate it but no thanks."

"If any of my guys quit, you're first in line. Is there anything else I can do for ya'?"

"Maybe, I have a car I need to sell. LT's. He left me the pink slip, said to sell it to cover his share of the rent he was sticking me with."

"What kind of car?"

"T-Bird, nice one, '66 in good shape."

Eddie started writing down a phone number. "Call this guy, he's a friend of mine, works down at Pierce Ford. I'll give him a call myself. He'll treat you right."

I thanked Eddie and left with no idea how to get right.

During the first week of January the Veterans Administration awarded former Petty Officer Kevin Martin a 100% Disability Rating due to injuries incurred while serving on active duty. The notification by mail came as a surprise and a shock to Kevin.

"Does this mean I've got to go back into the hospital?" A frightened, Kevin, not Butchie, asked his now brother-in-law Teddy Gianoulous.

"No," Teddy replied. "It just means the Navy is accepting responsibility for what happened to you, and you'll be getting a disability check and disability benefits from the VA."

"I don't want a disability check and I don't want to be disabled!" Kevin shouted.

"The check doesn't make you disabled, only you can do that, and the benefits are to help you get over the injuries the Navy is saying they are responsible for," Teddy asserted, forcefully. "You were in a coma for almost six months, Kev, that wasn't because of you that was because the Navy screwed up. Do you feel the same today as you did before that happened to you?"

Kevin shook his head, thinking hard about not thinking at all.

"I'm trying to do better," He answered weakly.

"You are doing better, Kev, but you are not who you were. It was drugs, the wrong drugs that disabled you. It's not just a check, it's a validation."

Kevin still looked skeptical.

"Look, I've got two Purple Hearts, two of 'em. Just scratches really compared to what happened to a lot of guys. I'm getting 30% disability from the VA. I earned it, so did you," Teddy asserted.

"I don't feel like I deserve it."

"Feelings aren't facts, Kev. Look you took a punch, a big punch. You went down, it's time to get up. Remember when that guy from Providence clocked you in the semi's?"

Teddy was referring to one of Butchie, not Kevin's Golden Gloves matches several years before. Kevin, not Butchie, shook his head in wonder.

"Felt like I got hit by a truck."

"You went down, it'd been me I would have stayed down till the ambulance arrived. What'd you do?"

Kevin, not Butchie, fought the fog in his head. "Took an eight count. Caught him trying to throw that overhand right again, knocked him into the cheap seats." Kevin smiled, the warmth of remembrance inside him returning.

"You've had your eight count Kev, time to get up."

"The Troubles, daughter are most bitter in the north, Ulster, County Kerry. Here they simmer and I fear will get worse," Sean stated as Margaret Mary packed in Dublin for her return to London. "And as yet it is difficult to say if your Bernadette Devlin will be a help or a hindrance to the ending of these sufferings."

"She's not "my" Bernadette Devlin, father. She is Ireland's hope, a voice for sanity and hopefully a messenger of compromise and peace."

"The Troubles" as they were called had plagued Ireland for well over a hundred years of pain, turmoil and strife. Protestant against Catholic, rich against poor, Orange against Green, the divisions ran deep and deadly. Bernadette Devlin was a firebrand college student who spoke out against violence and spoke eloquently about civil rights and negotiation between these warring parties. She made headlines throughout the world when she became the youngest member ever elected to the English Parliament as a representative from mid-Ulster at the age of twenty-one.

"Raise not your hopes too high my daughter. Many have come before, tried before, yet Ireland's Troubles continue."

Sean spoke from his experiences and impressions formed during his first semester at the University of Dublin where he now taught classical literature and poetry. Students dissented over separatism versus unionism, the Free Irish State over allegiance to the British Commonwealth. Tensions mounted and the hints of coming violence grew stronger. He worried that his daughter had become quite enamored of the latest young firebrand on her Christmas vacation in Ireland.

"Don't worry yourself, Da, I'll not be building bombs or standing barricades. I've my education to finish and my future to decide."

"In London, no less, where the troubles begin," Rose injected.

"In London where the University stands," Margaret Mary answered. "And it's to London I need to be going."

Hugs and farewells later Margaret Mary thought of The Troubles, here, there and everywhere or so it seemed.

Second semester registration was on a Saturday morning on the triple basketball courts of Boyden Gymnasium. A couple hundred tables with long lines of students in front of each of them, late sign ups for classes, like me. I got to the gym at 8AM, so did everybody else. Noise, confusion, frustration, chaos. Taking a deep, deep breath I got in line for two classes, waited thirty minutes to get to the head of the line and was told each was full. I got in line for a third when a group walked past me complaining that the course, I was standing in line for was already full as well. In all likelihood the majority of the popular classes were already full. The open courses sucked. I didn't have a job. I was broke. I couldn't afford the apartment I was living in. I didn't have a friend on campus. My not so far away war raged on. Fuck this. Alaska beckoned. Key West beckoned. I'd find a way to explain this to Margret Mary later.

I stomped out of the gym, threw my registration packet into a trash can by the door and stood on the stairs taking deep breaths, not sure what to do next.

"Hey, you a veteran?" A voice behind me asked.

"What's it to ya?" I snorted, thankfully to myself, as I spun around.

A guy about my age, wearing an Army field jacket, jeans and combat boots had my registration packet in his hand. He was smiling. I was curious.

"Yeah," I answered tentatively.

"Thought so. I saw you go by our table."

"What table?" There were lots of tables.

"Beta Chi, Veterans fraternity. My names Dick Gerson. When the guys let me, I'm the president of Beta Chi. Vet's don't have to stand in those lines. C'mon I can get you registered."

"I don't want to join a fraternity." I was still surly, cautious.

"You don't have to," He was grinning, "You want to sign up or not?"

I did. I followed Dick back in. He asked me what courses I was interested in. We walked to the back of the tables. He spoke with the registrars. They took down my information. I got every class I wanted, even the full ones. It took about fifteen minutes. I was dumbfounded.

"Thank you," I said, and never meant it more in my life.

"De Nada," Dick replied, holding out his hand for shaking. I shook.

"You ought to come out to the house, meet some of the guys. We meet Monday nights, 6:30," Dick offered.

"Uh'm yeah, I might do that," I replied. Not. The last thing I needed was a room full of vets telling each other war stories. Thanks, but no thanks.

"I saw on your packet you live in Squire Village. That's right down the road from us. He wrote an address on my envelope. "C'mon by, Monday night."

"I'll try," I lied. Dick excused himself to get back to his table and to saving vets. I left re-registered and grateful with no intention of looking these guys up on Monday night.

"Bounce around a little, move to your left, jab, duck, roll, jab. That's it, much better!" Kevin ruffled the hair of the young boxer working the heavy bag at the YMCA gym. The boy's smile lit up his face, lit up Kevin's as well. Across the room looking from his office door, Max smiled too.

Kevin had started coming to the gym three days a week, then four, now every day except Sunday. He coached the youngsters, sparred gently with the older kids and rocketed the heavy bag on his own between lessons. He was hardening back into shape, his shoulders and legs felt fit, ready, strong. His mind was starting to feel that way as well. At his sister Beth's, now Mrs Gianoulous, insistence he had started taking night classes, two of them, at Lowell Technological Institute. Sports Therapy and Nutrition being the subject matter, self confidence and purpose being the by product.

"Nix it! The cops!" One of the young boys shouted as Teddy entered the gym. Full police uniform belted and badged, Teddy headed straight for Max's office, waving across the room at Kevin. Teddy was volunteering at the gym as well.

"You up to something I should know about?" Teddy said to the boy who shouted the warning.

"Not me, Officer Ted," The boy responded happily. "You wanna' go a few rounds?"

"Tomorrow, three o'clock. You be here, we'll dance," Teddy said with a grin as he went into Max's office. Max was seated behind his desk looking tired, very tired. Age was catching up to the old fighter, but he was still here every day. Doing what he did best, doing good for a lot of young boys who needed something good done for them. Teddy noticed the years piling up on his old friend. Max erased them with his smile.

"That box of gear you got us came yesterday. Good stuff, you shoulda' seen the kids when I passed the stuff out."

Tape wraps, jock straps, head gear, bag gloves, all from Lull & Hartford, the locally owned and managed sporting goods store run by the Ryne family. Donated, Teddy pointed out by a good man running a good business.

"How you feelin' Max? Kevin working out okay?" Teddy asked.

"Practically runnin' the joint," Max responded. "The kids love him, I love him. He's doin' better than better."

"I'm happy to hear that, my wife is going to be happier than me."

"You guys talkin' about me?" Kevin asked from the doorway.

"Always," Teddy answered. "You hittin' 'em hard, Kev?"

"Only if they hit me first. Max, I gotta' leave about three today. School night. Hey, you guys are coming to dinner on Sunday, right? Ma's making pot roast."

Max nodded. Teddy said of course. Kevin went back to his young boxers. Teddy went back to his squad car and for now all was right with the world.

Eddie's buddy at Pierce Ford gave me eighteen hundred bucks for LT's T-Bird. More than enough to cover his share of the rent for the semester. I had my GI Bill money but still needed a job if I planned on eating regular. I was without a plan Monday evening when there was a knock on my door at Squire Village.

Dick Gerson of the Beta Chi Veterans fraternity was on my doorstep.

"Thought I'd see if you needed a ride to come out to the meeting," He began cheerfully. It was about 14 degrees outside and getting colder. I let him into the apartment.

"Look," he added. "I know you weren't coming. I also know you should. Give it a try, we're only a couple miles down the road. If it sucks, you can leave but give it a try. You owe me one."

I owed him one? I didn't like owing anything. But I did owe him one. I grabbed my coat.

"I'll follow you in my car."

And off we went. A few minutes later we arrived at a white farmhouse just off the road in Sunderland. There was a large barn out back and a roomy parking area. We parked and went inside. There was a spacious front room, three sofas, a couple of overstuffed chairs, and a good old-fashioned twenty-foot-long, well stocked bar. The lighting was dim, saloon style. And the room was noisy.

"Dick! Will you tell this asshole the Beach Boys ain't got nothin' to do with Rock & Roll!" A giant with a bushy black beard, leather biker vest, jeans and motorcycle boots exclaimed as we walked in the door.

"Dion & the Belmonts," a scrappy looking dude in jungle hat and cammos muttered beside him to nods of approval.

"Skinny Elvis," another guy added.

"Brenda Lee, Little Miss Dynamite," a fourth guy said. "What are you guys a bunch of homos?"

General laughter, camaraderie, greetings and then everybody was looking at me. Silently.

"The Everly Brothers," I said as assertively as possible.

"Yeah!" The giant roared again. "That's what I'm talking about."

And just like that I was in. Thanks to Don and Phil.

Introductions were made, beers were passed around. I struggled to remember names, nicknames, branches of service. The guy who voted for Brenda Lee handed me a beer. He introduced himself as Ron Crobek, Army, Vietnam, 67-68, Long Binh. He was an MP. Stockade duty. Tough tour.

The giant was named Lucius Verdanne. Army, Vietnam, 66-67-68. Eleven Bravo, Trigger puller. Delta, mostly. I was catching the others on the fly, and they were kind of running together when Dick banged on the bar and said, "OK guys, let's make a circle and get started." With that the chatter died down and everyone started migrating toward the sofa and chair area, forming a circle, everyone standing. I followed. Dick took the hands of the men on either side of him. Everyone else joined hands as well. Me too. I didn't know why until Dick bowed his head and intoned,

**For those of us who gave their all,
We remember.**

**For those of us who answered the call.
We give thanks.**

**For those of us who are here tonight,
We gather in the memory of the fallen.**

And with respect for one another.

Everyone sat down. I had tears in my eyes. Dick began, "All right, we made it another week. There are some new faces here tonight. Why don't you guys identify yourselves?"

And before I could speak (damn lump in my throat again) a guy I hadn't noticed before began, "My name is Jack Harrington. This is my first semester here. I transferred in from Mount Wachusett Community College. I was with the Air Force in Nam. Ton Son Nhut. Didn't see much combat. Lots of rockets, mortars, stuff like that."

"Why are you here tonight, Jack?" Dick asked.

"You invited me, Dick. At registration." There were several chuckles. Then Jack continued, "I don't know anybody out here. I walk around the campus, and I feel like a freak.

They're a bunch of kids. I feel like if they knew I was in Nam they'd shun me. I gotta' be around vets, you know?" Heads nodded. Jack sat back. Dick looked at me.

I made my introduction. Told the group I was with Dustoff in Nam. Instant approval. I told Jack I felt the same way he did walking around campus. I admitted I needed to be around vets myself. More head nods. I began to feel a little more relaxed.

Jack and I were the only new guys. When we were done the rest of the guys in the circle introduced themselves, name, rank serial number kind of stuff. There were fourteen of us in all. The same, yet different, but the same. Then Dick got down to business.

"Okay, who's had trouble this week?"

Shuffling of feet and squirming in seats started. Then Lucius spoke up, "My old lady's on my case again about drinking."

"Lucius, we've all been on your case about your drinking. You're a good guy until beer number three, then you're an asshole," Dick said.

"Not all the time," Lucius offered.

"Pretty much all the time," The guy in the jungle hat and cammos, who was the Dion & The Belmonts fan, added. His name, I now recalled was Mike.

"Fuck you, Mike," Lucius answered without malice.

"That's a buck, that's a buck." Several guys said at once. A rusty coffee can was produced. Lucius deposited a dollar into it. Dick dropped in a dollar as well then explained.

"For you new guys we're trying to keep the swearing down. Social graces and all that. Costs you a buck a swear."

"Geez, I gotta see a list," Jack Harrington said, "I could go broke here."

"No list, just pay the buck," Lucius stated.

"If you can't tell when you're swearing, you should have a pretty good idea about why we charge you for swearing," Dick pronounced.

The discussion returned to booze. There was beer at the bar, brown and clear fifths and pints behind it, lots of cans and lots of glasses.

"It's about choices," Dick declared. "This is not an AA meeting, good as some of their ideas are. It's about respect. If you can't have a drink and not get drunk, don't drink. It's that simple, or that difficult, however you make it."

The group discussion went on for another hour. We got off booze and onto isolation, depression, anger, truth and fiction. I gathered very quickly that these guys really cared for one another, looked out for each other and were experiencing problems not just similar to mine, they were exactly like mine. Maybe, I admitted to myself, I had found a place to belong to. By 7:30 or so the group discussion ended with a recitation of Alcoholics Anonymous' Serenity Prayer. Standing once again in our hands clasped circle we recited:

God grant me the serenity to accept the things.
I cannot change,
The courage to change the things I can,
And the wisdom to know the difference.

I was silent through this prayer. But I listened. Good words. Advice I could use. The rest of the gathering was social. A new phenomenon called Monday Night Football flickered from a battered 24 inch black and white TV with enough aluminum foil wrapped around the rabbit ears antenna to cook a turkey. Several guys paid attention. The rest returned to the bar.

"Anybody know anyone who needs a roommate? I'm sleepin' on my ex-girlfriend's sofa. It's scary," Ron Crobek implored.

Music to my ears. I had a hundred dollar a month bargain waiting to be bargained. In short order Ron was coming by my place tomorrow, Lucius was fixing Mike's car, and Jack Harrington found half the textbooks he needed but couldn't afford on an overstuffed bookcase against a back wall. Those were the benefits.

These were my questions: No dues, no secret handshakes, no requirements other than discharge papers and showing up for meetings sober. Meetings were every Monday night, 6:30 to eleven-ish. And there was a poker game. More music to my ears.

Dick Gerson went on to explain that Beta Chi was an unofficial, non-affiliated fraternity for veterans only. There were donations rather than dues, guidelines rather than rules with mutual respect and cooperation absolutely required. The buck a swear coffee can was well funded and the dollars were used for loans, gifts and emergencies. Whatever was left over, paid for a party on whatever holiday was appropriate and convenient.

Thus went my first meeting with Beta Chi, which was also the first real connection I feel I made at UMass. This could bode well for my time to come.

"Have you thought any more about how to tell your family about us?" Gianna asked as she and Margaret Mary walked hand in hand across the campus.

Margaret Mary blushed, as she still did, when talking about her new, romantic relationship with her roommate, Gianna. It had started innocently enough, a welcome back hug after the Christmas holidays, a beat too long. Shy smiles back and forth as they studied in their room, and then one night Gianna slipped into bed beside her and they hugged again, longer, each feeling safe and wonderful in each others' arms. They confessed to each other how they felt. They told each other their secrets. They told each other how much they cared for one another. But how to tell the world?

"I haven't," Margaret Mary confessed, "I'm afraid of what they may think."

Gianna Viscoli was from Verona, Italy, the fabled city where Romeo met Juliet. She was a child of wealth and culture and kindness. Like Margaret Mary she was studying classical literature and music. She was a talented musician herself, playing piano and harpsichord masterfully and viola even better.

"I have yet to meet these people whose thoughts you are afraid of," Gianna said, "But you tell me they are wonderful people who love you very much. Why should you be afraid?"

"They, we, are Irish, Catholic and very traditional in the way we think. We," and Margaret Mary blushed again, "are not traditional."

Their relationship had started slowly. Roommates, friends, confidantes, and one lonely night, lovers. Margaret Mary recalled a bright, crisp winter afternoon when she had returned from the campus sad and lonely. All afternoon she had seen couples strolling about the grounds hand in hand, arms around each other, stealing a kiss beneath a golden oak, laughing and enjoying life. Ever since Kendall, save two wonderful nights in York Beach with David, she had slept alone. Alone and hurt and angry and sorrowful. Until Gianna.

"Tradition once burned heretics at the stake, today we give them microphones," Gianna pointed out.

"I'm not ready for a microphone," Margaret Mary said, without blushing.

"And perhaps you are not ready to tell them. Is there not someone else you could talk about us with first?"

There was. She would. I was going to get one big surprise phone call.

Chapter Twelve

Messages, Fair, Foul & Fantastic

The call from Margaret Mary came on a Tuesday. Unfortunate, since my weekly veterans support group had come and gone the day before. It began friendly enough with our old familiar salutation that always preceded important news.

"You better be sitting down when I tell you this."

Then Margaret Mary dropped the bomb. The big bomb.

"You know I have loved you ever since we were in the fifth grade, don't you David?"

"Wait a minute," I said, "We met when we were in the third grade."

"You took some getting used to." Margaret Mary laughed her wonderful laugh from across the far away sea.

"Okay, fifth grade, but I loved you first," I half joked; half confessed.

"And I still love you now," she responded with more to follow. "But I've got to tell you something I haven't told anyone else, not even my Da or Aunt Rose."

A silence followed, a $7 dollar a minute, trans Atlantic phone call silence. Then Margaret Mary whispered, "I've found someone special, David. Someone I feel safe and good with."

Which was okay, I guess. After all I had an occasional Becca or a friendly waitress and such in my life. It was the next part that floored me.

"It's Gianna, my roommate. We're lovers," she said. The phone went silent. My head went boom. "Are you still there?" She asked.

"Gianna is a girl?" My talent for stupid questions almost never let me down.

"She is, and I care for her very much." Margaret Mary said this simply and I believed her.

"David, do you remember when we were on the ski trip, and we slept together?"

I told her I did. She continued, "I wanted to make love with you then, but I was afraid, and you understood. Do you understand now?"

I told her understanding might be a bit of a stretch for me right now.

"Ever since Kendall forced himself on me, attacked me, I have been afraid to ever have that happen again." Which I understood. "Even the physical part of being with a man, of being with you or anyone else, I couldn't do it."

I was struggling to digest what I was being told. I understood the physical part, the "care for her very much" part was harder. Finally, I was able to speak, "Is Gianna good to you?" Sometimes, just sometimes, I can ask the right question.

"She is, she understands, she comforts me. She makes me feel better."

Confused as I was, surprised as I was, I felt good hearing this.

"When are you going to tell Sean and your Aunt Rose?" I asked.

"I wanted to tell you first. They'll understand. Do you?"

"I'm working on it. But let me tell you this much, if you're happy and feel safe I'm glad and I still and always will love you. Thank you for telling me this."

There was another $7 a minute silence from Margaret Mary's end of the phone. Then I heard a sniffle, and a choked "thank you" as well.

On the practical side these phone calls were way beyond either of our present pay grades and we had to get off the phone. I promised to write to her soon. She promised to write me as well. When I hung up and stood up, I knew three things, another part of my childhood had disappeared, I needed to talk to Eddie at the China Rose about making some more phone call money and I needed to find a girl in a tight black sweater right away.

"Did you tell him? What did he say? Are you alright?" Gianna exploded with questions when Margaret Mary told her of the phone call to David. She wanted to throw her arms around Margaret Mary, to hold her tight, but sensed this was not the right moment. Margaret Mary was in tears.

"He said he hoped we would be happy and that he still loved me," She sniffled.

Gianna pondered this. "I think perhaps this David must be a very good person."

Which brought a fresh round of tears to Margaret Mary.

The phone call to Dublin did not go quite as well.

"This is the girl we had lunch with when we visited?" Sean asked, still digesting the information that his daughter was in a relationship which to him was a violation of his religious and moral beliefs.

"It is Da, and I love her."

Sean swallowed hard, counted to ten, twice. The silence was thunderous.

"Da, are you there?" Margaret Mary asked sheepishly.

"I am." Sean paused, measuring his words, his tone, "The world may judge you harshly for this daughter."

"But you, Father, do you judge me so?"

"I'll try not daughter. But I fear for you all the same. This is a harsh road you are travelling on."

"We're Irish, Da. We were made for harsh roads."

"Shall I pass this news along to your Aunt Rose or would you prefer to speak to her yourself?" Sean asked.

"I want to tell her myself, Da. I'll call later tonight when she's home. Do you think she'll be mad?"

"Your Aunt loves you as I do. She'll be surprised, as I am, but she will love you all the same. As I do."

Sean hung up the phone with a heavy heart. He knew that all the dreams he had for his daughter, all the fruits of her knowledge and kindness and wisdom could be overshadowed by her relationship with Gianna.

The world was not yet kind or understanding about such things and the hatred and ostracism she would face worried Sean to his bones. His very conservative, parochial Irish bones.

Max was not at the gym when Kevin arrived Monday morning. Kevin now had his own keys and opened the doors, switched on the lights and crossed to Max's office to give him a call to make sure he was alright. There was no answer at Max's apartment.

By noon Kevin was more than worried and about to call for help when Teddy arrived. He explained about Max and Teddy set off for a welfare check at Max's home.

When he got there the door was locked. There were no lights on inside. There was no sign of Max. Teddy used a triangle pick to open the front door. He found Max in his bed. He was cold to the touch, not breathing, silently, eternally, sleeping. He looked peaceful, serene and very, very dead.

Teddy sighed and sat on the edge of his bed. He remembered the first time he had met the grizzly old sailor at the gym. He recalled the old man's patience, tolerance and encouragement of a roomful of boys who wanted to be boxers. He gently touched the old man's head as another part of childhood faded away.

Kevin took the news hard. Max was his mentor, a surrogate father, a teacher and a friend. On Kevin not yet Butchie's perilous personal journey back into the world Max was a pillar to lean on. A guidepost.

No one seemed to know if Max had any family. A search of his apartment gave no clues. Teddy took control, with Beth's help, in arranging the funeral and the formalities. On one cold as hell February morning Max was laid to rest in Lowell's Edson Cemetery. I drove in from Amherst of course. Half a dozen kids from the YMCA gym were there with their families, Teddy arranged for an Honor Guard from the local veteran's hall. Teddy was in full dress uniform as were several other members of the police department. Standing off to one side, huddling in overcoats, scarves and mittens were three guys I didn't recognize at first.

When I got closer, I got smiles from Paco Barnes, Antoine Davis and Eddie Prince. All from the gym, the old Gym,

Nelson's, which Max had run back in the day. Time and tide had swept us all pretty far apart, but news of Max's death reunited us. At graveside. When I recognized them, I turned and called to Teddy. He gave me a puzzled look and walked over cautiously then broke out in a big smile as well.

"Whoa! Officer Dukie!" Prince proclaimed, stepping forward for a handshake.

"The Prince!" Teddie responded as Paco and Antoine stepped forward as well. We caught up, new jobs and old habits, good times and forgotten places. Then we remembered Kevin, not Butchie.

"That Butch over there?" Paco asked.

"Yeah," Teddy replied, "Max's death hit him hard. They were pretty close."

"Is it true what I heard 'bout him havin' some kind of breakdown in the Navy?" The Prince whispered.

"Yeah," I added. "He's doing much better now. We should go say hi."

And we did. And it went well. Taps was sounded, three rifle volleys were fired for the sailor who watched Japan's surrender from the deck of the USS Missouri. Each of us offered a clump of frozen earth into the open grave. Then Kevin stepped forward and dropped Max's red, white and blue ribboned New England Middleweight Champion 1939 belt atop the lowered casket.

As we walked away from the gravesite, I took one last look. The simple gravestone was engraved as follows:

Max Ginsburg

1919-1971

Always Our Champion

LT walked with his head down, shoulders hunched, gloved hands jammed into his Army issue, field jacket pockets. He was marching along the perm frosted, frozen stretch of Seward Highway which stretched fifty some miles along the coast of Alaska's Kenai Peninsula. LT barely looked up or bothered to wave his thumb at the passing cars anymore. He just marched. Another fist fight in another Anchorage bar put him, by local police request, on the road again. His destination was the tiny town of Homer, also called "The End Of The Road" at the furthest end of the Kenai Peninsula. The end of the road is what LT has been thinking about a lot since arriving in Alaska.

The dim winter sun over his shoulder told him it would be dark in less than an hour. The temperature now was somewhere under six below zero. Balmy for late winter Alaska. It would get colder when the sun went down. LT knew if he was out on this road after dark he would likely freeze to death. He didn't much care. He snorted through his frozen nose, kept his head down and trudged along. "Might as well enjoy the rest of the afternoon," he thought. "Likely to be my last."

And then the battered, rusted out, old red pickup truck stopped ten yards in front of him. LT moved to walk around the truck.

"Get in here young man or I'll come out there and drag your ass in," a rough and not even slightly friendly voice growled. LT looked into the truck cab and saw an old man. White bearded and grizzled behind the wheel. He had no one with him.

"No thanks old man. It's a nice day for a walk."

"Nice day my ass. Are you comin' in here or am I comin' out to get ya?"

LT smiled at the old man and started to walk on. As he passed the truck, he heard a creaking door open as the old man stepped out. Holding a Remington Pump shotgun which he had pointed at LT.

"First load of buckshot goes in your ass, Sonny. In this cold you won't bleed much but you won't notice that because of all the pain you'll be in."

LT knew two things at once. This old codger wasn't kidding, and he was going to get in the truck.

"You got any right to be wearing that U.S. Army issue field jacket?" The old man asked as he coaxed the truck back up to speed.

"Some," LT answered, "You got any right to ask?"

"Lieutenant Colonel Jacob Hackleberry, United States Marine Corps, retired. Semper Fi," The driver answered.

"First Lieutenant Baker, Robert. USMC. Semper Fi."

They shook hands and went silent. The frozen landscape drifted by.

"Jesus, it's colder in here than it was outside," LT mentioned.

"Got a pretty good size hole in the roof up there, right above the windshield. Wind blows in, cools things down a bit."

"The heater work?"

"Go ahead and try it. Didn't last time I fiddled with it."

LT pushed and twisted the heater controls. An anemic sounding fan blew more cold air around their feet. The last thing this cab needed was more cold air.

"You headed for Homer?" LT asked.

"Nowhere else out here to head for, Lieutenant."

"You live there?"

"Live there, most likely die there."

"That's sort of my plan too," LT said it with a grin. He was not grinning inside.

"You another one of them sewer-side fellas?"

"Another one?"

"We get them all the time in Homer. Mostly they just get drunk, stay drunk, until the police pick 'em up and send them home to their Mamas."

"So how did you end up there?"

"Wife died few years back. Came up here fishin', stayed."

"Fishin' that good here?"

"What the hell do you care?"

"Just askin'."

"Well don't ask. You come up here to die, I can drop you off at the cemetery or the hospital. Whichever you prefer."

"Is there a good bar in town?"

"Ain't no such thing as a good bar, sonny. Not for the likes of you anyhow. We got us a VFW Post, but we don't admit no sewer-sides," Lieutenant Colonel Hackleberry spat out the last words with contempt.

"No need to get riled, Colonel. I just thought I might buy you a drink to thank you for the lift."

"You want to thank me for the lift, get out at the cemetery. Hospital's too busy to deal with the likes of you."

"The likes of me?" LT was getting steamed.

"Quitter's son. Crybabies who don't want to live no more. You climb in here tell me "Semper Fi" and then you're gonna' lay down and quit? I reckon you never figured out what "Semper Fi" means."

"Semper Fidelis, Colonel. It means "Always Faithful." Maybe I've just run out of things to be faithful to."

"How about being faithful to yourself Lieutenant, or to the Corps we left behind? You ever have a man under your command killed Lieutenant?"

LT bit back his anger, swallowed his grief and sat silent, his eyes filling with tears. Lieutenant Colonel Hackleberry noticed and knew the answer to his question. In a softer, kinder voice he asked, "Do you think any one of those men wouldn't give anything to be where you are today?"

"Maybe I'd give anything to be where they are today," LT whined.

Which brought the truck to a screeching halt.

"Get out of my truck. You're a disgrace."

LT hesitated. It was getting dark out there.

"Out I said." Lieutenant Colonel Hackleberry pulled back the fold of his parka to show a very large, lethal looking handgun.

LT got out. The cold air hit him like a sledgehammer. Lieutenant Colonel Hackleberry drove away. LT could freeze or move. He moved. Far off the lights of Homer twinkled in the twilight. Pretty far off. LT started jogging.

Forty minutes later he reached the outskirts of town. The first building he saw with lights aglow was the Veterans of Foreign Wars hall. A one story, one room clapboard building. It looked warm. LT rapped at the door. The

Sergeant at Arms, a local named Bill Egard cracked open the door.

"Members Only," he grunted and started to close the door. Over Bill's shoulder Lieutenant Colonel Hackleberry noticed.

"Let him in Bill, my guest," He said from his corner table. Bill stood back, LT limped in.

"Better get a warm cloth for this feller," Bill said, "His face lookin' frostbit to me." And he went off to warm a towel.

"Looks like you decided not to die after all," Lieutenant Colonel Hackleberry said as LT approached his table.

"Thank you for letting me in," LT said. "Yeah, the closer I got to dying the worse of an idea it seemed. Mind if I sit down?"

Lieutenant Colonel Hackleberry nodded as Bill returned with the warm towel. "Best be holdin' that against your cheeks. Gonna' sting a might at first but you don't look too bad."

LT held the warm cloth against his face, and it felt like his whole head caught fire. He pulled the cloth away and gasped as Bill smiled and Lieutenant Colonel Hackleberry asked, "What are you drinking?"

"Double Jack, double anything, as long as it's a double." Lieutenant Colonel Hackleberry nodded again, and Bill went to fetch the drink.

"Before that drink gets here, you got anything that proves you were a member of the United States Armed Forces other than that jacket you're wearing?"

LT opened his field jacket and withdrew a carefully wrapped envelope. He pulled out a folded and creased DD-214, his discharge certificate and proof of service. He handed it to Lieutenant Colonel Hackleberry who said, "Driver's License?" after taking the paper. LT turned this over as well. Lieutenant Colonel Hackleberry studied them both.

"That is one crappy picture and one very nice DD-214." He announced handing them back to LT. "Our guest here got himself a Silver Star in Vietnam," Lieutenant Colonel Hackleberry announced as Bill returned with the double Jack Daniels. LT took the drink and finished it in three large swallows. He handed the glass back to Bill.

"Actually," he said, "my men won the Silver Star, they just pinned it on me."

Bill grunted and went to refill LT's glass.

"Now, what's all this 'lay me down and die' bullshit?" Lieutenant Colonel Hackleberry asked.

LT took the no longer warm cloth away from his face which was now glowing like a hot skillet. Blowing out a long, exhausted breath he answered, "I came up here for a fresh start, looking for some peace, looking for some answers." He shook his head and continued, "Turned out I was still asking the wrong questions, still getting the wrong answers."

"You thought coming to Alaska was going to change that, did you?"

Bill returned with LT's drink, another double. LT took a grateful sip and continued, "What I've been thinking is just about as wrong as how I've been thinking." He waved his glass at Lieutenant Colonel Hackleberry. "This isn't helping either."

"If it's not helping, why do you do it?"

"It's not hurting either." Lt smiled and drained the glass. His face stung like hell but there was now a warm glow in his belly.

"So, what's your plan now that you've made it to the end of the line?" Lieutenant Colonel Hackleberry asked.

"My plans haven't been working out very well of late, Colonel. I'm trying out the no plan method."

"The no plan method got you a place to sleep tonight?"

"There must be a motel in town. I've got money."

"Motel's closed, costs too much to heat it off season."

"There's an on-season?"

"Fishin's might good around here come summertime."

"That's not going to help me much tonight."

Bill interrupted, bringing LT another drink, this one a single. "You interested in a job?"

"Is it warm?"

"See that pot belly stove over there?" Bill asked, "And that one over there in the corner?"

LT nodded, Bill continued, "Them's what heats this place. If they go out it takes two whole days to warm this place up again. I'm lookin' for a feller to stay here, keep those stoves goin' and clean up a might. There's a cot in the storeroom you could sleep on."

"What's the pay?"

"'Bout what your bar tab comes to right now, at least for tonight."

Lieutenant Colonel Hackleberry said nothing while this exchange took place. But he watched LT, close.

"You go getting' drunk, start sloppin' up my liquor while I'm gone, I'll throw your ass out of here in the morning." Bill added.

LT took his now empty shot glass and turned it upside down on the table. "Sounds good to me partner. How about you show me to my quarters."

"Them stove's gonna need kindling before morning. There's a wood pile out back you should visit before you get shown to any quarters."

LT pulled on his gloves and followed Bill to the woodpile. Lieutenant Colonel Hackleberry finished his beer and headed for his home sure this young Lieutenant would be drunk or gone in the morning. He would be wrong.

"So, your girlfriend is like, a dyke?" Lucius asked with more wonderment than disdain.

"That's a buck! That's a buck!" Several guys shouted.

"What?" Lucius protested, "Dyke's not a swear word."

"Context," Mike LaPage argued, as several other members of the group nodded.

Dick Gerson, the group's voice of reason concluded, "The way you used it was insensitive to Dave, that's a buck."

The coffee can was passed to Lucius. He put in a dollar. "Sorry Dave," he said.

"De Nada," I answered, still dazed and confused. The Monday night veteran's group had become safe haven for me, and the others. When I told them about Margaret Mary I was as relieved as I was confused. And most of the group acted sympathetically.

This was my first Monday night group following Max's death. I had a lot on my mind. Margaret Mary not the least of it. It felt very good to have somewhere to go to talk about my troubles.

"I've known Margaret Mary since we were little kids. She's always been the smartest, the funniest, the kindest person I ever met. I can't remember ever not loving her."

"Even now?" Lucius asked cautiously.

"Even now," I answered. "She was raped guys, over and over by a guy named Kendall Prescott. It hurt her deep and she hasn't gotten over it. She told me this girl Gianna makes her feel safe and loved. How am I supposed to not like that?"

Which brought a silence to the group. Then Lucius muttered, "How the hell would we know? We're guys."

And in the laughter that followed my confusion ebbed and I managed to laugh with the others.

"Sure would like to meet this Kendall Prescott guy," My roommate Ron Crobek commented.

"Been there, done that," I answered without further details.

As the evening went on, I respectfully eulogized my friend Max and we discussed loss. Most of us had seen more than enough of that sort of thing in Nam. Grieving didn't hurt any less in the 'real' world. We discussed shared problems with intimacy, anger issues, loneliness, finances and families. Dick Gerson kept us out of the swamp of politics, religion and "fucking hippies." Something about, "Changing the things we can and the Wisdom to know the difference," from our closing invocation. Good words.

After the group Dick pulled me aside and asked, "You still looking for some work?"

I was, he continued, "The campus bookstore is being stolen blind. Shoplifters. Petty stuff that really adds up. The manager is a guy named Wynn Garrett. He asked me to hire a few security guards, unarmed, to walk the floors try to slow the theft down a little, or a lot."

"What's it pay?" I asked.

"Five bucks an hour. I get four more guys. We work two, three-hour shifts around our classes. You want in?"

I wanted in. Things were continuing to look up. Except for the Margaret Mary thing of course.

As second semester ground on I found that among the faculty there were a few exceptions to the pipe smoking, elbow patched, egghead academics I encountered last year. This time around I was lucky enough to draw a passionate, knowledgeable, committed English professor, Vincent Guardella. He brought literature to life, taught that good writers read a lot, and chose books that would have made Margaret Mary smile. Vince was my first academic mentor, introducing me to Steinbeck, Hemingway and Dashiell Hammett.

I also took yet another tentative peak at William Shakespeare, not a writer of note in Lowell, but apparently held in high esteem everywhere else on the planet. Even Margaret Mary found his plays ponderous, full of antiquated phrases and obscure dialogue. I memorized the mandatory passages in high school and went right back to Mark Twain and Edgar Rice Burroughs. I had a brief moment of insight with the Bard while at Suffolk University but it, like most of what happened there, had disappeared into my pre-military past. Once again, I was gifted, even blessed to find an instructor who knew and revered Shakespeare as the master he was and knew how to translate that devotion to others. Like me.

Beatrice Stockton-Powers was a force of nature in the UMass English Department. Known as a brilliant scholar but very strict taskmaster her classes on classical literature were assiduously avoided by slackers and praised to the skies by all others. I enrolled for Shakespeare 101, The Tragedies, on LT's recommendation, one of his very few good ideas.

One memorable Tuesday afternoon after an initial and tedious class or two I went to Beatrice's office to drop the class. I didn't understand it, wouldn't get it, and wasn't enjoying it. Her office looked like the world's smallest, most overstuffed library. Books crammed the shelves, the windowsill, the floor and the extra chairs. I found Beatrice to be a pleasant enough person, I just didn't fathom Shakespeare.

"Have you actually read any of the plays, David?" She asked.

"I tried Mrs. Powers, I really did. Othello, Hamlet, King Lear, I got lost in the wouldeth's and shouldeths' and pious perchances."

Which made her laugh. She had a great laugh.

"That's actually very good, David. Pious perchances indeed. I'll have to remember that one." She motioned me toward the least book infested chair and said I could relocate the stack to the floor and please have a seat. I sat.

"Would you do me, and perhaps yourself, one very great favor before you withdraw from my class?"

I nodded, she continued, "Would you go to the very pleasant library in the Emily Dickinson Museum here in town and listen to, as you read, Laurence Olivier's production of Hamlet which is available on long playing records there?"

This sounded vaguely familiar to me. "You want me to go to a library and listen to Hamlet on a record?"

"I want you to hear the words as they were meant to be spoken, to understand the rhythm of the language as it was written. I want you to dig a little deeper into the plays."

So, I did. Like I said, Beatrice was a very nice lady, brilliant in her speech and ideas. Sometimes, not often enough, I listen to good advice and follow uncomfortable suggestions.

Technicolor! Cinerama! 3D perfection! It took about ten minutes of listening to Olivier, to hear his Hamlet spoken aloud and in character for all my inner lights to come on, all my dulling senses to spring to life, and to finally understand the magic and majesty of Shakespeare. That first night I listened to all of Hamlet on four long play records running almost two hours. I was halfway through Macbeth when a kindly librarian told me they were closing, I could come back tomorrow. Which I did.

"And your impressions of the plays, David?"

I was back in Beatrice's office/library, happily this time, grateful for her suggestion.

"I think Hamlet had troublesome Mommy issues and Macbeth needed a Las Vegas divorce."

I was rewarded by Beatrice's wondrous laugh, but only for a moment. "Aside from the glib, but admittedly funny comments, what did you learn from the plays?" Beatrice knew her business.

"Too much introspection isn't necessarily a good thing, greed and ambition is contagious and dangerous, and human affairs are at best, complicated and convoluted." I replied more seriously.

"Very good," she replied, "I would like a five-page, 1200-word paper on each play citing examples from the play that support you opinions. By the end of the week please."

This was Tuesday. I'd been had, but in a good way. The rest of my classes were more standard generic introductions, Psychology 102 where students developed symptoms as fast as the professor could assign them, a Sociology course where we learned that society's problems were calamitous, inevitable and unsolvable and a European History course where I learned all wars are one war, with sporadic generational interruptions, usually all about money and inevitably futile.

Meanwhile I started walking the floor of the campus bookstore waiting for people to steal. Dick Gerson, Wynn Garrett, my roommate Ron Crobek, a guy I hadn't met before named Abraham Steiner, and a feisty, delightful girl named Jenny Long had been hired for the job which we sort of made up as we went along. First of all, we were not cops. We wouldn't be arresting anybody. We were sanctioned as security guards and backed up, if necessary, by the campus police department. But for low level shoplifting we all agreed the consequence should be kept in-house so to speak and not ruin a student's education or future.

First offense shoplifters were warned, fined and kept on record, informally, at the campus store. Second offenders were rare and the consequences more severe. They could be suspended, even expelled from school. After that it was arrest by campus police, arraignment in North Hampton court and all the legal repercussions that followed. The vast majority of the students we stopped were embarrassed, frightened and compliant. There were few second offenders and very rarely a third.

"You only stopped me because I'm black." The large, angry, black student with the Marvin Gaye record album hidden under his jacket proclaimed as I led him into the security office.

"No," I replied, "I stopped you because you stole. The record is under your coat, and you were past the last point of purchase in the store. You want to handle this legally or make a racial thing out of it?" I didn't reply angrily. I didn't want to argue with this guy. Right is right.

He sheepishly removed the album from inside his coat and placed it on my desk.

"You're right man. I did wrong, shouldn't have. I apologize."

Which was the reaction most of our shoplifters adopted.

"What happens to me now?"

"Now I write your information on a 3X5 card. We keep it here in the store. You'll pay a fine to the Student Council of three times the price of the article you took. You don't get the album. If this never happens again, we tear up the card, no record of this event. You graduate, this never happened."

And so, it went. Twenty or thirty shoplifters a week among the five of us. Three in a day by one guard was a hat trick, hockey style. Theft in the store rapidly went down. I was working twenty hours a week. I could talk to Margaret Mary a lot longer. I became good friends with everyone on the security team. Things were looking up. What could go wrong?

Chapter Thirteen

Confessions & Contritions

"It's na' proper, a woman sleeping with another woman! I'll not have it under my roof!" Rose's voice rose with her conviction and Sean struggled to keep his own from rising.

The phone call several weeks back when Margaret Mary had told her Aunt of her relationship with Gianna hadn't gone well. Since then, there had been a stony silence on the subject and much less communication between Aunt and Niece. A sad state of affairs with Sean in the middle. Now Margaret Mary wanted to come for a visit. With Gianna.

"This is my daughter, Rose. Your niece. Our family child whom we love very much. How can you not allow her decision?"

"It is God's law that does not allow it!" Rose exclaimed.

"Much sadness has been brought into the world by what is told to be God's law. I'll not have such a decree condemn my daughter."

"Then condemn her I will! She lives in sin! An abomination!"

Sean tried to put his arms around Rose, to hug her. She twisted away angrily.

"I cannot have you speak of my child as an abomination," Sean said sadly. "If that is truly how you feel she will not stay here, nor will I."

Rose fell silent, her anger tempering with the love of her brother. Sean waited. Rose spoke. "It is not just I," she began, "but it is the Church as well that says how she behaves is unnatural."

"And isn't that's what's wrong with this whole cursed country!" Sean exploded. "The Church Says! And families are torn apart! The Church Says! and the Protestants fight the Catholics! The Church Says! and The Orange battles The Greens and Ireland bleeds on. I no longer give a damn what the church says. Margaret Mary is my child; she has been gravely wounded and takes solace where she can. We are her family and should be solace to her as well."

Rose stood silent. The truth she was being told was sinking in. "They'll not sleep in the same bed. Not in my house," She proclaimed. Glenmere street rules. With a twist. This was going to be interesting.

"Two hundred dollars a week, Mr. Mayor? Max had that gym open at 8AM every day except Sunday. Trained fighters till 6-6:30 every day. That's ten hours a day minimum, fifty hours a week, that comes to about $4 an hour. Does that sound right to you Mr. Mayor?" Teddy was steaming. The city was offering Max's job to Kevin. Same salary as Max.

"Two hundred a week is what the city can afford, Officer Gianoulous. If that is not sufficient, we can close the gym, or it can be open fewer days, fewer hours." Mayor Tom Daley was not an unfair man. Neither was he generous with the city's funds. Not for boxing programs at any rate.

"Four dollars an hour is insulting to an honorably discharged veteran with a service-connected disability," Ted responded, angrily.

"Four dollars an hour is insulting to anyone for that kind of work, but four dollars an hour is what the city can afford." Now Mayor Daley was getting his back up. The temperature in the room was rising. Tempers were about to be lost.

"I'll take it," Kevin said quietly amidst the argument. Teddy and Mayor Tom both turned to look at Kevin who had been sitting quietly until now.

"Pardon me, Mr. Martin, what did you say?"

"I said I'll take it." Kevin stood up and faced Mayor Tom. "I ain't doing this because of the money, Mr. Mayor. I'm doing it because it's a good thing I know how to do and it needs doing."

Teddy started to interrupt. Kevin silenced him with a look.

Mayor Tom considered Kevin, considered Teddy. "I believe the city can make it $5 an hour. Congratulations Mr. Martin you are now a city employee."

Teddy and Kevin left City Hall and crossed to the police station where Teddy had parked his car.

"From now on you handle the money, Kev. I'll stick to police work." Teddy smiled. Kevin smiled. He was doing more of that lately.

Meanwhile back at UMass, Dick Gerson, myself and the rest of the store security team were bagging shoplifters like cheap groceries.

"This is the first time I ever stole anything! Honest!"

"I was going to pay for it, I just forgot."

"Everything in here costs too much. I was just ripping off the man."

"You only stopped me because I'm black, white, male, female, left-handed, right-handed, short, tall, or fat."

We heard them all over the course of the semester. Wynn Garrett, the store manager, was thrilled. Shrinkage went down. Campus outrage went up. I wrote a story for the campus newspaper, "The Daily Collegian," explaining that stealing from the store drove retail prices up. So did having to hire security guards to police the theft. Logic proved worthless, stealing continued. So did our arrests. Everybody was happy except the shoplifters.

"Miss, I am with store security, and you have left the store with items you have not paid for. I need you to come with me to the security office." Jenny Long saw the momentary panic in the shoplifter's eyes, the urge to run, the fear and panic.

"Please come with me. You are on camera. Don't make this situation any worse," Jenny intoned. The flight urge passed, the young girl put her head down and followed Jenny back into the store.

We didn't have cameras, but they were a great pacifier when we stopped the thieves. We, of course, knew they weren't there. They didn't. I was behind the desk in the security office when Jenny came in with the girl. The rule was don't frighten them, don't bully them. They were already scared, embarrassed, and sometimes even a little ashamed. Our job was to stop the stealing, not to humiliate them.

I got up and offered Jenny my seat. I excused myself and left the two of them alone. Jenny could handle the situation, she was tactful, polite and fearless. All of us were the same way. Do the job, don't escalate the situation. Reassure the shoplifter that if this is the lesson learned they would be fined, then forgiven. Unless they did it again. Too bad the whole world didn't work that way.

Almost Father Peter Rayburn had made up his mind. Secretly, painfully, after much prayer and consideration he had decided to leave the priesthood. The inconsistencies of Church doctrine and Church practices, particularly those of a financial nature, had charted his course. Faith he would always have, a vocation to the priesthood he would not.

Follow the money, he was once told. He did and he could not reconcile what he discovered. Peter learned that the Catholic Church is the wealthiest, most secretive, most shielded private institution in the world. Billions upon billions of dollars in assets, real estate, art, and treasures were stockpiled, stored and hoarded in the Vatican and all around the world while in Africa and in South America parishioners were mired in lifelong poverty.

After a year and a half living in the splendor of the Vatican, Peter decided he had had enough. He had spoken with his parents about his decision of course and they told him to follow his heart. His heart which was now heavy with his choice.

"I am, of course, gravelly disappointed in your decision," Monsignor Specio said as Peter turned in his formal resignation form.

"I've tried to make my reasons clear," Peter said, "It is the business of the Church that repels me not its doctrine."

"Yet if the business is not maintained there would be no way of conveying the doctrine, Peter."

"Every day I walk over marble floors worth more than the houses millions of our parishioners live in. In this building alone there are paintings, sculptures and statuary worth tens of millions of dollars. Why? Are we a circus? The other day I watched the ticket vendors selling Vatican tour passes, thousands sold every week. I often think of Jesus and the moneychangers when I see merchants selling a visit to our Church."

"Much of this money is passed on to the poor," Monsignor Specio argued.

"Much more of it isn't." Peter decided, handing his mentor his formal letter of resignation. He had purchased a plane ticket and packed the night before. Without another word Peter walked out of the Vatican, away from the Church and into his new life.

His letter read…

Dear Monsignor Specio,

First of all, I want to thank you for being a true and patient friend as I searched for a place for myself in the clergy. I will always cherish my time as a novitiate and my friendship with you. I have not lost my faith, not my faith in the principles and lessons of Catholicism I believe in Jesus Christ and all that he stood for and preached in his Gospels. I do not believe, or condone, what men have done with those teachings.

Why does the message of a poor carpenter require a cathedral? Where did all the pageantry and opulence of the Mass come from? How much commercial real estate should a church own, and why?

I have always been very good at asking why. I am also very good at finding out why. The more I find out however, the less happiness I have. So, it has been with my faith. My faith is in God, my happiness in the purity of his teachings. The rest, the fiscal, secretive, clandestine rest, is my misery.

In Matthew 19:24 does not Jesus say, "It is easier for a camel to pass through the eye of a needle than for a rich man to enter the kingdom of God?" Yet here we live in this palace of palaces. Beneath us is an Archive, filled with the most priceless of all things, knowledge. Yet this Archive is sealed, locked, secret. Why? I have found no answer.

I am therefore leaving the priesthood, but not the faith. This I will always have. I will retain my belief that man is more than his possessions, more than his baser instincts, more than his weaknesses. I wish I could say the same of the Church.

Respectfully and with deep regret, I resign my vocation.

Peter Rayburn

Margaret Mary and Gianna arrived in Dublin during the passing of the summer. They arrived by train and excited as Margaret Mary was to see her Father and Aunt, she was apprehensive about how Aunt Rose was going to behave meeting Gianna. Which was not going to happen right away.

Rose was not at the train station. Sean explained, "Your Aunt is at home preparing our lunch and, I suspect, huffing and puffing a bit about your arrival."

"What is 'huffing and puffing'?" Gianna asked.

"Father, you remember Gianna, she is my partner, my friend, my heart," Margaret Mary said.

"I am happy to see you, Gianna. 'Huffing & Puffing' is my dear sister trying to let go of her old beliefs and make room for new ones."

Gianna nodded and smiled and shook Sean's welcoming hand and they set off for home where Rose huffed & puffed.

"I'm an old woman and set in my ways, but it's welcome you are in my home as a companion of my niece." Rose stood stiffly in her kitchen after hugging Margaret Mary and offering her hand to Gianna.

Gianna took Rose's hand in hers and said, "I know how much you love your niece and how much she loves you. I wish never to lessen that. I love her too for the wonderful person that she is and for the better person she makes me."

And Rose softly relented, the huffing and puffing replaced by a smile and a semi-reluctant hug. Margaret Mary breathed a great sigh of relief, Sean set the table and the four sat down to a steaming shepherd's pie and a warm Irish welcome. The meal was delicious, the conversation easy as new tales supplanted old stories and new bonds were formed around the kitchen table. As well they should.

"We have a surprise for you," Margaret Mary announced as they finished lunch.

"I don't know that I could survive another surprise from the likes of the two of you," Rose responded with a smile.

"This surprise you'll survive," Margaret Mary promised as she rose from the table with Gianna to retrieve two bundles, they carried with them from London. Margaret Mary unpacked her bundle first revealing a fine, handmade Budhran, the traditional Irish folk drum. As she did Gianna unpacked a flat backed Irish Bouzouki, the 8 stringed, 24 fretted, guitar/mandolin/banjo of Irish folklore. She gave the strings a tuneful pluck as she and Margaret Mary resumed their places in the kitchen cradling their instruments.

"We've a song or two for you. Gianna taught me the music; I taught her the tunes."

With that Gianna's fingers flew over the strings of her Bouzouki and Margaret Mary thumped a happy tune on the Budhran as they sang,

"It's my dear Irish home, far across the foam,

Although I've often left her, in foreign lands to roam,

No matter where I wander, in cities near and far,

Sure my heart belongs in Ireland in the County of Armaugh."

After several choruses Rose hid a tear as Sean slapped his thigh and sang along. More music followed, Sean's favorite, "Carrickfergus" and Rose's, "The Ballad of Molly Malone." When their throats were dry, and their eyes quite wet Margaret Mary put aside her drum and Gianna played the "Tarantella Napolutana" from her native Italy as beautifully as it had ever been played.

As silence sang in the kitchen the music played on in their hearts. All prejudices put aside, all trepidations banished, the family cloth was rewoven, at least for now.

Peter Rayburn arrived back home a week after leaving the priesthood. He stopped in London and spent some time visiting Margaret Mary and her now "partner," Gianna. I heard all about it from Margaret Mary on our now lengthier phone calls on Sunday evenings.

"Please go see him when he gets back," Margaret Mary implored, "He's very confused, a little bit ashamed, which is how I feel most of the time."

Which I saw no need for either of them to be. Just maybe maturity was creeping up on me. So, I drove down to Lowell the following weekend and arranged to meet with Peter at Lefty's on Saturday morning. Old school, new problems.

I checked in at Glenmere Street Friday night and all was well with the family. We had a delightful fish dinner and caught up on each other's lives. My Mom was even in good spirits and my Dad was now a Boy Scout leader at a local church. My brothers were chugging along. Bob was a licensed electrician. John was driving a truck for our Uncle Artie at the box company. I was sensing direction, if not purpose in my life. All was well. So far.

Peter came into Lefty's Saturday morning looking more tentative than I had ever seen him. The swagger was gone from his step. He barely smiled when we shook hands. He wasn't wearing his beret. I missed the beret, and the smile.

"Look at us," he said as we parked ourselves at a back table. "Older, and wiser."

I knew sarcasm when I heard it.

"Older for sure," I answered, "getting wiser all the time." Mostly the hard way. "How you doin?" I asked. The classic rhetorical question.

"Doing alright, mostly. I'm twenty-two, living at home, a defrocked priest who didn't quite get a frock and I am currently unemployed."

"No, I mean beside that!" And I laughed and Peter laughed, and we got down to business.

"I heard you stopped to see Margaret Mary on the way back."

"I did, she's fine. She actually looks happy."

"Did you meet 'what's her name'?"

"I met Gianna and she's wonderful. They seem to be really happy together."

So much for feeling good and bad at the same time.

"How did your parents take the news about you're quitting the priesthood?"

"Resigning from the priesthood," Peter corrected. "And they took it very well. "Follow your heart' they said. I can't seem to stop following my head."

"Thought your way through another one, huh Peter? What was it like? Resigning I mean."

"Like getting kicked out of Keith Academy, times ten."

"Ouch! But this time it was your decision, right?"

"No, this time it was my attitude, just like it was at Keith."

"You know Peter," I admitted, "Keith sucked. An elitist snobatorium. I'm glad I got kicked out. I'm glad you got kicked out."

"So, say all of us," he replied taking a sip of his coffee. "You know Dave, it's crooked, the whole damn Church thing is crooked. The more I looked into it the surer I became. They're Billionaires, Dave! Billionaires! They live like kings among enormous wealth and run a worldwide charity scam to fund it."

Peter was getting his edge back. He went on.

"I tried, Dave. I really tried. I studied the Gospels, read the Bible, memorized the prayers and lived in a palace! Millions in, thousands out. I'm sure of it."

"Maybe a little harsh, no?" I suggested.

"Not if you look behind the curtain, Dave. I got a peek behind the curtain. I'm going to keep looking."

"That ought to make you a lot of friends." And we laughed again, whistling in the graveyard.

About then a Lowell Police Department squad car rolled up to Lefty's. Officer Teddy, hat, badge, gun belt and all joined us.

Teddy and Peter shook hands. Teddy punched me on the shoulder. I didn't hit back. Lefty himself brought over the free cop coffee Teddy always paid for and we sat back down.

"How's Beth?" I asked.

"Getting more pregnant every day. A little cranky. I work a lot," Teddy responded.

"I'm sorry I missed your wedding, Ted. Late, great congratulations." Peter added.

"Not a problem, Peter. It's good to see you. That must have been a hard decision you made."

"Hard, but proper, for me anyway. You ever arrest a priest?" Peter said half smiling.

"No, but I'm open to it," Teddy replied and once again we laughed, almost.

So, we sat awhile and caught up. An almost priest, an expectant father cop and a getting settled college student. We were a long way from the Little League, bike rides and spelling bees. Moving onward.

Back in Amherst my days were playing out peacefully. The Monday night veteran's meetings were my lifeline. There I shared my fears, anxieties, anger and angst with the guys and they with me. We were all in it together and it helped, helped a lot.

I had become good friends with my roommate, Ron Crobek. I learned he was a guard at Long Binh Jail during his tour in Vietnam. This was the military prison for US personnel under charges which ranged from drug and alcohol offenses to murder. Soldiers were held there before being shipped stateside for courts martial or prison. Not the kind of duty anybody would ask for. While he could sympathize with some of the prisoners, he had to be wary of them all. Not to mention the Viet Cong, North Vietnamese regulars, Saigon gangsters, and international drug dealers.

He was nineteen when he started his tour. Ron's opinion of humanity became somewhat skewered during his tour but he somehow managed to maintain a cheerful sense of humor and an optimism that went well with his deep desire for love. He was semi-engaged to a girl back in Peabody, his hometown, and went home to see her every weekend. Ron and I got along well. He thought flying Dustoff was dangerous, I wouldn't have traded places with him at the prison for the world. Such was Vietnam.

I probably spent a little too much time down at The China Rose with Eddie and an occasional waitress. Dating professionals wasn't exactly dating at all, no matter what I told myself. I rationalized this with the whole Margaret Mary situation. Like an idiot.

Eddie did get me back on the circuit hustling pool though. There was a bar named Mickey's which had an eight-foot pool table, a shuffleboard table and an electric bowling machine. Eddie could play them all like Beethoven. We would usually play partners, challenging the house players. I could stay close enough to allow us to win by a little, not a lot. The stakes weren't huge, and we never sheared the sheep too close. Eddie didn't need the money but loved the action. I needed the money and loved the action. Between hustling and the bookstore, I was getting by comfortably. My classes were interesting. I passed all my courses. And heard a tune echoing in my head,

As you brush your shoes
Stand before the mirror
And you comb your hair
Grab your coat and hat
And you walk wet streets
Tryin' to remember
All the wild night breezes
In your memory forever.*

Onward.

Lyrical Aspiration:

*Wild Night, Van Morrison

Chapter Fourteen

Machinations

When second semester ended, I stayed in Amherst for the summer. The lease on the apartment didn't end with the school year, Ron kicked in his share even though he was going home to Peabody, and we had LT's car money to make up the rest. I got plenty of hours in at the bookstore and Eddie and I played partners in a firehouse poker game once a week for a little extra pocket money. I even managed to get my 1964 Volvo sedan back and forth to York Beach, Maine several times to spend a weekend with my family.

The end of summer brought the beginning of fall football and Eddie still wanted an on-campus card man. I was game.

The semester started smoothly with veteran pre-registration, an interesting lineup of classes and an easy to manage work schedule.

By NFL Week Three I was making forty bucks a week dealing football cards and taking the odd football bet for Eddie. Low key, same customers, easy money. No more school bus. Here's the way I got started.

Every college has its on-campus jock/frat hangout. At UMass, just like at Suffolk, it was the Newman Center. Coffee bar, three pool tables, easy chairs and sofas, card tables. I was sitting in the lounge looking as studious as possible while pondering a football card. Looking around the room I asked, in general, "Anybody follow Notre Dame football?" I noticed a couple of interested nods.

"Who do you like in the game with Michigan State this week?" Now I had the attention of a couple of wannabe experts.

"Notre Dame will cream 'em'," frat boy number one chimed in.

"Notre Dame easy, Michigan sucks." Another expert heard from.

"What about the points?" I asked. "Notre Dame is a ten-point favorite."

"Take the points," says expert number one, "Michigan got no offense."

"Take Michigan and the points," says expert two, "Ten's a lot of points. My dad says always bet the underdog when they get ten points of more."

And that is what makes a horse race.

"Watcha' doin?" Expert one asks as expert two watches. So, I explain the cards. "I get mine from a friend and yeah, I could get an extra one if you want to bet. Even two." Word gets around. I'm in business.

"Ten cards Eddie, the boys are lining up for next week's games and I need a couple of winners. Good advertising."

So, Eddie, who's totally wired in to the Las Vegas line, clues me to a couple of sure things that I generously pass along to my customers. As long as they have a dog or two on their picks to cancel the payoff. The smallest bet I will take is two dollars on a three-team combo, biggest is ten dollars. Many are called, few are chosen, and the experts bring their friends. Pretty soon I'm invited to the Kappa Sig Saturday night poker game. I go. I win a little, lose a little, but mostly I win a little. I'm not Santa Claus. And I pass out a lot of football cards.

By Thanksgiving I'm dishing out forty cards a week. Eddie pays the winners and I console the rest. I get paid whether the card wins or loses. After Thanksgiving it's coming up on Bowl games season and the stakes, and bets go up. Life is good.

LT was polishing glasses behind the bar at the VFW hall when Alaska State Trooper Luke Dayber came in.

"Officer Dayber, have you lost your way again?" LT asked as the trooper took a seat at the bar.

"Coffee, cream, sugar and keep your greasy thumb out of it this time."

"I thought you liked my greasy thumb." LT placed the steaming mug in front of the Trooper. They had become friends, as LT had with most of the town's inhabitants. LT was six months sober, six months employed and six months happy for the first time in a very long time. He worked three days a week at the VFW hall where he used to sleep in the stockroom. Now he had a comfortable one-bedroom apartment over the best diner in town where he worked three more days a week as a line cook. That other day he was learning to fish for halibut with Lieutenant Colonel Hackleberry, now Jake, another newfound, greatly appreciated friend.

Christmas had come and passed and LT's attempt to reconcile with his father had ended once again, in dispute. A card, a letter, a phone call failed to help and the great silence between them continued.

Now Jake Hackleberry had stepped in, becoming a surrogate father with not so surrogate wisdom and advice in LT's life.

"Coffee, with," Now Jake ordered as he settled in at his table." "Coffee with" was black coffee, Bailey's Irish Crème and a shot of Tullamore Dew Irish Whiskey. It also meant Now Jake was done working for the day.

"I just filleted us about sixty pounds of halibut we caught yesterday. It's all iced down and ready to go." Now Jake said as LT set the "coffee with" on the table. "You going to be able to run that up to Anchorage today?" He continued.

"Soon as Bill gets here. And I'm going to get that hole in the roof of the truck fixed while I'm up there. I'm tired of freezing my ass off every time I gotta' go somewhere in that thing."

"Fresh air is good for you. Don't you go spending all our profits on some roof repair."

"Twenty bucks, Don at the garage is going to stuff a tarp or something in it."

"That does not sound aesthetically pleasing." Now Jake sipped his coffee.

LT and Now Jake had teamed up as fishermen several weeks back, LT going from theoretical Marine Biologist to bait and hook man on Now Jake's boat. They soon worked well together, fishing the shoals, partners and friends.

Bill Egard arrived to take over the bartending duties. LT slid into a chair at Now Jake's table.

"Truck up at the house?" He asked.

"Nah, outside. Loaded, ready to go. I'll catch a ride home later."

"I best get after it then. I want to be back by dark." LT rose to grab his coat and headed for the truck.

"Don't you be taking less than two hundred bucks from that bandit Delroy for that fish. Those are prime fillets," Now Jake warned.

LT waved and left, his day, his life and his future settling into some reasonable order. Sobriety was a large part of his recovery, so was Now Jake's advice and wisdom. The Vietnam war hovered in their pasts like a specter, becoming a manageable remembrance rather than a shameful recollection.

Lieutenant Colonel Hackleberry sipped his coffee with as LT drove away. He had been ashore as a military advisor when the 5,000 Marines of the 9th Expeditionary Force landed at Red Beach, northwest of Da Nang on March 8, 1965. These were the first official US ground troops deployed to Vietnam. Tragically they would not be the last.

"Goddamn cluster fuck then, bigger cluster fuck now," He growled when he allowed himself to remember. "We tried telling Command and Control this was never going to work. They wouldn't listen. The more men they poured in the worse it got. You inherited a meat grinder son; you never stood a chance."

LT would sit and listen when Now Jake began to talk about Vietnam. He didn't do it often, but when he did, he spoke from direct experience. Lieutenant Colonel Hackleberry knew a lot about the Vietnam War. Most of it not good. He resigned his commission following the debacle of the Tet Offensive of 1968. As he spoke it was not his anger that escalated, it was tremendous sadness.

"I knew once they killed that young President down in Dallas this country was in a lot of trouble. Old Lyndon Baines, he gave them boys the war they wanted, a war we never had a damn chance to win."

"Who were 'them boys?'" LT would ask.

"Pentagon, CIA, anti-Commie fanatics who happened to have huge government armament contracts, the usual collection of shysters and criminals," Now Jake would growl. Then his voice would soften, and he would say, "Young man, there is a lot you do not know about the war you just fought. Probably you never will and that may be best. Things were bad with LBJ, they're going to get a hell of a lot worse with that little crook Nixon in charge. I came here to put all of that nonsense behind me. I suggest you do so as well. Life's too short, the corruption is too deep, the outcome will be too damn heartbreaking."

Often this left LT craving the relief of the bottle and old friend Jack Daniels. It did so until he found the serenity of the Homer sunsets and the promise of the Homer sunrises. Colonel Jake could handle the whiskey, LT came to accept that he could not, and when he acknowledged this the community and Colonel Jake opened up to him as well.

As he drove sixty pounds of bait caught halibut to Anchorage he hummed as he drove, free in large part from the ghosts that haunted him. The Vietnam war raged on below, in the lower 49, LT would not allow it to disturb him in the place he had now come to call home.

Margaret Mary and Gianna marveled at the beauty of Florence. They strolled hand in hand through the Galleria dell Accademia which housed Michelangelo's breathtaking "David" among its other treasures after visiting the Duomo Cathedral with its famous bell tower engineered by Giotto and stunning terra cotta dome. What Margaret Mary didn't know about the fabled city Gianna did, whispering a narrative for only the two of them as they walked the streets and plazas.

"I can't believe how beautiful it is here," Margaret Mary said as they approached the Ponte Vecchio, the oldest stone arched bridge in all of Europe and the only covered bridge in Florence spared destruction during World War II. The Ponte Vecchio was lined with shops selling exquisite merchandise, gold, silver and leather goods of the highest quality, perfect for two strolling shoppers like Margaret Mary and Gianna.

"'Ponte Vecchio' means 'old bridge.' It has been standing since 1345," Gianna noted as they passed within.

"Ponte Vecchio will aways mean I love you and thank you for bringing me here," Margaret Mary responded.

They were both completing their second year of residency at Oxford University. Graduation beckoned as did another year of study if they so chose. Gianna had been offered a position as a docent at the Ubbitzi Gallery here in Florence which contained Boticelli's "Birth of Venus" and da Vinci's "Annunciation" among its artworks. The position was very coveted, very prestigious, a dream offer for Gianna.

Margaret Mary's heart however was for Dublin after graduation, an as-yet-unspoken rift which could leave them many miles and many tears apart.

But on this wonderful golden night in Florence all future aspirations were put aside as they walked the Ponte Vecchio to the 4Leoni restaurant in the Piazza della Passera where, in legend if not fact, the Mona Lisa is said to have lived. While the 4Leoni's homemade pasta dishes are legendary their cheesecake was said to be even better. Gianna promised, Margaret Mary imagined, and their pace quickened.

Kendall Prescott was parked four houses down from 57 Glenmere Street, my family home in Lowell. He was with a goon from some San Francisco Bay area biker club who called himself "Masher." Kendall was there at 6:30 AM when my Mother left for work at Raytheon. At 7 when my brother Bob backed his Austin Healy Sprite onto the street and left for his job. He watched my Dad drive off at 7:30, and still he waited and watched. My brother John left at 9:30 on his Kawasaki 350 and the house went silent and still.

At 11AM he moved the rental car further away but still in sight of my home's front door so as not to call too much attention to himself. At 1PM Masher took the car to get sandwiches while Kendall walked the neighborhood never taking his eyes of 57 Glenmere Street. Masher returned, they ate and watched. At 3:45 my Mother returned from work. An hour later John rolled in followed shortly afterward by Bob. My Dad got home around 6PM and thirty minutes later Kendall made his move.

"Good evening, sir. Is this where Dave Ferrier lives?" Kendall asked as politely as possible at my front door. My Dad answered, "I'm Dave Ferrier, can I help you?"

"I'm sorry sir, I mean your son. My name is Douglas Matte, I served with Dave in Vietnam. He saved my life. I wanted to come by and thank him."

John and Bob overheard the "served with Dave in Vietnam" part and came into the living room. My Father invited Kendall in. Masher watched from the car. My Mother came into the room drying her hands on a dishtowel. Kendall went on, "Dave was with me when I lost my arm. He bandaged me, pulled me to safety. I would have bled to death except for him."

Kendall now had the attention of my entire family.

"You were with the 571st Dustoff?" My Dad asked.

"Dustoff, yes sir. Until I got wounded of course." Kendall looked mournfully down at his shattered arm.

"Dave's not here. He's living out in Amherst, going to college."

Kendall looked as disappointed as he actually was.

"I was really hoping to see Dave. I'm only going to be in town for a couple of days."

"He doesn't have a phone in his apartment, or we'd call him," My Mother offered.

"Oh no," Kendall said, "Please don't do that I want to surprise him."

"I've got his address around here somewhere. Amherst is about a two-hour drive from here." My Father took my address down from the refrigerator door. "Here you go, Unit 12, Squire Village, Sunderland, Mass."

"Unit 12, Squire Village, Sunderland," Kendall repeated.

Are you going out there to see him?" My Mother asked.

"You bet," Kendall/Douglas said. "But I want it to be a surprise."

"We were just about ready to sit down and eat supper. Would you like to join us?" My Father offered.

"I can't really, thanks. I have to get going. I'll say hi to Dave for you when I see him."

"Tell him to remember to come home for his Aunt's birthday next weekend," My Mother said.

"I will," Kendall promised. "Thank you."

Kendall left. My family felt good that they were able to help.

I first met Ruth Tabura while she was sorting magazines in the campus bookstore. She was squatting down, replacing last week's Time and Newsweek with this week's Time and Newsweek. Tall, thin, with wild black hair and fierce green eyes, I had seen her in the store before several times doing what she was doing now. She was neither friendly nor distant. She was focused, somewhat intense and beautiful. I was slightly smitten.

"What happens to the old magazines?" I asked by way of making conversation.

"Recycled," she replied without looking up.

"Is that a nice word for thrown away?" I said.

She looked up. I was all the way smitten.

"You're the guy in charge of security here aren't you?" She asked. I nodded. "I was wondering when you were going to talk to me," She continued.

"What were you wondering I was going to talk to you about?"

"Asking me out of course, I've seen you seeing me."

Gulp. Things were moving a little fast but that's the way it was with Ruth, whose name I didn't even know yet.

"I'm Ruth," she said, standing up and looking even better than when she was squatting down. "You're Dave Ferrier, I asked, and the answer is yes."

I hoped I was answering the right question. "Would you like to grab a beer at the Blue Wall sometime?"

"I don't "grab beer" and the Blue Wall is full of noisy adolescents getting drunk. I drink wine, cheap wine is fine, with lots of ice, somewhere where it's quiet. Top of the Campus will do. Say four o'clock, I'll meet you there."

"Top of the Campus" was a sort of unofficial faculty bar on the top floor of the campus center. Prices were a bit higher than the noisy, adolescent Blue Wall, but they had snacks, hors'd'oeuvres to the faculty crowd. I was in. Boy, was I.

She didn't just look good when I met her at the Top of The Campus lounge. She looked fabulous. I don't think she had even changed her clothes from this morning. Tight, very tight blue jeans, lace up leather boots and a tank toppy, kind of muscle shirt with a blouse thing under that. But she had done something with her eyes, liner and such and combed a few tangles out of her wild black hair. Whatever comes after smitten, I was.

She smiled a nothing less than gorgeous smile when I arrived. She was seated in a secluded corner table next to the big windows which overlooked the campus. It was getting on to sunset, the sky was golden, she was gorgeous, but I already said that.

"Hi," she breathed when I got close and patted the chair next to her. She was sipping from a goblet shaped glass full of ice and Chablis. A carafe of the same sat on the table. With another glass. And an ice bucket.

"I ordered for us. Do you like wine?"

"Yes," I lied. I was more of a beer guy. Right now I'd drink gasoline if she ordered it.

"Liar," she laughed, "But go ahead and try it, you might like it."

I did, and I did. "How did you know I was lying?' I asked.

"I'm very good at those things," she replied, "and you don't strike me as a very good liar."

"That depends on what I'm lying about," I answered and was rewarded with her million-dollar laugh.

We breezed through the essentials, "Where are you from, What's your major? "What do you want to do after you graduate?" It was easy, frank, fun. Ruth was straightforward, confident and motivated. She was a year ahead of me in school, majoring in Physical Education, liked most sports and looked like she would be good at any of those she played. She was Jewish, fiercely Jewish, as it turned out. She was very proud and well informed about Israel and planned to move there after graduation. She was going to live on a kibbutz, enlist in the Israeli Army and dedicate herself to protecting what she proclaimed to be her homeland.

She surmised that I was a veteran and was curious about my military service. I told her briefly what I did in Vietnam and as usual, I started to choke up a bit. Dammit. She reached over and patted my arm; said we could talk more about that another time. I was embarrassed, on fire, and super smitten.

We finished that carafe, ordered another and started another one after that. Sunset became sundown and the room was starting to spin a bit as more and more stars filled the night sky. Ruth checked her watch and discovered it was 7:30. We had been talking for over three hours, it felt more like three minutes except for the fact that I was more than a little drunk. She appeared to be fine. Standing up she said, "Come, let's go to my house."

I wasn't that drunk. We went to her house.

Ruth lived in a delightful hippie-laden conclave just off campus called Puffton Village, or just Puffton. We walked there, arm in arm sort of, and once when we mutually stumbled over nothing at all, kissed, long and lovely under a streetlamp. We walked faster.

Ruth's one bedroom apartment had a loft. The bed was upstairs, in the loft. Almost instantly so were we. I did take a quick look around as we climbed the stairs. On one wall she had a poster of a Sherman tank, on another there was a feathered and Boa'd Janis Joplin poster. There were throw pillows and cushions, a stereo, stacks of record albums, all the standard apartment stuff, though I viewed it in a rush. In the loft was a good-sized futon bed. On one of the futon posts there was a bayonet dangling in a sheath. A comfy looking chair had a reading lamp and a rather large set of bar bells nearby. Any or all of these things may have been an alarm bell under different circumstances but went virtually unnoticed as Ruth began to slowly get undressed, with a very wicked smile on her face. I did too.

Sometime later I found the bathroom. Ruth was curled up, napping or asleep. I was panting like a run out hound dog. I enjoy sex. Ruth enjoyed sex. For the last hour or so we almost enjoyed ourselves to death. Ruth was enthusiastic, gymnastic, and very, very energetic. I wasn't drunk anymore.

"You ever going to come out of there?" I heard her ask from the futon. Ruth, it turned, out liked sex like I liked baseball. The only problem was she expected a full nine inning game. The spirit was strong, the flesh was weak. I'd be lying if I said I lasted five full innings. Eventually we both slept till almost noon the next day.

During the aftermath of such happenings, I often found myself feeling awkward, unsure of what kind of ongoing situation I had gotten myself into. What, if any, obligations did I incur? Was this love? Lust? A mistake? Kismet? I was typically clueless. Sadly, this was not to be a passing perception. But not this morning.

Ruth was up first, chipper and cheerful. I needed coffee, lots of coffee and a cigarette or three. Ruth made coffee. She didn't smoke.

"Good morning," she said, "Coffee?"

"Lots, thanks." She handed me a full cup and we sat down across the small kitchen table, waiting.

I sipped, sipped again and said, "I really enjoyed last night," I began, then stammered, "not just the sex part, I mean I really enjoyed talking to you, the Top of the Campus and all. I'm glad we've met. I hope we can be friends." Which was a long speech for me, with only a couple of sips of coffee.

She relaxed, I relaxed. We drank coffee and chatted until I vaguely wondered what day it was and what I should be doing. No classes, I remembered it was Saturday. I was on at the bookstore 2-5 PM. I needed a shave, shower, new clothes, the works.

"I have to go," I mentioned, "I'm working this afternoon and need to go home and freshen up."

Which made her laugh.

"David, I enjoyed last night too and if you didn't have to rush off to work, we'd be enjoying this afternoon as well. Don't worry, you be you and I'll be me. I'll see you during the week and we can talk, maybe more than talk." She had the same grin I saw last night when she was undressing. "Now go, be you, I've got work to do."

And then I was back on the street, heading home, no guilt, happy. It was amazing how fast all that would change.

It was only by sheer luck, random chance, that I saw Kendall in the Student Union cafeteria when I got to work that afternoon. He did not see me. He had Jesus hair down to his shoulders, a white headband around his head and a biblical looking cloak thing on. When he moved, I saw the missing arm. Tough shit. He was walking around with some biker looking goon, too much denim and black leather. I surmised they were looking for me. I found them instead. Good for me.

"Ron, come over here for a minute, will ya?" Roomie Ron, my roommate and store security compadre came over as I ducked out of sight of the cafeteria.

"See that Jesus looking dude over there in the cape?"

"With the biker?"

"Yeah, that's Kendall Prescott."

"The guy who raped your friend?"

"The very one," I answered grimly. "You parked in the garage?" Ron said he was. "If they have a car they probably are too. Will you stay with them, find out where they're staying?"

"Easy," Ron said. "I'm on it."

"I'll be at the bookstore. Call me when they go to ground."

"You gonna' do what I think you're gonna' do?" Ron asked.

"Probably much worse," I answered.

"I'm in. You should get a hold of Lucius."

"I will."

"I'll call."

Two hours later Ron called me at the bookstore.

"They're staying at the Hilltop Motel outside of town. Looks like they're in for the evening. They bought take out from Hardees."

I checked the clock. 4:30 PM.

"Stay with them. I'll be there in an hour. With Lucius. If they leave stay with them. Call me when you can at the bookstore phone."

As I waited for Ron's call, I did some figuring. How did this guy find me? I wasn't too confused about why this guy came looking for me, the goon answered that. I also had to figure what I was going to do about this. I was more curious than angry, so far. Slowly a plan emerged.

An hour later I rolled up at the motel with Lucius. Ron reported they had not left the room. The flickering TV winked from the curtained window. We waited.

By 8:30 things had settled down at the Hilltop Motel. Only three other units were rented, and the lights were out in two of them. None were close to Kendall's room. Ron went to pick up a large pizza. He came back with a white and red pizza box the size of a card table. We moved.

Ron banged on the door of Kendall's room holding the pizza. The goon's head peaked out the corner of the window.

"Who is it?" Kendall asked from somewhere back in the room.

"Some guy with a pizza."

"Tell him to get lost. We didn't order no pizza," Kendall commanded.

As the goon opened the door Ron stepped aside and I rammed the goon right between the eyes with the butt end of a four-foot 2X4 plank. His nose exploded like a bloody rose, and he staggered backward. I hit him again, right above the ear with the broadside of the wood. He went down like a stunned buffalo.

Lucius rolled the goon onto his belly and slapped on a pair of stainless-steel handcuffs I brought along for the occasion.

He cuffed his wrist to his ankle with one set and then did the same with another. He pushed a soggy chloroformed rag onto the goon's face and now he was sleeping soundly, face down on the floor.

Kendall meanwhile was watching in horror from the bathroom. He was only wearing some girly looking orange underpants and combing his Jesus hair. Until I came in. I leaped across the bed and grabbed Kendall by his neatly combed Jesus hair. He started to squawk like a chicken until I rammed my 2X4 into his solar plexus as hard as I could. He folded in half, gasping for air as I threw him onto the bed. Lucius tossed me the chloroform rag and I put Kendall to sleep. Ron closed the door. Lucius hog tied Kendall and stuffed a rag in his mouth. We ate the pizza and waited for them to wake up.

The goon came-to first. Ron threw some water on him, and he rolled around a bit until Lucius stepped on his neck.

"Easy big guy," Lucius crooned, "We just want to have a word with you."

The goon's name was Emmett Still. I knew this because I had his wallet in my hand and was carefully looking through it. Lots of pornographic pictures, greasy looking garage cards, $200 bucks cash and a California Driver's License. Also, tucked in the back, the name and number of his probation officer, current. One of the cards was the clubhouse address of his biker buddies. It had a Nazi swastika and helmet atop a red skull with flaming eyes and lettering. Charming.

"Emmett, I'm Dave Ferrier," I said as I sat down next to him on the floor. "Look I want you to know you never had a chance once you opened the door. Sorry I had to hit you so hard but you're a big guy and I couldn't take any chances."

Emmett glared pure hatred at me but couldn't say a word. He still had a filthy red rag jammed down his throat, two very colorful raccoon black eyes and his bloody nose looked kind of permanently squashed in. I'm sure his head was still ringing and his ear looked like cauliflower. That's what you get for keeping bad company.

"Emmett, I don't know but I bet old Kendall here neglected to tell you I'm a cop." Of course, I was exaggerating a bit but Emmett didn't know that.

Emmett's beady little eyes got wide, and he struggled to see Kendall atop the bed. Kendall was awake now watching us very closely. Ron was sitting next to him.

"If he makes a sound break his nose," I said to Ron. Ron smiled and patted Kendall on the cheek. I think Kendall peed on the bed. Disgusting.

"He didn't tell you, did he?" I said as I turned my attention back to Emmett. "Well, anyway we're maybe going to let bygones be bygones and maybe let you get out of here. I'm guessing you got hired to do a job and it was nothing personal. Am I right?"

Emmett nodded his head slowly. I shook a brown paper bag under his nose making sure he could see what was in it. He looked alarmed.

"You know what that is don't you Emmett?" In the bag were several tied off bindles of a powdery brown substance in clear wrapping. "That's very pure Mexican brown tar heroin,

Emmett." It was actually Canes Granulated Brown sugar wrapped in cellophane. But he couldn't know that.

"There's going to be a lot of this scattered around this room in a little while, Emmett. That's the little while when all the other cops get here. Good old Kendall here is going to have a lot of explaining to do, if he's still able to explain anything when the other cops get here. You, on the other hand, may just catch a break."

I now had Emmett's undivided attention.

"I noticed that's a rental car you've got out there. Rented at Logan Airport two days ago, it's good for another five. I also found your plane tickets back to Frisco. They're no good anymore, I tore them up. Now, here's the deal. You are going to get in the rental car and drive. Go west young man, very west, very fast. Nobody ever needs to know what happened to you here. I've talked this over with my friends. They won't tell, I won't tell, you drive away. Deal?"

Emmett nodded his head.

"There is one more thing," I added. Emmett waited. "We're going to take all of your clothes. We are going to put them in the trunk of your car and then we are going to let you go. This is so you don't get any second thoughts about getting out of the car any time soon. There are lots of nice, dark roads between here and the Massachusetts Turnpike where you can stop and get dressed. There may also be a bindle or two of the Mexican brown hidden in the car. You won't know where, but I guarantee you the cops will, so don't get pulled over. Deal?"

We had a deal. Lucius and Ron stripped off Emmett's boots, socks, jeans, jacket, vest and underwear. It was not a pretty sight.

"We are going to take the rag out and the cuffs off now Emmett. If you give us any trouble, I am going to whack you with this board right where you make babies. You get up, you get in the car, and you drive away. We keep our secret."

Emmett nodded. We released him. He stood there, buck-naked, embarrassed. He actually tried to cover himself up with his hands. It was kind of cute.

"Emmett," I added as he looked to the door, "I found some dough in Kendall's suitcase. Here's three hundred more to get you home safe and sound. I gave him the money and his driver's license.

"I'm going to hang on to your wallet for a while Emmett. I promise I'll get it back to you though. Now you can leave, careful you don't scare the neighbors."

As he scuttled out the door and dove into the rental car, Lucius waved goodbye, and the car disappeared into the darkness.

Now to deal with Kendall.

"Would you guy's mind giving Kendall and me a minute or two alone?" I asked Ron and Lucius. Ron checked Kendall's bindings and stood up. He gave him a goodbye pat on the cheek. Lucius followed Ron out into the parking lot.

"Alone at last!" I said and dragged Kendall off the bed onto the floor. He hit with a thud. Tough shit. I straightened him up and crouched very close to his face. My anger was building now, white hot, remorseless, dangerous.

"I couldn't figure how you knew where I was at first. Then I called home, and they told me all about my Army buddy who had been there. They hoped I was happy to see you." I smacked him across the face, hard.

"You went to my home and spoke with my parents! You stood in the living room of the house I grew up in and told my parents we served together in Vietnam?" I smacked him again. He fell over on his side. I straightened him up. "Do you notice anything different about this meeting as opposed to our last one Kendall?"

Kendall couldn't answer but he could look terrifically scared.

"There's no Jesus here this time Kendall. And no Sherlock. It's just you and me."

This did absolutely nothing to make Kendall look less scared.

"Do you remember how bad I wanted to kill you last time, Kendall? Jesus saved you, remember?"

Kendall looked like he remembered. Then his eyes got as big as dinner plates when I pulled the .38 caliber Police Special revolver out of my belt.

"In fact," I added, "There's nobody here to save you this time."

I opened the cylinder of the pistol and showed Kendall the six cartridges. Locked, loaded and ready to go. Kendall started to whimper. I snapped the pistol closed.

"I want to kill you this time even more than I did last time, and I didn't think that was possible," I said, playing with the gun. "However, by nature I am not a killer. Not without giving a guy a fair chance anyway. You want a fair chance, Kendall?"

Kendall started nodding his head furiously. Nodding his head, whimpering and crying. He was a busy boy. I cracked the pistol open again and took out three bullets. The three I left in were dummies, no powder, no firing cap. Kendall, of course, didn't know that.

"Here's your fair chance, Kendall. I'm going to spin this cylinder three times. I'm going to fire the gun into your fucking head three times. You got a fifty-fifty chance each time of not being dead when I do."

Kendall was shaking head to toe. By the smell and the stain, I noticed he was now sitting in a puddle of very stinky, runny shit. I jammed the pistol, hard, into Kendall's ear.

"Now you are either going to hear a click or a big fucking bang. There is a school of thought that says you won't actually hear the bang, but who knows?" I pulled the trigger. A very loud Click. Kendall fainted and fell over into his puddle of shit. I straightened him out and slapped him around a bit until he came to.

"Congratulations, Kendall, you're alive. I think I'll try an eyeball shot this time."

I pressed the barrel of the pistol hard into Kendall's closed eye. The puddle beneath him got bigger, and smellier. Click. He didn't faint this time but was panting very fast.

"Wow! Congratulations again, Kendall. Calm down, only one more to go. Tell you what, I'll go back to your lucky ear."

Click. Kendall passed out. I called Ron and Lucius back in.

"Pew! What the fuck did you do to the guy!" Lucius asked. Ron was holding his nose as well.

"Not as much as I wanted to. He's fine. He just fainted."

I went to the bathroom and got a glass of water and threw it on Kendall. He came to, crying.

"Help me stand him up, will you?" We got Kendall to his feet stained and stinky.

"I'm going to take the rag out of your mouth now Kendall. You make so much as a sound, say one fucking word, and I'll chop your other fucking arm off. You got me?"

He got me. I pulled the rag out of his mouth. He looked from me to Ron to Lucius. Like a terrified rabbit in a cage.

"Now you go into the bathroom and wash that shit off yourself. One of my friends here is going to go with you so you don't miss a spot. Then get dressed."

Kendall came out of the bathroom, spritzed but still very frightened. He stood still, remained silent.

"You're going on a trip. Now the only way you can travel in our wonderful country with no identification, no luggage and very little money is…you guessed it, The Hound. We are going to drive you to the Greyhound Bus terminal in Springfield. Here's your ticket, you are going to New York City. From there you catch a bus to Chicago, St. Louis, Tulsa, I don't give a shit, just catch another bus."

I handed Kendall the ticket. He did not look me in the eye when he took it.

"Also," I added, "Here's two hundred bucks, travel money. I'm guessing you're heading back to San Francisco, that's where your driver's license says you live. I'm keeping that by the way. In case I want to get in touch, which you better fucking hope I never do."

I handed Kendall the money and as I did, I jammed the pistol up under his chin, hard.

"One more thing. If I ever see you again, if I ever smell you again, I will fucking kill you. No Jesus, not fair chance. I swear, I will kill you dead. You understand me?"

Kendall didn't speak. He nodded his head and kept looking at the floor. Ron took an arm; Lucius took the stump, and we shuttled Kendall out to the car. We drove him to Springfield, about an hour away. Nobody said a word on the trip. We dropped him at the curb outside the bus station and drove away.

"Thanks guys, for backing me up," I said to Lucius and Ron.

"De Nada," they both said at once.

"Guy's a major scumbag," Lucius said. "My pleasure."

"Me too," Ron added. Then we too were silent for the rest of the ride home.

I realized that same icy anger I felt during my last session with Prescott was within me still. Scary, harsh, murderous, present. I was going to have to learn how to live with that. Prescott had pushed me close. I didn't want to go there again.

No wonder shrinks love talking to me.

You can shine your shoes and wear a suit
You can comb your hair and look quite cute
You can hide your face behind a smile
One thing you can't hide
Is when you're crippled inside

You can wear a mask and paint your face
You can call yourself the human race
You can wear a collar and a tie
One thing you can't hide
Is when you're crippled inside

You can go to church and sing a hymn
You can judge me by the color of my skin
You can live a lie until you die
One thing you can't hide
Is when you're crippled inside

John Lennon, Lyrics from "Crippled Inside"

Chapter Fifteen

Destinies

Peter Rayburn led the Freshman Debate Team at Suffolk University. The beret was back, so was the wolf grin. Peter was pre-law, near the head of his class and feistier than ever.

"Would it be true to say then that Appeasement did not work in Munich in 1936, did not work at P'anmunjom in 1951 and is not likely to work in Paris in our negotiations with the North Vietnamese?" Peter posed the question to the Brandeis debate team leaving them on the defensive on a topic no one wanted to address.

Since entering Suffolk Peter had flourished. His natural contentiousness coupled with his insatiable curiosity and literate speech made him stand out and above his class. He was active not only in Debate but in the Student Government, the Civic Action Forum, the Criminal Justice Council and the Student Voice. Peter had found his calling.

"Great call, Peter. That question really tilted the scales in our favor." Chuck Desmond was the captain of the debate team. Chuck realized Peter was the heir apparent. The team would be in good hands.

"You going to be at Woodside tonight? Cindy's going to be there," Chuck asked. Cindy was a classmate currently pressing Peter on his celibacy issue. Woodside was the off-campus watering hole. Celibacy didn't last long there.

"Can't," Peter replied, "Crim Justice meeting tonight. Those things go on forever."

"And yet they say there is nothing criminal about justice." Chuck took his leave, saying over his shoulder, "Cindy's going to be disappointed."

I am too, Peter realized as his celibate road got a little longer. With Rome and the priesthood behind him Peter realized he was also behind the social skills and habits of his peers. Dating was faster, looser than he remembered. Sex had become recreational and lacked the enhancement of intimacy he desired and feared. Marijuana was new to him as well, though not only socially acceptable to his classmates, but it had also become practically socially mandatory. But not for Peter. He preferred to keep his wits about him and saw little attraction to being stoned or drunk. The sex thing was different though, and there was Cindy.

"Peter, I want you to spend the night with me tonight," Cindy had whispered in his ear after some serious social cuddling at Woodside last week.

Cindy was a classmate, bright, pretty, friendly and definitely not behind her peers in social skills and habits. Yet Peter had hesitated. Despite his disaffection with the priesthood, he still harbored the whole Ten Commandments thing and intercourse outside of marriage was a barrier he had yet to cross.

Maybe he decided he could get away from the Criminal Justice meeting early after all.

"It's baby time!" Teddy announced in a joyous phone call to me at the bookstore. "I just took Beth to the hospital. Her water broke, she's in labor, little Wolfgang Elvis is on the way!"

I was still smiling as I made the two-hour drive from Amherst to Lowell. Teddy was still clinging to the whole baby boy thing, even though the medics had confirmed that he was going to be the father of a bouncing baby girl weeks ago. Wolfgang Elvis was Lefty's drive-in, Lowell Police Department consensus for the as yet unnamed and un-gendered Teddy baby, though cooler heads would undoubtedly have prevailed.

"You're the god father, you and Kevin, so you have to be here to make it official," Teddy declared, though there was never any doubt that I would be on my way, right away. "Saint Joseph's Hospital," Teddy continued, "the clock is ticking."

The clock was still ticking when I rolled up in my 1964 Volvo sedan recently purchased from a Beta Chi brother when my MG Midget finally became too expensive to maintain. The Volvo was Rust Red, had two hundred thousand plus miles on it, no passenger side window, and a set of mis-matched, bald tires. "The Sleigh" as I had named her, had a top speed of 45 miles an hour, which I had just maintained for the entire two-hour drive from Amherst.

Teddy was pacing around in the hospital parking lot with Kevin and three Lowell cops I didn't recognize when I arrived. Teddy was puffing on a cigarette. He didn't smoke.

"What's the good word?" I asked.

"No word yet," Teddy said as the three Lowell cops went over to inspect the non-safety features of my rusting Volvo. Kevin looked as nervous as Teddy; I was getting ready to join the club.

"Beth's Mom is inside with the doctor's," Teddy said, "Beth's been in labor almost three hours." Which is where Teddy's worry lines came from.

Then a doctor came out, looking grim.

"Mr. Gianoulous, we need to see you inside please," the doctor said. We all started heading for the door. "Just Mr. Gianoulous at this time please," The doctor added, grimly.

The rest of us went mute. We stood still, didn't look at one another. Fifteen minutes later Teddy came out. He was crying.

"What happened? Are you okay?" We all silently asked as Ted collapsed against the railing of the concrete steps of the hospital. I stood stock-still, paralyzed. So did the others, except Kevin. He crossed to Ted and asked, "Is my sister alright?"

Ted nodded his head.

"The baby?" Kevin added.

Ted shook his head as his heart broke into a thousand pieces. Kevin's mom, Alice, came out of the hospital then and put her arms around Ted. Kevin put his arms around them both.

We watched, dumbstruck, silent until Alice looked up at us and said, "Beth is alright, resting. The baby was born with spinal bifida occulta and a cleft palate. She is having difficulty breathing and is on a respirator."

While I had no idea what spinal bifida occulta was and only a vague notion of a cleft palate knowing Ted's baby was struggling to breathe numbed me. The pain was too big to feel. I learned to do that in Vietnam, in Phu Bai, in the back of bloody helicopters. It was a skill that would not always serve me well in life. There was nothing to say, nothing to add or comment on. Ted, Alice and Kevin went back inside the hospital. I stood in the parking lot with three cops I didn't know, wishing I could have a word with Father Coogan or Margaret Mary or somebody. After another hour I drove away.

I slept at Glenmere Street that night. My parents were surprised to see me, even more surprised when I told them what had happened.

"I can't imagine what they are going through," my Mother said as we sat at the kitchen table. "I remember when each of you were born, I went over every inch of you making sure you were all there, all right."

I could hear the sorrow and concern in my Mother's voice. While there may have been nothing practical, we could do for Teddy and Beth the sorrow and concern was genuine and heartfelt.

The tone changed when my Dad asked how the reunion went with my friend from Vietnam. I was stumped. No amount of lying, no sense of cover up or consideration for their feelings could smother the rage that I felt that Prescott, that piece of shit, had been in this house, spoken to my parents, and could have done them any possible harm when he was here. I swallowed the rage hard and lied instead.

"It was fine. He couldn't stay long."

"He said you saved his life," My Dad added. Irony abounds.

"Well, I guess you could say I did that."

"I'm proud of you for that, we're proud of you." My Mom nodded as my Father proclaimed.

Just when I thought I couldn't feel any worse.

"Would it be alright if I called Margaret Mary? I'll keep it short," I asked.

"You go ahead," my Mom offered, "and don't worry about the cost, it won't break us."

So, I did. I knew from experience that London was four hours ahead of Lowell. It was 7:30 here, almost midnight in London. I called anyway. There were the usual clicks and buzzes at the trans-Atlantic call until the ringing began. A sleepy voice answered. It wasn't Margaret Mary.

"Hello?" which sounded vaguely Italian. Another picture I didn't need in my head.

"Is Margaret Mary there?" I asked.

"This is who?" the vaguely Italian voice asked.

"This is Dave Ferrier. I'm calling from Lowell."

A panicked but familiar voice came on immediately.

"David? Is everything all right? What's wrong?"

I told the tale. Teddy and Beth's tale. I left out the other part I need to talk about most. The Kendall part. I'd have to save that for Father Coogan, if and when he was available.

"Will you tell Teddy how sorry I am and that I will say a prayer for his daughter?" Margaret Mary asked.

I told her of course I would and then struggled for words or topics to move on to. I was beginning to realize that there was more than the Atlantic Ocean separating us now and this was not doing a lot to make me feel better. There was a bit of an awkward, unfamiliar silence between us, one that was never there before and I rang off, promising to be in touch immediately with any news.

When my numbness wore off my sorrow at what had happened to my friend turned to anger as to why such things happened. That would become much, much worse when I discovered why, in all likelihood, Ted's daughter had been born with such infirmities. I really didn't need any more reasons to get angry, be angry or remain angry. I said a silent good night to Margaret Mary as I hung up the phone and went to lay awake in bed.

LT and Jake were once again sharing a table and a conversation at the Homer, Alaska VFW Hall. Homer felt more like home to LT every day, every week and every month that he remained there. The troubles "down below" in the lower 49, as the States were called up there, seemed far away, sad, tragic and distant. But troubles have a way of traveling as they would do this very evening.

"Got us another set of runaways," Trooper Luke Dayber said as he brushed a light dusting of snow off his hat and took a seat at the bar. Bill Egard put a mug of coffee in front of him. "Stole a car up in Anchorage, abandoned it just outside of town," he continued. "Probably trying to get to Kodiak if they can get aboard a ferry."

"Sounds like a great escape plan, Kodiak being an island in the middle of nowhere where a stranger is going to stick out like a pink sailboat," LT answered.

"Girl's only sixteen, boy is seventeen. The girl is probably pregnant, scared of her parents. Boy's gotta' be poppa. They're just runnin'." Trooper Dayber had seen such foolishness before.

A subject I once knew a lot about myself, LT thought as Now Jake added, "Careful of those two, Luke, runnin' is running scared and running scared can be dangerous."

"Life's dangerous Colonel. That's why they pay me the big bucks."

"You wanna' be around to spend those big bucks you best be careful anyways." Now Jake answered, "I best be getting myself home, we got those desperadoes running loose and all. You coming by later, we'll play some cribbage?" He asked LT.

"About an hour or two. I've got some cleaning up to do around here then I'll come by."

Now Jake pulled on his hat and coat and went to the parking lot. LT cleared the table. Trooper Dayber sipped his coffee. Two shots rang out from the parking lot. Everyone inside scrambled outside.

Jake was lying in a puddle of blood in the snow. A young girl was screaming. A young boy was backed against Now Jake's truck with a gun in his hand. Trooper Dayber pumped three bullets into the gunman. The young girl screamed louder. LT rushed to Now Jake who was breathing and bleeding.

Trooper Dayber kicked the now dead boy's gun out of his hand. LT pressed his bar apron onto Now Jake's entry wound. The Colonel's eyes were clouding over.

"Look! Look! Look at me!" LT pleaded. "Focus, look at me! Don't you die on me old man!" Now Jake managed a smile and wink. LT hovered between panic and purpose as he willed his friend alive.

Trooper Dayber knelt beside LT with his prowl car first aid kit. He replaced the bar towel with a large gauze pad.

"Keep pressure on this," he told LT. "I'll call for the ambulance."

Now Jake closed his eyes. LT kept pressure on the wound as his world spun around. Moments later the ambulance slid into the parking lot. Now Jake was placed on a stretcher and whisked away to the Emergency Room, LT in the back of the ambulance with him.

Trooper Dayber dealt with the fiasco in the parking lot. The very dead boy and the still screaming girl were the runaways from Anchorage. They had been trying to steal Now Jake's truck. It was now known the runaways had murdered a storekeeper outside Anchorage the day before.

Trooper Dayber put the girl in the back of his prowl car. The funeral home hearse took away the dead boy's body. Bill Egbert reverently swept new fallen snow over the large puddle of Now Jake's blood. Officer Dayber started the prowl car. He could not keep his hands from shaking. And he heard in his head the words to a Bob Dylan song he knew by heart:

> **Oh what did you see my blue eyed son?**
> **And what did you see my darling young one.**
>
> **I saw a newborn baby with wolves all around it.**
> **I saw a highway of diamonds with nobody on it.**
> **I saw a black branch with blood that kept dripping.**
> **I saw a room full of men with their hammers a-bleeding.**
> **I saw a white ladder all covered with water.**
> **I saw ten thousand talkers whose tongues were all broken.**

I saw guns and swords in the hands of young children.

And it's a hard, it's a hard, it's a hard rain a-going to fall.[*]

I was supposed to drive back to Amherst the day after Teddy's daughter was born. My classes and my job were waiting. I called Teddy twice before I had to leave. No answer. I drove to Saint Joseph's Hospital. Teddy's car was still there. Inside, Ted, Kevin and Alice had spent a sleepless night. Beth was awake, cradling her baby. Her family was around the bedside. I did not want to intrude. Teddy saw me in the hall before I could slip away.

"Dave, wait up," he called. I stopped. Teddy joined me in the hall. We walked out onto the back stairs in the parking lot. Teddy's eyes were red and swollen. He looked exhausted. He was.

"Beth is going to be fine," he said before I could ask. "Our baby is off the respirator but is going to have to have surgery this morning." Then he choked up, couldn't talk anymore. Neither could I. After several long minutes of silence, us just standing there, Teddy asked, "What do you know about Agent Orange, Dave?"

I racked my brain. Agent Orange was a defoliant used in Vietnam. Killed the little trees, killed the big trees. It was used to clear jungle the enemy used for cover. They sprayed it a lot out in the A Shau Valley, around airfields, around firebases, around everywhere. They told us it was harmless to humans.

"Not much," I finally answered, "Saw a lot of it in Nam."

"Me too," Teddy said. "Whole lot."

"Why?" I asked.

"There's this Doctor, Doctor Gleason his name is. Beth and I saw him before she had the baby. He is a Nam vet, served down in Vung Tao, big hospital. He said they were starting to see a lot of birth defects in the children of Nam vets. He said there was something about gene mutations and chromosomal aberrations and it might have something to do with Agent Orange. I didn't know what he was talking about, and he told me I probably didn't have anything to worry about because my blood work all looked normal. Now I'm thinking about what he said a lot. Could you talk to him for me? You know more about that medical stuff."

I could and I would. School could wait, my job could wait. Teddy is my buddy.

I found Doctor Robert Gleason in the Lowell phone book. I called his office, and he answered the phone himself. I told him I needed to see him right away. He remembered Beth and Teddy. He'd see me at noon.

We met at his office. I told him about Ted and Beth's baby.

He sighed and told me what he knew.

"Agent Orange was the most widely used of three herbicides utilized by the military in Vietnam. The others were Agent White and Agent Blue. Orange and Blue were only soluble in diesel fuel. White was soluble in water."

So far so good. I understood colors and soluble.

"Agent Orange particularly was composed of two herbicides 2,4, D and 2, 4, 5, T both of which were contaminated by a highly toxic poison called TCCD."

He was losing me.

"Did the military know this?" I asked.

"TCCD was first reported to be toxic by the Monsanto Chemical Company in 1962. This was reported to the Joint Chiefs of Staff that same year. The military continued to use it anyway."

"They told us it was harmless, it only killed plants," I said.

"They lied," He answered.

And the world changed for me once again. Changed for the worse, with worse yet to come.

"Spinal bifida occulta is an incomplete closing of the spine," Dr. Gleason went on to explain. "It can be partially corrected by surgery followed by physiotherapy and mobility aids. There is no cure but with treatment patients can live fairly normal lives."

He went on to explain something similar regarding the cleft palate. I had trouble listening and understanding after hearing they knew it was toxic and sprayed it on us anyway.

Dr. Gleason said that the medical community was still accumulating data about the effects of Agent Orange and that he would personally check in on and help Teddy and Beth however he could. He said this was a national tragedy and a disgrace that should end up in a court of law. He was sure a legal team would be founded to look into this.

So was I and I knew just the person to talk to about it.

I found Peter Rayburn's Boston phone number and called. No answer. I drove back to Saint Joseph's to find that Teddy and Beth's daughter was in surgery. Kevin, Alice and Teddy were awaiting the result. Beth had been sedated and was sleeping. Teddy and I went out to the parking lot. Kevin came with us.

"I talked to Dr. Gleason," I began, "He's going to come over later today. He knows a lot about this Agent Orange stuff. He said your daughter's condition is treatable with surgery and that should she be alright." I wanted to stop there but Kevin asked,

"What about this Agent Orange stuff?"

So, I told them what Dr, Gleason told me. Teddy looked like he had been punched in the stomach, hard. Kevin became furious.

"What, what, what kind of shit is that! They knew and they did it anyway?" He half shouted; half cried.

I nodded, speechless. I told them I was going to contact Peter Rayburn and have him find out more about this. Teddy explained to Kevin that Peter was in law school and was the smartest guy we knew. I told Teddy I spoke with Margaret Mary and that she was going to say a prayer for them. I didn't know what else to say or what else I could do. Teddy said I should go back to school, and he would call me when something happened. I couldn't go, not until I spoke with Peter, not until I spoke with someone who could help me understand. I had no idea who that could be. So, I drove to the early morning silence of the immaculate Conception church. I sat quietly in a back pew and waited. Nobody was home.

Lieutenant Colonel Jake Hackleberry hovered between life and death for three days. LT never left his side, sleeping in a chair next to his friend's hospital bed. On day two the Colonel awoke, weak and thirsty. LT held his head while he sipped water. The Colonel blinked his thanks and waved LT closer.

"Bring me a pad and paper," he whispered, "I have to write to someone." His head fell back on his pillow. LT fetched a pad and a pen. He sat back down in the chair as the Colonel wrote slowly and for a long time on the pad. When he finished, he folded the pages and called LT to his bedside. "For after, just in case." Then he closed his eyes. He would never again open them.

Through the cold winter air, a bugler sounded Taps. LT heard the music. He knew the words.

Day is done.

From the lakes, from the hills, from the sky,

Rest in peace,

Soldiers Brave,

God is nigh.**

After Lieutenant Colonel Jacob Hackleberry had been honorably interred there was a gathering at the VFW Hall in Homer. Bill Engel hosted, LT helped out behind the bar, most of the town was present. Respect, regret and remorse were the order of the day.

Trooper Lucas Dayber, in full dress uniform, walked to the middle of the room and called for the gathering's attention. When the room quieted down, he raised his glass in toast, "To Colonel Jake, Semper Fi."

And the room saluted another fallen hero.

"Luke, could I have a word with you?" LT asked as the room full of people dispersed.

"Sure, LT, let's sit."

Colonel Jake's table was reverently set with an overturned coffee mug, a bottle of Bailey's Irish Cream and a fifth of Tullamore Dew. Luke and LT sat near, but not at, the remembrance.

LT pulled a sheaf of folded yellow lined pages from his pocket and handed them to Lucas.

"The Colonel gave me this in the hospital. I don't know what to do about it."

Trooper Dayber spread the pages on the tabletop and read,

This is my Last Will & Testament

My mind is clear though I feel my body is, at last, failing me. It is my wish that my home at 35 Harborside Lane be passed to former Lieutenant Robert Baker, who is in possession of this document. Likewise, my boat, The Mary Anne, I hereby bequeath to Robert as well. Those personal possessions of mine he should want, he should have, the rest to be given to the Rescue Shelter. I have bank accounts at First Federal in Anchorage, and I want those assets passed to Robert as well. He should also get my truck. Please honor my wishes. I have no other relatives or family that need be notified. Bless you all,

Lt. Colonel Jacob Hackleberry (Retired)

The document was dated and signed two days after the shooting.

"Looks like you're a homeowner, there LT."

"Is it legal?" LT asked.

"Will be, I'll take care of it down at the station. If this is what the Colonel wanted, this is the way it will be. I'll need to hang on to this." Trooper Dayber carefully refolded the document and put it in his pocket. There was another page, yet unread on the table.

"What's this one?" He asked.

"A letter the Colonel wrote to me. It's kind of personal but I'd like you to read it as well." The letter read,

Young Man,

When I found you walking along the highway way back then, I didn't see you, I saw myself, a shavetail second lieutenant with the First Marine Division retreating, along with my men, along a frozen highway from the Chosin Resevoir in Korea in 1950. My Division lost over four thousand men during that battle and afterward I was just as lost and just as hopeless as you were stumbling along that road.

We were soldiers, young man. We could not choose where we fought, or when we fought or who we would do battle against. Soldiers trust those decisions to their country in the hope their country will not send them into harm's way for improper reasons. Sadly, our country let us down in both our wars. Korea ended badly; Vietnam will end worse. This is not the fault of the soldiers who fought those wars but of the leaders who sent us there to fight.

I came to Homer because if was "the end of the road." I found peace there, not from my country but from the community. I hope you will do the same. This pencil is getting heavy now and I must stop. I want you to take my Will to Luke Dayber, he's a good man and will see that it is handled all legal and proper. I've done what I've done and now you know why.

Your friend, Jake

Lyrical Aspirations:

*A Hard Rain's A-Gonna Fall, Bob Dylan

**Taps, Daniel Adams Butterfield

Chapter Sixteen

Gatherings

“You disappeared!” Ruth said quite forcefully when I saw her at the bookstore after I returned to school. She sounded disappointed.

I told her about Teddy, about the tragedy of his daughter's birth. I choked up, she hugged me. All was well between us again.

“I'll make dinner for us tonight. My place, bring your jammies and a toothbrush,” She said with her wicked smile. I did, and we did. All night.

“What the hell happened to you? You look atrocious!” Roomie Ron Crobek announced when I arrived at work the next day. Two- or three-hours sleep will do that.

“Ruth happened,” I muttered. “I stayed at Ruth's last night. I need sleep and vitamins.”

Roomie Ron had a crush, a massive carnal crush on Ruth he made no secret of, except to Ruth. Whenever she came to the store to replace magazines Ron watched her like a hawk, a love-struck, lust struck hawk. Ron had an almost-fiancée and was faithful, except in his fantasy-stricken head.

“Details! I must have details!” He pleaded as I sipped, no, gulped coffee.

"Ron, I like Ruth a lot. She's smart, funny, beautiful and very, very energetic. She has a poster of a Sherman tank in her living room. She says it's her favorite tank. How many girls have you ever met who have a favorite tank?"

"I don't care about her favorite tank!" He pleaded. "Tell me about the good stuff!"

Just then Karen Abreau, who worked at the store's jewelry counter, stuck her head into the security office and announced, "Hey you guys, there's some bozo out here stuffing his pockets full of magic markers. You might want to do something about that."

So, we did. Magic Marker boy was sure we only stopped him because he had a ponytail. And eight unpaid magic markers. Life goes on.

Opening the gym each morning without Max brought a solemn melancholy to the start of Kevin, not Butchie's, day. Kevin lived in a gray, solitary world of work, home, sleep, and repeat. He continued to live with his Mother. He rode the city bus to work every day, spoke to no one, ate lunch in his office and rode the city bus home every evening.

He interacted well with the kids who came to box. He was cordial but distant to the rest of the staff at the YMCA. He was, for the most part, alone. This routine made him feel safe.

His brother-in-law, Teddy, had not been coming to the gym much since the birth of his daughter. A revolving schedule of doctor's appointments, surgeries and physical therapies kept him away and perpetually sad, as was his wife, her mother, and himself.

Teddy and Beth named their little girl Samantha and despite her physical ailments she was a happy, smiling, beautiful child. Which broke everyone's heart even more.

Dr. Gleason, the obstetrician who knew of Agent Orange, came by Teddy's house often. He coordinated care, made referrals and kept Teddy and Beth up to date of Samantha's progress and prospects. Her spinal affliction could be eased, but not healed. Her cleft palate was surgically repaired but not erased.

Peter Rayburn too came by. After speaking with Dave, he had begun researching defoliation projects in Vietnam. The numbers and statistics were adding up, horribly. A class action suit against the government was forming and Peter intended to be right in the middle of it.

The only person not grieving daily over these circumstances was Samantha, who knew only that she was loved, and a lot of people were paying extra close attention to her. Which made her feel safe.

Margaret Mary and Gianna were arguing once again. When not arguing there was a stony silence between them which Gianna broached this morning, "It is a wonderful opportunity for me. The Ubbitizi offers me this position, I cannot say no!"

The famous art museum in Florence had made a firm offer for Gianna to work there as a docent. The position would be open in six weeks. They needed an answer right away.

"Of course, you can say no! What you really mean is you won't say no!"

"If you loved me you would come with me to Florence." Gianna would argue.

"If you loved me, you would not put a job ahead of our happiness," Margaret Mary would reply.

And they would go to their separate corners and mourn. Gianna wanted the docent position in Florence very much. Margaret Mary's roots and heart and family were in Dublin.

Two hearts an ocean apart. Until Gianna had a proposition.

"We must go to Paris," She announced one gloomy afternoon. Margaret Mary had never been to Paris. Gianna had an older sister in Paris. They had talked about visiting there often.

"A vacation is not going to resolve anything between us," Margaret Mary replied sadly.

"Not a vacation. My sister Lucia, she is to me what your David is to you. She is wise and thoughtful. Perhaps she can see a solution that we cannot see."

"Does she know about us? Why haven't you spoken of your sister before?"

"We had a difficulty, three years ago. It was foolish, very foolish. We speak only sometimes as this difficulty heals," Gianna answered.

Margaret Mary was fully attentive now. She assumed her patient, thoughtful, hands in lap posture and said, "You must tell me about this difficulty."

Gianna hesitated, embarrassed. Without looking at Margaret Mary she whispered, "It was about a man."

Which doubled Margaret Mary's interest.

"Three years ago, in Verona my sister was in love with a man, an aviator, very handsome, very charming. They were to be engaged." Gianna struggled with revealing the next part. "This man, one night he comes to me, tells me I am beautiful, tells me I have his heart. I am young, I believe him. He says we must not tell my sister of our love. We are passionate together. It is my first time. My sister discovers us. I was very ashamed. This man, Giovanni was his name, tells my sister it was I who seduced him. She believes him. She hates me."

"That must have hurt terribly," Margaret Mary commented.

"Later she finds out there are others, like me. She comes to me, apologizes, but the hurt for me is still there. I love my sister, there is no more anger between us, just regret."

"We must go to Paris," Margaret Mary declared, "Didn't someone once say, 'Paris is always a good idea?'"

That someone was Audrey Hepburn and Audrey Hepburn was never wrong.

I was back in Lowell for the weekend, something I was doing more often since the birth of Teddy's daughter. I was there to comfort Teddy, he's, my buddy. Sometimes we would go to Lefty's and have coffee. Others we would go to a familiar bench at Shedd Park and remember when a bike ride or a good throw to first base or a line drive in the gap was all we needed to be happy. Whatever or whichever we did, we did together then, even though our lives were taking us farther and farther apart now.

But I had another, very secret agenda for returning to Lowell on weekends. On Saturday mornings, very early, I would go down to the Immaculate Conception church. It was typically very deserted at this time of day. I would go in, sit in the back and wait. I would wait for Father Coogan.

Nothing ever happened. No Father Coogan. No Father anybody.

Eventually the further I got from my ghostly experience the less real it seemed. I know it happened, at least I think I knew. Father Scanlon knew what happened but only because I told him so. I needed Father Coogan to return. My conscience needed him. I harbored a beast within myself I was afraid to talk to anyone else about. I needed someone to hear about my demons, someone who might understand. Margaret Mary was far away, becoming another person, one I did not know. I could never reveal to her what I most needed to acknowledge. There was only one other person I could think of to tell these things to. The Father I should have talked to in the first place. So, I did.

"Dad, I need to talk about something."

We were, at my request, seated at Paradise Donuts, just him and me and all my secrets. The secret I most needed to talk about was Kendall Prescott. As was his nature my Dad was open, receptive and ready to hear what I had to say.

"That guy who came to the house and said he was my buddy from Vietnam, he wasn't. He wasn't my buddy, and he wasn't with me in Vietnam. His name is Kendall Prescott and he is the guy who raped Margaret Mary."

My father's eyes went wide. "What the hell was he doing at our house?"

"Most likely looking for some payback," I admitted.

"The arm?"

"Yeah." And for the first time I was ashamed of doing it.

"How?" He asked.

"Slammed it in a car door. Big block Buick."

"On purpose?"

"Absolutely."

And then we were quiet for a while.

"You are absolutely sure he was the one who hurt Margaret Mary?"

"She says so."

"Then he deserved it." My Dad sipped his coffee closing that subject, opening another. "What happened out at UMass?"

"I found him before he found me. He had a guy with him, biker, supposed to be the muscle."

"And?" My father waited patiently.

"No Buick this time, I scared the shit out of him though." Literally, but I didn't say that.

"And the other guy?"

"Banged and bruised but he's alright. I doubt either of them will be back."

"You don't think either of them will go to the police?"

"Not likely, they came in from San Francisco, they went back to San Francisco."

"I don't need the details, David, I don't want the details, but I do want to know you won't be taking the law into your own hands like this again."

"The law had a chance to do something about this guy. They let him go."

"And you are not the Lone Ranger son. You could end up in trouble the law won't let you go for."

"I know that, Dad. It won't happen again, if this guy shows up again, I'll find some other way of dealing with it. I promise."

"Good, and don't swear." We sipped coffee.

I wasn't done. My real problem wasn't what I did to Kendall, either time. "Masher", the biker dude, was collateral damage. His fault, not mine. My real problem was how good I felt when I did those things. Not that I would do them to just anyone, but that I did it to them. Focused, intentional, targeted revenge. The violence didn't bother me in the least. That is what I hesitated to tell my Dad. But I did.

"Dad, the worst part about the whole Kendall thing is I wanted to hurt him, truthfully, I wanted to kill him."

"But you didn't."

"I really wanted to."

"Son, wanting something that isn't right and not doing it is called character. I'm not saying what you did to this fellow was alright, but what you didn't do, that you wanted to do, would have been far worse. And you chose not to do it."

"Not by much, Dad."

"By enough. What you have to decide as you go forward is to concentrate on your ability to do the right thing, not your temptation to do something else."

I would. We sat back and enjoyed our coffee. The whole Father Coogan thing seemed much less important now.

On my way back to Amherst I stopped and mailed Emmett, "The Masher's" wallet back to his biker clubhouse in California. With the wallet I put a note telling The Masher Kendall had called him a pussy for not fighting back that night at the motel. Fuck him.

"I'm finding out about something called Operation Ranch Hand," Peter explained. Teddy listened. "It was run by the Air Force primarily. Exact figures are hard to come by right now, but estimates are that between 1962 and 1971 they sprayed over 19 million gallons of this poison over more than 5 million acres of Vietnam. Most of the spraying was done by C-123 cargo planes with thousand-gallon tanks of the stuff. You know what these assholes used as a motto? "Only you can prevent a forest."

Peter struggled to keep the anger out of his voice as Teddy struggled to keep the sorrow out of his. "They knew this was going to mess guys up?" Teddy asked.

"They knew. High command decided the tactical advantages outweighed the risks of toxic exposure among the troops," Peter quoted, with disgust.

"Didn't do much good anyway," Teddy observed.

The war in Vietnam was indeed not going very well, not going well at all. President Nixon was rapidly withdrawing US troops as North Vietnam poured thousands more troops south. The poorly trained, poorly led South Vietnamese forces were no match for the soldiers of the North and doom and defeat hovered in the air. To date over fifty thousand US troops had been killed in the war, well over two hundred thousand wounded, and it was all going to hell.

"I promise Ted, something is going to be done about this. There is an alliance of Vietnam Veterans, activists, students, lawyers, parents, like yourself getting organized to take this to the courts. I'm going to be part of this, I want you to be as well."

"For my daughter?"

"For all the daughters," Peter replied. Ted agreed. The war in Vietnam ground on. Samantha continued in treatment. The country looked elsewhere. For now.

Paris is called, among many other wonderful things, "The City of Lights." This was because, at least in part, Paris was the first city in Europe to illuminate its streets with gas lamps at the turn of the nineteenth century. The larger part of the "Ville Lumiere's" reputation stems from its magnificent palaces, museums, boulevards, cafes, restaurants and shops all glowing golden in the night, every night.

Margaret Mary was swept away, overcome at first sight of the city's elegance. Gianna had insisted they arrive by train, "Airports are so commercial" she said. After taking the ferry from Dover to Calais, they rode the train, from Calais to Paris. And the magic began. Arriving in Paris at the Gare du Nord train station Margaret Mary was immediately, perpetually, entirely charmed by the city. They rode the Metro, Paris' version of London's Tube, to Colonel Fabien Circle and walked to Gianna's sister Lucia's apartment.

"Bonjour, ma petite soeur," Lucia sang in flawless Francais when they arrived. There was no trace of animosity, or tension between the two, only joy at seeing one another.

"And you must be Margaret Mary who has captured my sister's heart," Lucia continued in unaccented Anglais as she opened her arms for a welcoming hug. Holding Margaret Mary at arms length she commented, "You must be very special to capture my sister's heart. She has been very shy for too long."

They had lunch at Café de Dames, a delicious quiche with fresh salmon and a shared bottle of white wine. Margaret Mary watched fascinated by the ballet of the motor scooters, bicycles and cars rounding the Colonel Fabien traffic circle, the sartorial elegance of the passers-by, the gentility of their surroundings, the romance of their associations.

"Marie has never been to Paris before; we must show her everything!" Gianna exclaimed as Margaret Mary's name transformed once again to her surroundings.

"Then we must start where all of Paris must start, "Le Tour Eiffel!" Lucia decided as they finished lunch and descended into the Metro.

The Eiffel Tower was built between 1887 and 1889 as the showpiece for the 1889 Exposition Universelle, the World's Fair. Named after and designed by Gustave Eiffel the Tower stands 984 feet tall, and for four decades was the tallest man-made structure in the world, surpassed in 1930 by New York City's Chrysler Building and Empire State Building. But neither entranced the public and no one had ever built a structure of such elegance, such romance and beauty as Le Tour Eiffel.

Margaret Mary, now Marie, stood transfixed, speechless and delighted. "It is more beautiful than I ever imagined," she swooned gazing up at the structure. As twilight deepened the tower was bathed in golden lights enhancing by monumental degree the magnificence of Paris' premier landmark.

They walked arm in arm in arm about the landscaped commons surrounding the Tower. They passed the Musee de Orsay and the Rodin Museum, strolled the Left Bank of the Seine before descending once again into the Metro for the day's last adventure.

"Montmarte," Lucia announced, "Les Tres Petit Couchons' for our dinner and then home. You two look exhausted." Which they were, exhausted, exhilarated and enchanted.

Thrilled as they were, Margaret Mary found herself falling asleep on the Metro. It had been a long day, London to Paris by boat, train and subway. But Margaret Mary, now Marie, was elated with the knowledge that tomorrow she would wake up in Paris! As the great mystery of life went on.

The grand tour of Paris went on for three blissful days. All personal troubles were put aside as Margaret Mary drifted down the Seine, scoured the book stalls and art shoppes of the Left Banke, walked hand in hand with Gianna down the Champs Elysee and wandered wide eyed and worshipful through the Louvre, Mussee d;Orsay, and the gardens and ballrooms of Versailles.

On a side street near the Place Vendome Lucia proudly displayed her own Gallery, "The Premiere Expression." She explained that she had opened the gallery with a friend three years ago. Her friend had moved on and Lucia was now sole proprietor. The gallery had wall space for only forty-five paintings carefully selected and curated from an ever-growing inventory of appreciative artists.

"I have over a hundred paintings in storage I have no room to display. I must have more space but I cannot manage this by myself."

They were talking over a lunch of croissant and café at a small sidewalk bistro near the gallery. "There is no room here and I do not want to move. I have looked at a space in Montmarte, very suitable. But I have no one to manage it."

As an expectant silence fell over the group Lucia continued, "Unless of course you two would be interested in managing it for me."

And the world once again turned.

"Higher! Higher!" Ruth commanded, "Now push it in as hard as you can!" She was out of breath. I was out of breath. I pushed it in.

You wouldn't think installing a new shower curtain could sound so erotic but with Ruth everything was erotic, sooner or later, usually sooner. The shower rod in place Ruth clipped on the plastic curtain, turned to me and said, "That's that. What do you say we take this thing out for a test drive?" Then we were naked and wet.

My pathetically enamored roommate Ron Crobek had taken to referring to Ruth as "Rootin' Tootin," a nickname she would probably have laughed at and with had she heard it. So far, I had not had the courage to use it to her face. But it fit.

"David, you have not talked about what you are going to do after you graduate," Ruth declared after we toweled off and lounged about in her living room. Which was true. I was still wandering through classes that caught my interest without declaring a major or even envisioning one. I was taking several Sociology courses, bunnies, as LT used to call them, along with some literature and English Lit courses. Nothing seemed to stick but the candle was burning. Ruth was right, I was creeping up on decision time.

"I kind of like the Criminology courses I've had," I whimpered.

"David, you sound like a child when you say things like that. You are a junior in college. Pick a major, grow up."

Ruth pulled no punches. And she was right.

"I'm thinking of some form of law enforcement, maybe a cop. I've even thought about going back in the Army, Military Police or Army Security Agency."

"You would make a good police officer, but I think you are done with the Army," She observed.

Which was regrettably true. I had gotten a look at how the military operated. On the ground, with good leadership, like Dustoff, the best. Headquarters and command behind the front lines and isolated from the men in the field was often out of touch, overly cautious and poorly led. A military career, once a proud warrior's vocation, was an ash heap now. Burned to the ground by the Vietnam War.

"How about you?" I asked, "Still going to Israel?"

"I have all my paperwork in order. My uncle Daniel and aunt Rachel live in Tel Aviv. I will stay with them before entering the kibbutz and joining the IDF."

I didn't know what IDF stood for.

"Israeli Defense Forces," she explained, "within this is the Sayaret Matka, like our Special Forces, I will join them as well."

"Ruth," I tried to explain, "Special Forces, any special forces, only means one thing, killing people, often and up close. Do you think you are ready for that?"

"For my country, yes, I am ready for that."

"And Israel is your country?"

"It will be David. It is my homeland."

"There are other ways of serving your homeland."

"Sayaret Matka is how I will serve."

"It will change you," I stated as simply as I could.

"How? How will this change me?" She implored.

"You must hope you never get used to the killing. Each time, each incident must stand out in your mind as horrible, a waste, a tragedy."

"They are the enemies of my people."

"They are people just like yourself fighting for something they believe in as strongly as you do. When they die part of you will die with them."

"You have done this? You have killed people?"

"I hope not, Ruth. I fired my weapon a lot, mostly at random during fire fights or evacuations. Things were moving a bit too fast to count who did what, but I saw the dead, lots of the dead, ours and theirs. They looked very much alike."

"Alike how?"

"Heartbreaking, Ruth, they looked heartbreaking."

She put her head on my shoulder. I put my heart in her hand.

Chapter Seventeen

Farewells & Not So Wells

About the middle of our junior year Roomie Ron mostly stopped going to classes. First, he asked me not to schedule him on Mondays or Fridays at the bookstore. This was not a problem; I could work around the guy's schedules. He started leaving Amherst early on Friday, going to Peabody where his almost fiancé waited. He would return on Monday, usually in the afternoon. He put in more time working at the bookstore than he did attending mid-week classes all of which led to my getting a phone call from Ron's Dad, a good man named Fabian Crobek who also happened to be the deputy chief of Immigration and Naturalization for New England. I had met Fabe, as he liked to be called, on his several visits to Amherst to visit and check on his son. Fabe told me early on,

"Ron's a good boy, a good son, but he's a flake. He's head over heels in love with this Alice woman, she's divorced and has a child. He's putting a lot more effort into being with her than he is into his education. I would appreciate anything you could do to help."

Which so far hadn't been much. Until this phone call.

"There is a Federal Service Entrance Exam coming up in a few weeks. It's going to be given in Amherst. I want Ron to take the exam. I've signed him up for it but I doubt he'll go on his own. Would you take the exam with him? I've signed you up as well. Just get him there, as a favor to me, and to him, maybe even to yourself. I would appreciate it very much."

I said I would though I had no idea how I would. So, I talked to Ron.

"Your Dad called," I began, "He wants you to take the government service exam next month."

"Yeah, I know. Why'd he call you?"

"He wants me to make sure you get there. He signed us both up for the test."

"Dave, I worked for the government once, it didn't work out so well."

"This isn't Nam, Ron."

"Don't kid yourself, Dave, Uncle Sam should never be your favorite uncle."

Which meant Roomie Ron had given this much more thought than I had.

"I'll take the exam," Ron decided, "I never did test very well anyway."

I did. I should have known this wasn't going to turn out the way Fabe expected.

"We must talk of my sister's office in Paris," Gianna said over dinner one night. Her relationship with Margaret Mary had remained strained after their visit to Paris. For Gianna the lure of the Florence museum called to her, for Margaret Mary the ties to her father and aunt in Dublin beckoned. The road before them was parting with separate paths leading to sadness.

"What about Florence? The Ubbitzi."

"This I would give up, for you, for us."

"And for Paris?"

"For us," Gianna stated conclusively. "The Ubbitzi is a career, my career, I thought. I love you and I want us to be together."

"I love you as well, but there is my family in Dublin."

"Children must outgrow their families," Gianna pleaded. "We cannot remain children forever. I am not asking you to give up your family. Your father and your aunt will always be there for you. I am asking you to place us ahead of them as I have with my career. You can come with me to Paris or go to Dublin and remain a child."

And in that moment Margaret Mary shed her childhood skin and stepped into adulthood. They were going to Paris.

"I can't believe he threw that poor woman under the bus!" Cindy was outraged at the latest Watergate development. In another futile, stupid, dishonest attempt to cover up his complicity in the Watergate break in besieged and battered President Richard Nixon declared that his personal secretary, Rosemary Woods, had accidently erased critical and incriminating Oval Office audio tapes while transcribing them.

"That poor woman has been a political hack and henchman for Nixon since he was a freshman congressman in 1951. She's as crooked as the rest of them," Peter replied over studious coffees at the Travis Coffee Shop.

"Are there no depths that man will not sink to?" Cindy asked.

"Not so far," Peter replied, "but he's still digging."

Things were looking grim for the 37th President of the United States as the Watergate scandal widened and deepened. Peter, Cindy and most of the sophomore class at Suffolk University pored over every word and debated every new revelation. Sleaze abounded with political rodents like John Mitchell, John Dean, H. R. Halderman and the like scurrying to get off Nixon's sinking ship.

Cindy and Peter were now a couple. Sharing classes and ambitions at Suffolk University had brought them together. Both were law students, bright, energetic and at the top of their class.

"Are we still on for this weekend?" Cindy asked.

"Nantucket by midnight. We can catch the last ferry out of Woods Hole, dump our bags at the Inn and be having dinner dockside by 8PM." Peter declared.

"So, what's the midnight part?" Cindy asked.

"That's you and me on a very sandy, secluded beach, naked as jaybirds," Peter leered.

"It's true what they say," Cindy answered, "Once you've had a priest you never go back."

Which was a private joke only she and he could laugh about. While Peter had few regrets about leaving the priesthood it was not part of his past he shared with many people. While the numbers show that the Catholic church loses an average of a thousand priests a year by resignation, most of these are generated by the celibacy restrictions. Peter resigned for far different reasons but had discovered the joys beyond celibacy to be more than a compensating reward.

"And we take no work with us?" Cindy implored.

"No work. No newspaper. No evening news. Just us, I promise."

Later that evening, after the lobster and other assorted shellfish Peter and Cindy bundled up in a wisely chosen sleeping bag on one of Nantucket's more secluded beaches. The sleeping bag not only insulated them from the cool autumn evening it kept their shiny white, naked Caucasian bodies from being seen by ships at sea and trans-continental aircraft.

"Why did you want to become a priest?" Cindy asked for the tenth time after receiving nine prior partial answers.

Peter took a deep breath and began again, "It was my attempt to replace reason with faith. I could never fully understand the 'why' of many things. I thought faith would ease my doubts and make life more understandable for me. I was wrong."

"Does that mean you no longer have faith?" Cindy asked.

"I still have faith; I just have faith in different things."

"Do you still believe in God?" Cindy teased.

Peter did. Cindy didn't. This was a familiar topic with them. Cindy described herself as an agnostic. She claimed she neither believed nor disagreed with the existence of a God.

"I'm going to be the best person I can because I choose to be, not because I'm stacking up brownie points with a god who's going to reward me after I die," She declared, often.

Peter would counter with his belief that there was a God, though not necessarily the Holy Trinity of the catholic church or even the divinity of Jesus Christ. Parables, he learned, were not facts and he had determined through his own research that the Gospels of the New Testament were just that, parables. The church would admit such, just not publicly.

"Yet you believe you have a soul," Pet recalled from earlier conversations such as this.

"I have a conscience therefore I believe I have a soul. I do not believe a bunch of ritual hocus pocus is what I need to access my soul. On this Cindy was steadfast, as Peter was also learning to be.

"I am actually clearer on why I no longer wanted to be a priest than I am on why I became one in the first place," Peter admitted.

Cindy began to cuddle up closer to Peter in the sleeping bag. "I think I know what one of those reasons was," She teased. "Perhaps, but it was more than that. Celibacy was a compromise I may have been willing to make. The much more important issue was the wealth, the staggering, uncountable, hoarded wealth of the church."

"I know, I know, the cathedrals and the chalices, the statues and the paintings, the stained-glass windows," Cindy recited, "You've said all this before. You have not talked about what made you decide to enter the priesthood. I understand why you decided to leave it."

"I was looking for answers. I got rituals and superstitions and fairy tales."

"Those are the things I believe are the most important contributions of organized religion, especially the catholic church," Cindy answered.

Peter was surprised, almost shocked by Cindy's answer.

"Can you please explain that?" He asked.

"People love a circus; people need a circus. Religion is the oldest surviving circus we have. Lots of candles and incense, pointy hats and silky vestments. You think people would just go to church to hear some guy pontificating about being good? C'mon Peter, it's a shit show. People like shit shows."

After a moment passed when Peter half thought she might be struck dead for blasphemy he began to acknowledge the truth in what she said.

"You are a very smart girl, you know that?" He whispered.

"I am also a very naked girl who is tired of talking and wants to run on the beach."

Which they did to the amusement of ships at sea and trans-continental aircraft.

Cop cars. Lots of cop cars. I counted four Amherst PD cruisers and three black Crown Vic's with cheap hubcaps, which meant they were Feds. There was crime scene tape across every door of the China Rose and the upstairs casino doors were wide open with cops carrying out boxes of evidence. This was not good.

I looked for Eddie and found Tom Marrett, an Amherst copper who practically lived at the China Rose. He was looking very bashful.

"Tom? What the hell?" I asked.

"Feds showed up with warrants, lots of warrants actually. We're just here as spectators."

"What about Eddie?"

"Tried to take him into local custody. The Feds backed us off. He's over there in the back of that Vic."

"Can I talk to him?"

"Yeah, sure. Come with me." Tom walked me over to the car where Eddie sat handcuffed in the back seat.

"Nick," Tom said to the US Marshall standing by the car. "Do you mind if my friend has a word with Eddie? He's, his cousin."

Cousin was a nice touch. Nick opened the rear door of the car and stepped away.

"Dave!" Eddie looked very glad to see me. "I need a favor," He whispered.

"You look like you need five or six favors. What the hell?"

"Don't know. They haven't charged me with anything yet. They're emptying the casino and detaining all the girls. I need you to do something for me, it's important." Eddie lowered his voice and checked to see that Tom and Nick were out of earshot. "I got a bag, big bag, stashed. I need you to get it for me, take care of it."

"Bag of what, Eddie?"

"Cash, about sixty grand. If the Feds find it, it's gone."

"Where?" I asked, not sure I was doing the right thing, but I was probably going to do it anyway. Eddie was a good guy, at least to me.

"Boyden gym, on campus. In a gym locker, says "Murphy" on it, number 3774. It's got a combination lock on it. 12-24-32. Got it? 12-24-32. Got it?"

I'd get it. Eddie is my buddy.

"Times up you guys, my boss is coming," Nick said.

I backed away. Eddie looked grateful and very scared. I walked away with Tom.

"Where are they taking him?" I asked.

"Probably to the Fed lockup in Springfield. I'll let you know."

I thanked Tom, waved an unseen goodbye to Eddie and got the hell out of there before someone became interested in me.

A week later I was able to see Eddie at the Metropolitan Detention Center in Springfield. It was a contact visit, no phones, no recording.

"Didja' get the bag?" Eddie asked.

"Hi Dave, good to see you. Thanks for coming," I suggested.

"Sorry man, I'm a little uptight, you know?"

I knew. I also had the bag.

"What do you want me to do with it?"

"Take five grand for yourself, I mean it. Then find me a good lawyer. Can you do that?"

"Don't the people you work for know any good lawyers?"

"Getting g a lawyer my people know is like admitting you're guilty. I need outside help."

"I'll see what I can do, and you can keep your five grand."

"Why? I want you to have it."

"You offered me a friend loan once. This is a friend favor. Besides, taking your five grand would be like me admitting I'm guilty of whatever it is they think you're guilty of."

"You got somebody in mind?"

"Yeah, if I can find him." I was remembering a Captain type lawyer who got Harry Giles out of trouble years before. Horatio Marks, if I could find him.

First, I tried the post locator at Fort Meade, Maryland. They had no Captain Horatio Marks assigned to the post. The Judge Advocate general's office told me the same thing, but they remembered him. A chatty Spec 4, the backbone of the Army, told me Captain Marks had been discharged, end of service and had returned to his home in Baltimore. He did not have an address, but I was willing to bet the Maryland State Bar Association did. They did.

"Remind me," No longer Captain Marks said.

"Ferrier, as in Terrier, we worked on getting Harry Giles out of stupid jail at Fort Meade a couple of years ago."

"Giles? Two wives, no brains?"

"That's him."

"So, Nam didn't get you?"

"Not all of me. I'm up at UMass finishing my bachelor's degree and I've got a friend in trouble."

"You need a better class of friends, my friend."

"Until then, I'll call you. How have you been? What kind of law are you practicing?"

"I'm doing fine, almost got married, smartened up. I'm doing paid for in US currency law. What kind of trouble is your friend in and is he in possession of US currency?"

"He's charged with desertion and a bunch of immigration violations, false passport and the like. There are also a bunch of state charges, mostly gambling and civil stuff."

"He deserted from the Army?"

"He was never in the Army or anything else. He didn't show up for his draft physical and took off to Canada. He got arrested in Amherst running a casino, sort of."

"You can't 'sort of' run a casino."

"Eddie is an interesting guy, you'll like him."

"Five thousand, up front, plus expenses. I'll come up, meet with him and we'll see. Can you do that?"

"Done deal. I'll see you when you get here."

The Monday night veterans meeting had become a very important part of my campus life. We met as a group of troubled individuals who were very much alike. The Vietnam War remained a polarizing subject on campus. Much of the blame for the war dumped on the returning veterans, like me, like us. We were all coping with the stigma in different, yet similar ways.

Steve Price was one of the group regulars. He lost an arm in Nam. Street fighting house to house in Hue Citadel with the 3rd Marines he had his arm torn off at the shoulder by a rocket propelled grenade. Only the burning phosphorous on the shell which seared the wound kept him from bleeding to death. Now he was here, among us, coping.

"I was walking out of the Student Union yesterday afternoon, heading for the library," He began, his voice choked with emotion, staring at the floor, both of his legs shaking furiously, never looking up. Every one of us in the room leaned forward to listen. "This girl comes up to me, cute chick, kind of a hippie, you know?"

We knew. The campus was full of them.

"She asked if I lost my arm in Nam." Steve was choking on his words now. "I was really surprised because most people don't ask, you know?"

We knew.

"I kind of nodded and said yeah and she looked at me and said, 'Good!' and walked away."

Silence thundered in the room. Ten guys who thought they heard it all were hearing it once again. Steve was stone silent, still staring at the floor.

Dick Gerson broke the silence. "The world's not fair, not always kind, Steve. Bad things happen to good people, good things happen to bad people. When you can accept that, you can hang on to the fact that you can be a good person who's had something bad happen to them and move on."

"Yeah, what's that little bitch know about anything, anyway?" Lucius growled, then put a buck in the can.

"Steve," I offered, "whenever I look at you, I don't see a guy without an arm. I see a guy who is handling himself with grace and courage in a way I don't know if I would be able to do myself. I look up to you because of who you are, not because of what happened to you."

To my relief several heads were nodding in agreement. Steve looked up. "I know you guys know. The RPG that ripped off my arm missed my head by about two inches. A good thing. I know I'm lucky I survived. I just wish somebody else would care."

"We care Steve," Dick added.

"Yeah," Steve responded, "but I don't want to fuck any of you guys."

"She was that cute, huh?" Roomie Ron asked.

"Yeah, she was," Steve answered, smiling as he put a buck in the can. Nobody could say Vietnam Vets aren't resilient.

And a tune whispered…

They say the blues went out of style.
To cry is to act just like a child.
Smile each day that we're apart.
But I can't agree I never will.
Since You Broke My Heart.

They say the best way's not to care.
Just play a few hands of solitaire.
Read a book or study art.
All the remedies don't work for me.
Since You Broke My Heart.*

God Bless America.

Lyrical Aspiration:

*Since You Broke My Heart, Don Everly

PROUD
VIETNAM
VETERAN
ALL GAVE SOME
SOME GAVE ALL

Chapter Eighteen

Consequences

On this Monday night, after we had joined hands and said our opening prayer, several members of the veteran's group, including myself, had something to add. Dick Gerson, our leader, our friend, our guide was graduating. This would be his last meeting. He was taking a job in Hartford, Connecticut, moving there with his wife and child, leaving Amherst and us a better place and better people.

Lucius went first. "I'd probably be in jail right now if it hadn't been for Dick. He saved me from myself. I just want to say thanks Dick, thanks for everything."

Which was a huge speech for Lucius without costing him a buck or two.

"I feel the same way," Jack Harrington added, "except for the jail part. I was lost, no friends, no plan, no future until Dick brought me here and gave me all three. Thanks Dick."

"I came here the same night as Lucius, two years ago. Since then, Monday night has been my salvation. No matter how sour things might go during the week I always knew that if I could make it to Monday night I'd be alright. You did that for me Dick, thank you." This speech was from Gary, one of the quiet guys who never missed a meeting.

I waited till last as several more sentiments were expressed. Over the weekend Dick asked me to take over the Monday night meetings. At first, I didn't want to, but how could I say no to a guy who almost literally saved my life? Like Lucius I would have been long gone had Dick not followed me out onto the back stairs of Boyden Gym two years ago and rescued me. When it was my turn I began,

"Dick, I know everything these guys have said comes from their hearts. I can identify with every word. I just want to add that my thanks comes from my heart as well. All I've ever learned how to do was suit up, show up and hope for the best. For me you were that best, you are the reason I'm here tonight. Thank you."

Then I added, "There is one more thing. Everybody chipped in, and we drained the coffee can to get you something. This is a small thing to try and tell you what a big thing you have been to all of us."

Roomie Ron Crobek stepped forward with a plaque we had composed and had mounted and engraved. The plaque read…

Presented To

DICK GERSON

For your years of caring, understanding and devotion. For helping others to help themselves. For restoring faith and hope where none existed. For Being a friend to men who thought they were friendless.

Thank You.

The Veterans of Beta Chi, Amherst Mass. 1973

Dick read the plaque, wiped away a tear and said,

"I learned in Nam that I was not going to make it through there on my own. My survival, my mental, physical and emotional well-being wasn't strong enough, nobody's was. I needed help. I found it by seeking out the company of the good guys, the smart guys, the guys just trying to do their duty and get through another day. What they did, I did.

It was the same when I got here. I was alone. My wife and child were living with my parents in Worcester. I didn't know anybody, I had no friends, I was lost.

When I met the guys who were renting this farmhouse, I didn't know they were vets, not at first. I just knew they needed another guy to split the rent. Stu Randall, George Binnder, and Steve Loucraft are all gone now, graduated, moved on. But they left something behind. They left fellowship, understanding, support and kindness. Those guys were vets, like us. They were the kind I learned to hang with in Nam. We sat, we talked, we supported one another and that is what I have tried to pass on to you. We started calling this place Beta Chi after the Base Exchange on Air Force posts. The BX is where you went to get the extras, the things the service didn't give you. Then it was toys for the boys, civvies, and junk for your bunk. Here it's fellowship, friendship and support. Beta Chi, where you can get what you need. We can get it from each other.

Helping others is the best way I have ever found of helping myself. That is what I have tried to do for you and what we have done for each other. So, I want to thank you guys as well. Dave is going to take over for me. Keep doing what we've been doing. Help yourself by helping others. I'll always remember what we've done for each other here and I hope you will as well."

And that is one small example of how the Monday night veterans meeting saved my life and got me through the University of Massachusetts,

"21-14, Game."

I hated it, in a very good way, when Ruth beat me at Racquetball. She was good, very good, quick, coordinated, clever. While she was being very good, I was getting better. Ruth taught me the game. I endured multiple losses of 21-0, 21-3, 21-6, then the worm turned. The first time I lost 21-10 I saw a look on her face I hadn't seen before. Not worry, respect. 14 was my high score so far. It was going to get higher.

"You know it would have been 21-18 if I hadn't been staring at your ass in those shorts."

"Wait till you see my ass out of these shorts," She replied as we started another game.

I lost 21-11. Preoccupied by the shorts.

Later as we sat in her living room across from the poster of her favorite tank she announced, "My immigration papers arrived, I leave for Israel on June 6."

June 6 was three days after her graduation, two weeks from now.

"This means it is time for us to make our goodbyes," She said, ever practical, practically sad. So was I. I was not in love with Ruth, not like I was in love with Margaret Mary. But I liked Ruth a lot. I enjoyed her company, and I knew she enjoyed mine. Our sex life was phenomenal, our friendship was just as valuable, perhaps even more so.

I haven't had a lot of luck figuring out the whole love thing yet. Forever and ever, till death do us part, only you and you alone had not happened for me yet. There was the whole Margaret Mary thing of course but that had taken a left turn that left me even more confused. I was too uncertain about my own future to involve somebody else in mine yet. Ruth, on the other hand, always knew what her future held. She was going to live on a kibbutz in Israel, serve in the Israeli army, settle in and defend Israel from all enemies. There was no space for me in that future and somehow that was alright with me. I envied her the resolution, the firmness of direction she possessed. I didn't just like Ruth, I admired her. Which was the best I could manage short of love.

"Can I ask you about something we have never spoken of before?" She asked, looking me straight in the eye, politely.

At this moment there was no way I could ever refuse her. I turned to her on the sofa, she moved closer against me and asked, "You have been a soldier. I am going to become one very soon. What must I know?"

Short question that was going to take a very long answer. We had never spoken about my time in the Army, my tours in Vietnam, the consequences of being in a war. More new ground. As much as I often struggled to find the right words, I knew what I wanted to say.

"The first thing I learned was sacrifice. I know that sounds strange but once I was in the military, once I committed to doing the best I could, I had to sacrifice my opinions, my preferences, my choices and obey the orders the Army gave me. This was very hard. I have always tried to be independent, to follow my own instincts when I could. I think you are exactly the same way. Soldiers sacrifice the right to do that. They obey orders without questioning them. Sometimes, many times, this is very hard. They used to say, "There is a right way, a wrong way and the military way." You don't get to pick. You sacrifice the freedom of choice. You obey."

This was wearing me out. I had never spoken of this before, not to a civilian anyway. The Vets at my Monday night meetings understood this, Ruth would have to learn to comprehend and accept this.

"I need a drink," I decided while I chose my words.

"I've got Chablis, or Chablis," She replied.

I sipped on the Chablis and continued, "When you become a soldier you become part of a machine. Everybody has a job, you do yours right, the machine keeps everybody alive. Naturally the same goes for those around you. You have to trust them; they have to trust you. That's the most important thing. Trust, respect and responsibility. That's what you must learn."

"What about being in combat? The fighting?" She asked in a voice I had never heard before. Uncertain, tentative, fearful.

"The fighting, for me was controlled terror. You will be afraid, so will everybody else who has a brain in their head. You control the fear and try not to get yourself or anybody else killed or injured. You must never think there will be no fear. Courage is overcoming fear, not being without it.

There is one more thing, one I found only after the danger has passed. You cannot afford to hate your enemy. They are the same as you, fighting for a cause they believe in, following orders. They too are soldiers like you and deserve respect. When they are down, bleeding on the ground they are just men, men who do not want to die, men who are as frightened as you are trying not to be. Do not let your fear of them turn to hatred. It will dishonor you."

Then she kissed me, and I kissed her. And so on. The rest of the night when we spoke, we spoke of other things. Plans that would never occur, reunions that would never take place, promises we would not keep. We knew that life was sweeping us away to far and distant places in the very near future. When we made love that night there was a tenderness that overrode our considerable passion, and I caught a passing glimpse of what real love must feel like.

Ruth and I decided the best place for us to say goodbye was the place where we had first said hello. So, we met at the Top of The Campus lounge, 4PM, the night before she was leaving Amherst, moving to Israel, marching out of my life.

"I ordered you a beer," She said, sipping her Chablis.

"I'd drink gasoline if you ordered it. Did I ever tell you that?"

"No," she replied, "But you've showed me that."

We sat, we talked and one hour later we hugged and said goodbye forever.

Ted watched from the living room sofa as Dr. Gleason showed Beth how to fit the tiny spinal brace onto Samantha. Neither the lump in his throat, the ache in his heart nor the tears in his eyes provided any relief from the pain he felt as his daughter wiggled and giggled as the brace was fitted into place.

"All night, Doctor?" Beth asked.

"The longer she has it on the better," Dr. Gordon replied. "We'll fit her for a walking brace when the time comes but for now she should sleep in this and keep it on as much as possible during the day."

Beth turned to look at Ted and saw the pain radiating from him. He would not look her in the eyes, his inner rampaging guilt denouncing him for being the cause of his daughter's infirmities.

"Ted? Do you want to see how this thing works?" Beth asked hopefully.

Ted could only shake his head, get up and walk out of the room. Dr. Gleason followed.

"You can't keep blaming yourself for this, Ted."

"Why not?" Ted answered bitterly. "Is she going to get any better?"

"Yes Ted, she is," The doctor answered. "With the proper therapy and medication, she will walk, talk and have a life as near to normal as we can manage. I wish I could say the same for you."

Which triggered a flash of anger in Teddy, an increasingly dangerous flash.

"She's not your daughter, Doc! She's not your daughter who is not going to have any brothers or sisters, not going to ride a bicycle or put on ice skates. You call that getting better?"

"Yes Ted, I do." Dr. Gleason struggled to control his own anger and frustration. "Her cognitives are perfect, she responds appropriately to stimulus, her digestion is normal, she is beginning to recognize faces, smiles and moves without obvious discomfort. It could have been a lot worse!"

"It damn sure could have been a lot better too Doc!"

"Who are you feeling sorry for Ted? Yourself, or Samantha?" The doctor replied, which almost got him a strong left hook and right cross from Teddy. Cooler heads prevailed when Beth brought Samantha into the room.

"What are you two growling about?" Beth asked as Samantha wriggled happily.

Tempers cooled instantly, reason returned, Ted apologized, Dr. Gleason accepted, Beth hugged her daughter and Samantha smiled knowingly.

"So, it's to be Paris then?" Rose asked.

Margaret Mary sat trembling, her hands clasped together on the tabletop as she told Sean and Rose of her plans with Gianna.

"Are you disappointed in me then?" She asked in an unnaturally timid voice.

Rose threw her head back and laughed, Sean smiled, Rose continued, "Darling girl, do you think I have always been a doting dowager as I am now?"

Margaret Mary shook her head cautiously as Rose went on, "When I was a lass, much the same age as you are now, I couldn't be kept away from Paris as no one ever should!"

Rose reached across the tabletop and took Margaret Mary's trembling hands. "I was in love you see. With a dashing young Capitane in the Legione Entrange. We were devoted to each other, enthralled the poets might say. It is a miracle you do not have at least a dozen cousins of the French/Irish nature romping about today!" Rose laughed as Margaret Mary blushed.

"Tremaine was it not? Jean Paul as I recall," Sean added.

"A Celt to be sure, but raised in France, a French mother and a French soul."

Margaret Mary had never heard her aunt speak of Jean Paul Tremaine before, though she recalled whispers as a child of a long-lost love in Rose's past.

"What happened to him?" Margaret Mary asked with excitement and curiosity in her voice. And for a moment the room filled with sadness.

"In the spring of 1954, the 7th of May it was, Jean Pierre was killed at a far away place called Dien Bien Phu. Heaven rest his soul."

Margaret Mary knew her history. Dien Bien Phu was the final defeat of the French forces in what was then called Indochina. Today it was called Vietnam, and the killing was still going on.

"Jean Paul." Sean raised his glass, Rose and Margaret Mary did the same. They drank, the sadness settled.

"A Gallery of Art you say? And in Montmarte?" Rose asked.

"On the most wonderful street corner. It has cobblestones!" Margaret Mary exclaimed. "The street I mean."

"Of course, the street, my dear. Cobblestones are seldom an indoor thing," Rose said.

"And when shall this relocation be made?" Sean asked.

"Gianna is there now. I will join her when I go back. We have an apartment only a short distance from the gallery. You will come, and see?"

"Nothing could keep us away, daughter. We shall be there often as we are with you always," Sean said.

"And I always with you," Margaret Mary answered through
happy tears.

Chapter Nineteen

Destinations

"Fuck this!" Marty Kagle threw his registration packet toward an open trash can in Boyden gym and stomped out.

I picked up the envelope and followed him outside.

Marty Kagle was Dave Ferrier two years ago. This time I was doing the saving; he was being saved. Perhaps.

"Excuse me, you a vet?" I asked.

"What's it to ya?" He replied. Music to my ears.

Thirty minutes later Marty was registered for what would be his first semester at UMass. He had been home from Viet Nam for two years. A rough two years. He decided to give school a try after learning the hard way that his military training as an artilleryman had little cache on the civilian job market.

After getting registered for his classes Marty was appropriately grateful and promised to come to our Monday Night Vet group. Yeah sure. I would pick him up.

When we joined hands in support the following Monday evening Marty was there. He looked as surprised as I was all those years ago when Dick Gerson showed up at my apartment to bring me here. Marty was going to be fine. He had that characteristic about him. He was a survivor and a seeker.

Roomie Ron had not registered for senior year. He was now full time with his almost fiancé in Peabody and I was once again looking for a rent splitting roommate. I spoke with Ron's Dad and promised to accompany Ron to the government service test we had missed twice already. Fabe said he would stay in touch. So did Ron.

My roommate dilemma was solved, sort of, when one of my security guards at the bookstore, Jenny Long, announced she was looking for an apartment with her boyfriend. Two for one and living with a female roommate was going to be an adventure. I soon got used to finding my living room shoes and socks placed on my bed and having the kitchen counter tops wiped clean every hour or so. Jenny left only a series of mournful sighs after her compulsive cleaning. Her boyfriend, Andy Hillman, was an affable sort whom I rarely saw in or out of the apartment. The couple provided financial stability to my rent situation and the consolation of learning one female roommate could leave a bathroom in much more chaos than two not overly fastidious guys. Life is learning.

Lucius had also disappeared over the summer. The drop out rate among veterans was far higher than among the rest of the student body and only the rumor of his going to New Mexico was left behind. Steve Price was back and a few of the other regulars. We were banding together for another school year, my last.

"Your friend is going to have to do some jail time."

Former Captain Horatio Marks declared after several visits and a series of negotiations with prosecutors on Eddie's case. "I think I can get the State of Massachusetts to drop the gaming charges, so the Feds can prosecute on the draft evasion issues. He's probably looking at three years total, eighteen months in with good behavior."

"That long? I thought the government was backing off on the draft evasion issues?" I said.

"That little prick Nixon wants to stand them all up against a wall and shoot them. Supreme Court says no. Nixon's days are numbered. He might be in prison himself before Eddie gets there."

Such was the doomed atmosphere in the White House as the Watergate allegations became Watergate facts. Venal dishonesty and corruption had sunk to new lows under Nixon and the public had grown weary, very weary of the Washington political shenanigans. Which might work in Eddie's favor.

"Why would the state be willing to drop the gaming charges?" I asked as I learned.

"First of all, the working girls, the "waitresses" know half the cops in Amherst by their first names. Also having a full-scale casino and cat house running for almost two years without any official notice is a bit embarrassing if you're a law-and-order type. Eddie kept the place pretty drug free, which is good, and he did not cater to the college crowd a lot, except for degenerates like you."

"I object to the term degenerate." I was gathering my legal chops.

"What I need is something good to tell the judge about Eddie. Does he love his mother? Did he ever save a drowning puppy? Was he a Boy Scout? I need you to do a background report on him. Make it shine. Then I can press for a reduced sentence." Horatio, who now liked to be called 'H', for brevity, proclaimed.

"How?" I asked. "What's a background report look like?"

"Ask your friend Peter, he seems like a pretty sharp guy, that girl he's with Sandy? She's natural, have them help you. Pay them," 'H' advised.

Cindy and Peter had been picking 'H' up at Logan airport when he came to visit Eddie. They got along. Peter drafted motions. Cindy edited Peter's motions. 'H' filed Peter and Cindy's motions with the court. Eddie's dark skies brightened.

"Get me the background report. Write me a check and drive me to the airport." 'H' was heading back to Baltimore. I was heading into legal land.

The poachers were hoping to slide past Fritz Creek and land their illegal catch at Voznesenka, on the upper section of Kachemak Bay. That is where LT caught them and placed them under arrest.

LT had been employed by the Alaska Department of Fish and Game for a little over a year. When not bagging poachers, he issued fish and game licenses, oversaw reports of any invasive species on the Kenai Peninsula, and monitored the welfare of any endangered wildlife like the blue and humpback whales which frequented the region.

LT had found peace and a place for himself in Homer, Alaska where he had inherited the home and property of his good friend and mentor, the late Lieutenant Colonel Jake Hackleberry. For the first time since he left Vietnam he lived with purpose, without anger and among people whom he trusted and who trusted him.

"LT, you comin' to the soiree tonight?" Hack Benson asked while he pumped gas into LT's ancient and inherited pickup truck.

"Wouldn't be a soiree if I wasn't there, would it?" he answered.

"Thinkin' a little highly of yourself this mornin' ain't ya?" Hack asked.

"Finally caught them Roper brothers poaching out near the Pavilion. I've got thirty pounds of impounded flounder to toss on the grill tonight."

"You gonna' keep them Ropers locked up this time?" Hack asked.

"Third time's the charm. Shipped them off to Anchorage."

"Good riddance to bad garbage," Hack added. "Thirty pounds you say?"

LT smiled.

"That's a lot of tartar sauce." Hack grinned and finished pumping gas.

"You got some mail." Zack Turner tossed an open package to Emmet 'Masher' still at the Diablos clubhouse in Oakland, California.

"You opened it?" Masher said.

"Why not? It's my fuckin' clubhouse ain't it? And what's this shit about some guy named Kendall calling you a pussy?"

Masher read the note in with his wallet. He was not happy.

"You were sent back east to represent. Getting' called a pussy ain't representin', Mash."

Zack didn't sound happy either.

"I'll talk to him about it," Masher replied, and then he won't be talking to anyone else, he added, in his head.

"You do that," Zack answered, "or I'll talk to him for ya'"

Soon Kendall would not be happy. Fuck him.

"Do you remember Emily Kazantaros from high school?" Teddy asked as we sat having coffee at Lefty's.

"Emmy K? Major spinner, year behind us, nose in the air a little?" I responded.

"That's her. I saw her at church. She asked about you."

"You were at church?"

"Beth wants us to go. For Samantha." Teddy's voice dropped in sadness. I changed the subject.

"Why was she asking about me?"

Emmy K, was a very pretty, very popular girl at Lowell High back in our day. Always dressed well, dated the captain of the football team, prim, proper, polite. She didn't mix well with Shedd Park boys, but we knew who she was and where she was, a step above us on the social ladder.

"You should maybe ask her out," Teddy suggested.

"Out where? She never struck me as a few beers at the Whipple type girl. What happened to her and Jack O'Brian? They were the golden couple."

"Jacks in jail. Walpole, ten years. Ran a stop sign, killed some lady drunk driving."

"Wow! I didn't know that."
"Happened when we were away. He's got a ways to go."

"We've all got a ways to go Teddy."

"Yeah, but at least we're not at Walpole. She's in the phone book. She asked me to tell you."

"Maybe I will sometime, not now though. I have to get back to Amherst. You sure you're, okay?"

"I'm doing the best I can, Dave. But I wouldn't say I was okay."

Teddy could not stop grieving after the birth of his daughter. He held himself responsible for her infirmities, no amount of reasoning would shake him from his conviction. He was by himself alone, convicted.

"Teddy," I began, not knowing exactly where I was going, "Medicine these days, operations and such they can do miracles. Samantha is the best behaved, happiest little baby I've ever seen. As long as you love her, and Beth loves her she'll be fine."

I hoped.

On the way back to Amherst I added up the score. The girl I loved since grade school was living in Paris with another woman. My best friend couldn't stop grieving over his daughter's birth defects. Rootin Tootin was in Israel joining their special forces. Another buddy was in jail and my friend who used to be a priest was now an almost lawyer. I had two roommates who thought I was a bigger slob than both of them put together and my favorite waitress from the China Rose had been deported back to Taiwan. What could go right? I made a mental note to get my car radio fixed. I needed some rock & roll to give my brain a rest.

Just let me hear some of the Rock & Roll Music.

Any old way you can choose it.

It's got a backbeat you can't lose it,

Any old time you use it,

Gotta be rock & roll music,

If you wanna dance with me.*

I suddenly badly needed someone to dance with.

"The first time we cover these walls it shall be me. I have my favorites, I have made promises, so I select," Lucia began, "Then it shall be you. You must discover the art, love the art you discover, and place it on your walls."

Margaret Mary and Gianna followed Lucia from room to room in the gallery of "La Premiere Expressione II" like geese. This was all new to them, new and exciting and life changing.

"And we must open on La Toussaint?" Gianna asked.

"The Day of All Saints," Lucia answered. "A day to remember our past and the beginning of the autumne, the prelude to La Noel."

"La Noel is Christmas?" Margaret Mary asked.

"Mais oui, mon chere, we sell a lot of art at Christmas." Lucia laughed and the uncertain mood lightened.

"How many pieces?" Gianna asked, looking at the gallery walls.

"Here we will have sixty. More or less as you prefer after we premiere, but sixty at first," Lucia declared. "Come let us go look and choose."

There was much to be done before the November 1st grand opening. The art had to be selected, the décor decided, the apartment perched above the gallery to be furnished, their wardrobes to be assembled, their lives to be re-ordered. Margaret Mary's head was swimming with delight and anticipation though at night, just before she fell asleep, she reflected on the life she was leaving behind.

A month earlier she had moved, with Gianna, to Paris. Their completed studies in England behind them, their future in France ahead. They lived, quite underfoot, with Lucia, until their apartment in Montmarte was ready. Margaret Mary's weekly or semi-weekly phone calls to David had dropped off. Lucia had no phone in her apartment, she and Gianna would have none in theirs. Private phones in residences were still a luxury in France and a host of more pressing items had to be paid for. Sean and Rose gifted fine Irish linens. Lucia found them a luxurious feather bed. Table and chairs from a Left Bank flea market, pots and pans from the same. One life was taking shape, another was fading into the past.

Eddie had a court date. Horatio, with yeoman help from Peter and Cindy, had bartered a deal. In exchange for a guilty plea Eddie would receive no more than eighteen months in prison. This sentence could be lowered at sentencing at the judge's discretion.

"You know him best, he's your friend. This is what I need," Horatio announced as we gathered for what had become a team meeting. "Tell him Peter."

"Every defendant facing a judge for sentencing receives a state or federally funded probation report, or background paper which helps the judge decide how big a hammer to hit the defendant with at sentencing," Peter explained while Cindy nodded. I listened.

"These probation reports are prepared by cynical, overworked court employees who get most of their information from prosecutors and police reports. They invariably produce an unflattering and even biased view of the defendant and harsher sentences," Cindy added.

"Which is where you come in," Peter interjected. "Eddie is your buddy. Cindy and I have classes, exams, and internships to take care of. Spend some time with Eddie, learn about his background, his family life, education, his political ideas, his good deeds. Write them up, you always were a talented writer. We've got to show the judge he's not a degenerate criminal."

Cindy continued, "We want to show the court Eddie is an expatriate, forced to flee his home and his country due to his political aversion to what he believes to be an unjust war. What the court sees as crimes, Eddie believes is political protest."

Peter and I looked at Cindy in disbelief after her somewhat flowery speech.

"Have you ever met Eddie?" I asked. "His only political beliefs are nine-ball, draw poker and point spreads."

"Now that is something it would be hardly helpful to tell the judge, would it?" She replied.

"Just write a bio, interview him, family, education, goals, the right stuff. We'll legal it up later," Peter advised.

So, I continued to gather my legal chops. Horatio went back to Baltimore. Peter and Cindy said they would be in touch.

Eventually, and with a lot of help from Peter and Cindy, I constructed what Horatio submitted as a Motion in Mitigation on Eddie's behalf. It read like this…

FAMILY HISTORY AND BACKGROUND OF EDWARD LEGRAND

Edward "Eddie" Lagrand is the only child born to Harold Porter Lagrand and Hazel Lois Cobb, nee Lagrand. Eddie's father was killed in an industrial accident at Chelsea Naval Shipyard when Eddie was a sophomore at Boston University.

Eddie's mother, Hazel, is 68. She attended Elizabeth City State Teachers College completing her educational degree in 1936. Hazel was permanently disabled in an automobile accident when Eddie was twelve and is largely housebound. She resides in Chelsea, Massachusetts with her sister, Camile Cobb.

EARLY EDUCATION AND FAMILY LIFE

Eddie recalls his childhood as a vast intermingling of grandparents, aunts, uncles, cousins and neighbors in a tightly knit, religious and moral community which stressed religion, education, arts and sports. Eddie states that he flourished in school from an early age receiving encouragement and support from his widely extended family and community. Eddie recalls…

> I loved school, to me it was like learning a game. I studied math, science and the Red Sox, and always had plenty of time to play ball. My mother taught piano, we often sang together after meals and especially during weekly church services. The phrase, "It takes a community to raise a child" applied one hundred percent to the manner in which I was raised.

Eddie's attended parochial grade and high school in Chelsea. He established a highly successful scholastic career at St. Jude's High in Chelsea where he lettered in baseball, hockey and track while singing with the Glee Club and playing xylophone in the school band. Eddie reports…

> I graduated with Honors, in June of 1963 and was recruited for a full baseball scholarship to Boston University. My parents were instrumental in my choice, insisting that I balance sports and academics. BU is close to home and family which allowed me to continue to live where I had grown up and intended to spend my life.

Eddie's life was permanently altered when his father was killed during Eddie's sophomore year at BU. A construction crane collapsed in the Chelsea shipyard. Harold Lagrand was killed instantly. Eddie chose to leave Boston University to care for and contribute to the support of his mother.

In an interview conducted for this report Eddie's mother, Hazel, states…

Eddie has always been a hard worker. When he was ten, he had a Record American paper route in the morning, then he delivered the Globe in the evening. He always brought me his earnings and asked only for an allowance back. He did this right through high school. When his father died, he wanted to quit school and work fulltime. I begged him not to, to stay in school, but he knew we needed the money. He never complained about leaving school and we were always able to pay our bills.

DRAFT HISTORY

Eddie became eligible for the draft in March of 1965. He received a student deferment while enrolled at Boston University which he forfeited upon withdrawing in the spring of 1966. He was notified to report for a draft physical in August of 1966 and chose not to answer this summons. Eddie explains…

My father and uncles were all in the service. Military service, like strong religious convictions and family values are a tradition in my family, not quite an obligation, but an honorable, respected choice. I couldn't make that choice. I was, at this time, the sole support of my Mother. My aunt Camille had not come to live with us yet and she would have been all alone. We talked about this, and my mother encouraged me to enter the service, insisting she would be alright. I disagreed. At this time my best friend came home from Vietnam. Tommy Marks was his name. He lost both his legs to a land mine in a place I never heard of called Da Nang. Tommy was all-city football when we were in high school. He could switch hit, power from both sides of the plate in baseball. He weighed 165, all muscle. When he came home, he weighed around 90 pounds. He wouldn't talk about Vietnam except to tell me "Don't Go!"

Thomas Marks could not be interviewed for this report because he committed suicide in 1967, ten days before Eddie left for Canada. Eddie recalls...

After Tommy's funeral my Mother stopped saying I should go in the Army. She was frightened that what happened to Tommy would happen to me. Going to Canada, avoiding the draft was not an easy decision for me but I believed it was the right one. I couldn't understand why we were fighting that war, and I couldn't fathom leaving my mother to go there. In Canada I could work and send money home and when I came home it wouldn't be in a wheelchair.

Eddie reports that he received the information and support to go to Canada from a host of draft resistant organizations who assisted him in leaving the country. Arriving in Canada he immediately went to work at two jobs, short order cook and bartender. He sent as much of his pay home to his mother as he could. Current estimates from the Canadian government suggest that around 40,000 young men have sought asylum from the draft in Canada thus far.

Despite the risks Eddie made several visits to Chelsea over the past four years to visit his mother. Wages in Canada were low however and the cost factor became as much of an obstacle as the risk of arrest. Two years ago, Eddie was offered a job in the United States that would pay more than he was able to earn in Canada. This job would also make it much easier for him to visit his mother, which he did often.

Eddie's Mother, Hazel, states…

When Eddie came home my heart would be in my mouth all the time he was here. But I was so glad to see him. He always came with money that he left with me and told me I must buy something nice for myself. All I ever wanted was for my boy to be able to be home without fear of arrest. For that I would have given all the money I would ever have.

Eddie's aunt Camille adds…

Eddie is devoted to his family. What he did, he did for her. He knew the risks he was taking when coming to see us and he came anyway. Life would have been much harder on Hazel and me without Eddie's help but we both would have done without a penny of it to keep him safe.

Eddie Lagrand was working as the manager and head bartender at the China Rose restaurant in Amherst, Massachusetts when he was apprehended by Federal authorities and charged with draft evasion. At this time no other charges are pending against him.

SUMMARY

Eddie Lagrand's life is marked by extraordinary achievements and tragic, though necessary choices. He has been an outstanding student of promise and a fugitive from the law, all before his twenty first birthday.

Like thousands of youths of his generation he was torn between love of country and love of family. Eddie has voiced no strong political opinions of the Vietnam War, only admirably strong devotion to his disabled Mother and aunt. He made the choice to avoid military service only after the death by suicide of his close friend Tommy Marks and his overwhelming consideration for the effects of his absence on his Mother.

The current political climate favors the complete withdrawal of US forces from South Vietnam and considerations of a general clemency to those draft resistors who could not in good conscience agree to serve there.

Edward Lagrand chose to risk his freedom for his family while his country fought an unpopular and ultimately unwinnable war. That decision has already cost him several years in political exile, and life as a clandestine fugitive in his own country.

As the war in Vietnam winds down we are asking the Court to consider that Edward Lagrand has paid the price for his freedom of choice in exile and trepidation of the effects of that choice on his family and his future.

CONCLUDING REMARKS

I have attempted to show that by all historic, personal and behavioral factors available, that a causal link between Eddie Lagrand's decision to flee his country and avoid military service was predicated by genuine family concerns and not his personal well being.

In his letter to the Court, Eddie writes…

Your Honor,

I have not contested the charges levied against me and understand that my decisions have consequences. I love our country and did not flee as an act of protest against it. I fled to Canada to continue to help my Mother who needs me and to honor my obligations to her welfare. I have paid a considerable price for that decision. I have lived for the past four years looking over my shoulder at every siren, living in fear of my ultimate and unavoidable arrest. I have already spent considerable time in custody. I am asking you to allow me to go home to resume my family obligations and to make amends in any way I can for my actions.

Thank You,

Edward Lagrand.

This report was the result of a lot of editing, cropping, polishing and highlighting of the factual, but selective highlights of Eddie's past and motivations. When the State Of Massachusetts agreed not to charge Eddie with any of the China Rose gambling allegations the activities at the restaurant were deemed inadmissible in the Federal case, which helped Eddie enormously.

In a sentencing hearing on November 4, 1973, Eddie was found guilty of the draft evasion charges, sentenced to time served, three years probation and set free. A celebration was in order.

"Cheers, Beers and No More Tears!" A more than a little drunk Horatio Marks proclaimed as we gathered and guzzled in the closest bar to the Federal courthouse. Eddie was being out processed from custody. Everyone else, Hazel, Camille, Peter, Cindy, Horatio and I were stuffed into a corner booth, celebrating. Three pitchers of beer were on the tabletop. Three empty pitchers had just been taken away. Three more were on the way. Nobody would be driving anywhere after this party.

"For the love of all of ya!" Hazel toasted, her mug of beer waving above her head.

"A fine day!" Horatio exclaimed, happily. "Dave, the judge referred to your report twice at sentencing. Fine job, well done."

"Peter and Cindy helped me a lot," I replied. "To them!" I shouted, my mug over my head. We kept drinking, it was going to be a long night.

"Peter, Sandy, I want you to stay in touch. I enjoyed working with you both and I believe, if we survive this night, you will both become fantastic lawyers." Horatio was laying on the praise, well deserved.

"If you call me Sandy one more time, I'm going to wrap your balls around your ears," Cindy declared. She was more than a little drunk herself. Everyone erupted in laughter except Horatio who spilt his beer all over Camile who was dozing off in the corner of the booth. She never stirred.

"To Cindy, never Sandy, let justice prevail!" Horatio acknowledged.

I was really enjoying gathering my law chops.

Eddie was released from custody the next day. Horatio went back to Baltimore, with a massive headache. Peter and Cindy returned to Boston with mutual headaches of their own.

Hazel and Camille swooned over Eddie. Eddie was speechless with gratitude.

I went back to Amherst wishing I could share these wonderful happenings with Margaret Mary. But she had no phone in Paris, I had no phone in Amherst. We had not spoken in three weeks. I missed her voice. I missed her laugh. I missed her.

Thanksgiving weekend came and went. Once very profitable football games were played but Eddie, and me, were out of business. Three years probation was going to be a real challenge for Eddie. No football cards were going to be a real challenge for me.

"It means you have to keep your nose clean, Eddie. No gambling, no football cards, no booking bets," I explained.

"I don't know how to keep my nose clean!" Eddie proclaimed. "What am I supposed to do? Get a job?"

"Unless you want to go back to prison," I suggested.

"There's always Canada," Eddie quipped, I hoped. The next thing I heard Eddie was driving a cab in Boston. He confided that he took a lot of fares to Suffolk Downs racetrack and the like. Eddie loved thin ice.

The school year wrapped up without a crisis and I went back to Lowell to see my family. All was well and pretty much unchanged at Glenmere Street. I did a little shopping for the folks and one day I checked the phone book. Teddy was right, Emily Kazantoros was in the phone book. I called. She answered. We had a date.

"Have you ever been to York Beach, Maine?" I asked.

She had not. Emily was a Hampton Beach girl. Lots of Madras skirts, bright yellow sweaters and penny loafers with a smattering of Beach Boys music and surfboards nobody knew how to ride.

"I'd like to take you there," I suggested, "it's a bit of a ride but worth it. We can do dinner and see the sights."

"York Beach has sights?" She asked.

"For sore eyes," I answered. We were on.

Nubble Lighthouse was frosted with snow as were the rocky beaches of York. The town was pretty much abandoned as it was every year after Labor Day but as familiar, calming and comfortable as ever.

"It's really pretty here, thanks for bringing me," Emily said as we crunched through the snowy parking lot at Nubble Light. On the one-hour ride here we had caught up on old times and old friends, played "What ever happened to?" and got to know one another. Emily was substitute teaching. She had her degree from Lowell State Teachers College and was hostessing three nights a week at a local restaurant.

"Actually, I like hostessing more than teaching," she admitted, "truthfully, the kids drive me crazy. I'd quit in a minute if I didn't have the degree."

I laughed and told her of my one semester as a school bus driver that nearly turned into life in prison for homicide.

"I've got no patience with kids," I admitted. "And truthfully, I don't even like them very much."

We had our first good laugh and discovered our first common ground. I put my arm around her as we walked through Nubble park. It was nice.

After Nubble we drove to Perkins Cove and were seated at a table overlooking the harbor in one of the nicest restaurants on the Maine coast. I ordered a lobster. Emily hesitated, reading the menu.

"I want to help pay for dinner," she said, "this place is so expensive."

Wow, I thought, this one may be a keeper. I explained that I had come into some healthy Christmas money and insisted dinner would be my treat. I told her about Eddie and how he insisted on paying me for my work. I told her I agreed to take his money to end the haggling and firmly decided I would never let money rob me of the satisfaction of doing a good deed ever again. She then agreed but only if I allowed her to pay next time. Next time? Things were looking up.

Our first date went fine. We kissed goodnight when I brought her home, rather primly I thought, but that was just me. I liked Emily. I enjoyed her company. I promised to call her again before I went back out to Amherst. What could go wrong?

Christmas on Glenmere Street that year just wasn't the same. John and Bob both had places to go, girlfriends and such. There were gifts of course. I spent as much of my Eddie money as I could. I received as generously as I gave. We ate a fine meal. Yet something was missing. The whole thing felt like a gift exchange, this for that. I sat with my family and thought about things far away. Life was moving on. I couldn't know then that this was the last Christmas I would ever spend on Glenmere Street. Life is mysterious.

The road which was parting me from my friends now included Lowell. Home would always be home, I hoped, Dad always Dad, Mom always Mom and my brothers near but far as well. Yet I felt the drift and knew I would once again be far away from this place, from these people when Christmas came around again.

And once again an angel whispered a song in my ear…

I'll be home for Christmas,

You can plan on me,

Please have snow and mistletoe,

And presents by the tree.

**Christmas Eve will find me
Where the love light gleams.
I'll be home for Christmas,
If only in my dreams.***

Lyrical Aspiration:

*I'll Be Home For Christmas, Walter Kent and Buck Ram

Chapter Twenty

Finales

Fabian Crobek got a hold of me a week after I got back to Amherst. This was my final semester, senior year. I stacked up a few Criminology courses, a Psych Course and a Comparative Literature seminar. If all went well, I would have a degree in Sociology/Criminology in June. All would not go well.

"Dave, I set up the government exam for next Saturday. Can you get Ron there?" Fabe asked.

"I'll try, Mr. Crobek. Ron's kind of sailing his own course these days."

"I know but he trusts you. He'll go if you go."

"I'll go. Where and when?"

When and where turned out to be the Amherst Post Office, Saturday morning, 8AM. I was game and Ron drove out and stayed with me Friday night. We Blue Wall'ed a few beers Friday night, got home early and were "up and at 'em" on Saturday morning. We stopped on the way to the Post Office and got a couple of large coffees. I tried to carry mine into the exam room and was stopped by a matronly type who informed me I could not carry beverages into the exam room.

"Okay," I answered, "Ron, I'll wait out here for you. Good luck."

"You mean you are not going to take the exam?" Matronly one said.

"I mean I'm going to stay out here and drink my coffee," I answered.

She huffed and puffed a bit and then decided I could bring in my coffee if I was careful not to make a mess. I always make a mess, but I went in anyway. I was mainly there as a favor to Fabe and Ron. Government service was not on my radar. Not much was.

After plowing through a few challenging pages of questions like "How many eggs in a dozen?" and "Who won World War II?" I handed in my exam. It was a one-hour exam. I finished in twenty-five minutes. Ron was right behind me. Whatever will be, will be. We went for more coffee.

"What are you going to do after graduation?" Emily asked.

She started coming out to Amherst after our third or fourth date in Lowell. We saw a lot of each other over Christmas, exchanged gifts and attended her family's infamous and hilarious New Year's Eve party together.

The Kazantorus family, now known affectionately as "The Barking Greeks" gathered at Emily's mother's house at year's end and argued, benevolently, until the New Year rang in. They were a large group of hard working, badly dressed, outspoken aunts, uncles and cousins who had accumulated more money than they ever anticipated and were at a loss as to what to do with it. So, they argued, good naturedly, compared inaccurately, and bellowed, loudly.

I had a ring side seat to this circus and enjoyed it immensely. Sitting in Emily's mother's plastic wrapped living room I listened and learned.

"You're an asshole!" Uncle Nick would shout at Uncle Joe.

"I'm an asshole? You're an asshole!" Uncle Joe would answer. Then they would hug each other and drink more Ouzo. Meanwhile the ladies would compare how much eye makeup they could wear without actually going blind and who could tease their hair the highest. Emily and her sister, Georgia would float benignly between the two groups with the other children and young adults, enduring head pats and loud, smacking kisses on the cheek.

I was sitting quietly, discovering Metaxa, when another uncle, Vinnie, planted himself beside me.

"You're here with Emmy, right?"

I nodded and smiled, getting as much Metaxa in me as I could.

"You her new boyfriend?"

It was beginning to look that way. I nodded and smiled. The interrogation continued.

"What do you do?"

I explained that I was in college, graduating in June, thinking of becoming a cop, law enforcement of some kind, I confessed I hadn't really decided yet.

"You good to her, our Emmy? I'm gonna' check on this you know."

I said I was. Vinnie seemed temporarily satisfied.

"You ever been in in the Navy?"

"Army," I replied.

"You do good?" He demanded.

"Honorable discharge, Spec 5, two arms two legs," I answered.

"Hey Nick, come over here! We may not have to kill this one."

Nick came over. He asked me the same questions Vinnie did. I drank more metaxa. The night wore on. The New Year came. I drove drunkenly back to Glenmere Street avoiding herds of equally drunken drivers on the way. Such was life in Lowell, New Year's Day, January 1, 1974.

Emmy's question still hung in the air. "After graduation" was an inevitability now. I had to think beyond the bookstore, bunny classes and cute girls in black sweaters. Nothing particular came to mind.

Ever since being back from Nam I had a very hard time planning for the future. If I wasn't dead when I woke up in the morning or imminently dead by noon, I had no plan. Just get through the day. Suit up, show up, adapt. This worked well in Southeast Asia, not so well in the World. Emmy was coming to know this about me and worried about my, and maybe our, future. I was starting to worry myself.

The world around me, off campus, was in a shambles. Lyndon Baines Johnson, the man I firmly believed was directly complicit in the murder of President Kennedy, died in Texas. He was 61 years corrupt and old. Good riddance. President Nixon was hanging onto the White House by his fingernails. New Watergate charges were being levied against him every day. The accusers were no better than the accused. Nixon's vice president, Spiro Agnew resigned in disgrace for taking bribes while in the White House. Career sleazebag Henry Kissinger signed something called the Paris Peace Accords with North Vietnam midway through 1973, while our soldiers kept dying in the jungle. The Supreme Court, in a decision titled Rowe vs. Wade, overturned individual state's bans on abortion. Porn went mainstream. Elvis got fatter.

In Israel the Yom Kippur War killed over 2,500 Israeli soldiers and brought the US and Russia closer to a nuclear confrontation than any time since the Cuban Missile Crisis. I hoped a girl I would always remember as "Rootin-Tootin" wasn't one of the Israeli casualties. The Toot had been in Israel over a year now, in the Army, I was sure. I had not heard from her, except in my heart.

I often wondered how LT was doing in Alaska. Maybe he had the right idea. Leaving the straight life behind. I had not heard a word from him either. I hoped he was okay. He deserved to be.

"David, you haven't answered me," Emmy insisted.

I hadn't because I truly had no answer. I did notice that Emmy had begun to leave more and more of her things at my apartment. She came out every weekend now and had her own key. Did I do that? We began sleeping together right after New Year. The sex was not exactly earth-shaking, but pleasant. Emmy was very shy about nudity and always wore one of my shirts to bed. Initially. I liked her, wasn't sure if I loved her, and owed her an answer. As soon as I had one.

"Officer Gianoulous, you are being accused of using excessive force in the arrest of two individuals at the Centerville Tap last Saturday evening. I'm ready to hear your side of the story." Sergeant Kane was Teddy's immediate supervisor. This was not the first excessive force complaint brought against Teddy.

"I responded to a call about a brawl at the Tap around 9PM Saturday night. When I arrived Karmer and Toomey were rolling around on the floor kicking the shit out of each other. The crowd inside the Tap was cheering them on. I broke up the fight, separated the assailants and put them on the wall. Karmer cooperated. Toomey had a bit of an attitude. While I was cuffing Karmer, Toomer made a break for it, exited the bar, turned left on the sidewalk and ran, full speed, into the city mailbox right outside the door. Knocked him out cold. I scooped him up, handcuffed him and put him in the back of my squad car. Karmer too. I brought them in and booked them."

"And that is how Toomer broke his jaw?" Sergeant Kane confirmed.

"Lucky he didn't break his whole head," Teddy responded.

"And Karmer filed no complaint?"

"Karmer was too drunk to file his own fingernails."

"And they each blew a 2.0 plus at the station?"

"Blood draw on Toomey. He won't be blowing on nuthin' for about two months."

"Thank you, that is all Officer Gianoulous."

Teddy saluted and left his supervisor's office. His sometime partner Mike Dumars was waiting for him in the hall.

"You good?" Mike asked.

Teddy answered, "Hell yeah. Buncha' bullshit anyway."

"They bought the mailbox story?" Mike said.

"I told you it would work better than the truth," Teddy laughed as they left the station house.

Teddy had been getting mean since Samantha's birth, never at home, but especially on the streets. He had broken Toomer's jaw with one quick punch. Toomer wasn't about to say otherwise, or anything. Street justice, Teddy called it. Smoldering suffering is what it was.

"You sold 12 paintings, I have offers for six more. Three of my artists are madly in love with the two of you, and Le Monde magazine is sending out a reporter to do a story on you both. So yes, your opening was successful. Tres bon, trois tres bon."

Lucille was ecstatic with her new partners, her new gallery and her new year. Margaret Mary was thrilled beyond speech, Gianna as well. Parisian society had welcomed them as heartedly as they had embraced Paris.

"Now we must work," Lucille added. "We have walls to fill, artists to coddle, buyers to seek out."

"Where? How do we start?" Margaret Mary's head was spinning.

"First the walls. We must choose. Then the artists, they are like children and need constant attention. The buyers will bring themselves to your door. Come let us begin."

"La Premiere Expression II" soon became the toast of Montmarte. Its weekly wine and cheese evening in such demand lines formed at the doors. Sales prospered; demand increased. Inventory dwindled. Margaret Mary had an idea.

"I want to go to Dublin to seek out Gaelic art. I have not seen a single canvas in all Paris from Ireland."

Gianna agreed. Lucia agreed. Margaret Mary travelled to Dublin.

"Daughter! So happy to see you!" Margaret Mary exploded into Sean's arms while Aunt Rose impatiently awaited her turn for an embrace. Three sets of smiles were watered with tears of joy as they left the train station for their home.

"I spoke with the chancellor at the University. There will be a showing of student art this weekend. The entire campus is ablaze with the news," Sean announced. "I peeked I did, yesterday evening. Glorious it is."

And glorious it was. Margaret Mary returned to Paris with thirty-six pieces or art. Thirty-six potential starts of careers for young, deserving artists, thirty-six Irish dreams destined for Paris and the world.

"These are beautiful!" Gianna exclaimed. "We must find space immediately. I can't wait to show Lucia what you have done!" They hugged, they kissed, they celebrated. And their new lives moved forward.

Cindy and Peter took the Amtrak train from Boston's South Station to Baltimore. They were spending the weekend with Horatio and his fiancé. Peter was laden with stacks of discovery, recently obtained from the Dow Chemical company which was going to make some Pentagon official or two very uncomfortable when brought before the burgeoning Agent Orange class action suit's proceedings. A nationwide network of lawyers, activists, reporters, clergymen and women, many of them Vietnam Veterans themselves were demanding answers. Peter's papers would hold those answers to the banner of truth and a shameful set of lies would be disclosed.

Cindy was laden with two quarts of New England Clam Chowder straight from Boston Wharf, still warm Parker House rolls purchased at Parker House and a pair of red, silky pajamas she had no intention of wearing in bed. All work and no play was not an option.

"Did you bring the declaration from the Air Force colonel?" Peter asked.

"Does the Pope wear silk underwear?" Cindy confirmed, enjoying pushing Peter's Vatican buttons whenever possible.

Peter knew better than to comment. "How about that Operation Ranch Hand unit patch? That thing is dynamite." He was referring to the "Only You Can Prevent A Forest" insignia worn by members of the units who defoliated Viet Nam's jungles and people. The patch was given to them by the terminally ill colonel they had interviewed in Worcester. Colonel William Parkman was dying of chronic B cell Leukemia and stage 4 bladder cancer. He was 51 years old.

"Got it," She answered. "I still can't believe how remorseful that man was."

"He has a lot to be remorseful for," Peter answered.

"He was following orders just like any other soldier in Vietnam," Cindy offered.

"He was following the wrong orders," Peter declared.

They held fast to their opinions, as the country was. And that's what makes a horse race.

My final semester was rolling along uneventfully until Saint Patrick's Day. Always a day of considerable debauchery, when somehow everyone on campus, black, white, Asian or Native Indian became Irish for twenty-four hours. Green beer, shamrocks and hangovers were the order of the day. I was a little more than half gassed and happy when I stumbled home that evening. That didn't last long.

The apartment was half empty. My junk was still there, my mattress and box spring still on the bedroom floor, the three-hundred-pound purple, overstuffed sofa still in the living room with the 24-inch black and white Zenith TV. The jelly glasses were still in the kitchen with the chipped and mismatched tableware but everything, everything Jenny and boyfriend had brought to the party were gone. Their bedroom was bare, no bed, no clothes in the closet, no rickety bookcase, no junk in the bathroom. Cleaned out, all gone.

The less inebriated part of my brain realized this was a cause of some concern but there were two beers left in the now half empty refrigerator which I drank before I went to bed. This was a tomorrow problem not a Saint Patrick's Day problem. Erin go Bragh.

Order had not been restored when I woke up the next morning. Grateful that I had my own coffee pot and fixings I sorted my options. I had a three bedroom, three hundred dollar a month apartment, scantily furnished, with five months left on the lease. Without roommates my nut has just tripled. Eddie was out of the football card business. I was going to have to spend a lot more time at the bookstore. A class or two were going to have to go. Graduation was going to be set back a bit. Man plans, God laughs.

To her credit Emmy immediately offered to pay some rent. "I'm here almost every weekend, I don't mind, and I want to help," She offered.

Another check mark in the keeper column. But I did not want to get in that deep, keeper or not. As much as I had come to enjoy her company, how much I enjoyed hearing her rickety, yellow, Volkswagen convertible rattle into the parking lot, I wasn't ready for an obligation of that sort. I assured her I would be fine, financially. She assured me she would help however possible.

I never found out what happened to Jenny and boyfriend. She never picked up her last paycheck at the bookstore and they did not attend classes. In the wind they were. I hoped that was a good thing for them but couldn't understand how it could be.

Despite generous offers of forbearance and latitude from my professors I dropped two courses and planned to pick them up in summer school which would make me eligible to graduate in August. So be it. It's not like I had big plans or a tight schedule.

As these events unfurled Ron and I received letters congratulating us on passing the government service exam. Ron's dad, Fabe, had arranged for us to be interviewed in Boston for positions as United States Border Patrolmen. I wasn't at all sure what exactly a Border Patrolman did, but a phone call from Fabe implored me to attend, with Ron, for his sake. I agreed. Experience is better than lethargy.

Three weeks later I found myself sitting in front of a selection board for the Immigration and Naturalization Department. Three guys with crew cuts were conducting interviews for the position of Border Patrolman which I discovered meant guys who patrolled the US Border, primarily the southern border between the United States and Mexico.

Selected candidates would attend a 17-week academy in Los Fresnos, Texas and then be assigned along the Texas, New Mexico, Arizona and California borders. Even though I was not particularly interested, the job sounded interesting.

"It says here you are a Vietnam veteran, Mr. Ferrier," One of the crew cuts commented.

"I am." Short answers are best.

"What, exactly was your job in Vietnam?" Another inquired.

"My primary duties were those of a helicopter crewman on air ambulances, Dustoff. My position was patient protector. My job was helping save lives."

This went over very well with the board.

"Honorable discharge, Good Conduct Medal, couple of Air Medals." He read. "You did two tours?"

"Volunteered for the second. I believed what my unit was doing was important."

Apparently, he was reading from my military records. The board seemed to agree about the importance of my job. Lots of head nodding, a smile or two.

Ron had been interviewed just before me. Strictly a formality I guessed. Fabe had the juice. Like it or not I figured I was in as well, if I chose to be. It was high time I made a few choices.

I started summer school, took two courses, spent lots of hours at the bookstore, made my nut and coasted toward graduation. Emmy had started hostessing at a very nice restaurant five nights a week in Lowell and came out to Amherst fewer weekends. My indecision about my own future created problems about my indecisions about our future. Emmy didn't press, but she was backing away.

Ron and I got the official word that we were accepted in the Border Patrol and given an Academy start date in October. Ron said he was going, with little conviction or credibility. I thought I might as well give it a chance as well. My options were not that abundant. I applied for, and was turned down by the Massachusetts State Police, no juice. Teddy offered to sponsor me for the Lowell Police Department. I declined. There was nobody else knocking at my door. It looked like Roomy Ron and I were headed for Texas. Man plans, God laughs.

I finished my last undergraduate examination at 11:45 AM Friday morning, August 9, 1974. A celebration was in order but there was nobody around to celebrate with. Margaret Mary was in Paris. Emmy was in Lowell. Teddy was in mourning. Most of the Beta Chi veterans were home for the summer. I had not been dating anyone beside Emmy for the past eight months. I could celebrate alone, or not at all. I voted for alone and headed for the Blue Wall Bar.

When I walked in the air was electric. People were stomping, cheering, celebrating. I had the distinct feeling this had nothing to do with me finishing my finals. Most of the attention in the room was focused on the wall mounted televisions. There was a helicopter on the front lawn of the White House, blades turning. A small, rat-like figure in a dark suit was scurrying aboard the chopper followed by an ashamed wife and meager entourage. Richard Millhouse Nixon had resigned as the 37th President of the United States. He was the first President ever to have done so. He was fleeing impeachment and possible imprisonment. He was done. So was I.

My college education was complete. Life beckoned. Decisions awaited.

Thinking back on it all a goodbye song whispered in my head…

There are places I'll remember

All my life, though some have changed

Some forever, not for better,

Some have gone and some remain.

All these places have their moments
With lovers and friends I still can recall.
Some are dead and some are living.
In my life I've loved them all... *

Lyrical Aspiration:

*In My Life, Lennon/McCartney

THE END

If you enjoyed Wired For Sound, I would really appreciate a short review, your help in spreading the word is highly valued and reviews make it much easier for readers to find the book.

To get your FREE copy of the first book in *The Mountaintop Series:*

1. Click on the Free Book link below.
2. Enter your **name** and **email**.
3. Click **Send** and the book will be emailed to you. Enjoy!

Free Book Link:
https://battlepress.media/?page_id=13

BORN ON A MOUNTAINTOP
(Book One of The Mountaintop Series)

Available from Amazon and Battle Press:

https://www.amazon.com/dp/B09ZYW5FXT

https://battlepress.media/?product=add-title

RAISED ON ROCK
(Book Two of The Mountaintop Series)

Available from Amazon and Battle Press:

https://www.amazon.com/dp/B0CC3MHMY2

https://battlepress.media/?product=raised-on-rock

FORGED IN FIRE
(Book Three of The Mountaintop Series):

Available from Amazon and Battle Press:

https://www.amazon.com/dp/B0C8Y7Y8XV

https://battlepress.media/?product=forged-in-fire

CALIFORNIA DREAMING:
Coming in 2024!